ABIGAIL
PADGETT

THE MYSTERIOUS PRESS

Published by Warner Books

A Time Warner Company

Copyright © 1997 by Abigail Padgett
All rights reserved.

Mysterious Press books are published by Warner Books, Inc., 1271 Avenue of the Americas, New York, NY 10020.

A Time Warner Company

The Mysterious Press name and logo are registered trademarks of Warner Books, Inc.

Printed in the United States of America

ISBN 0–89296–614–9

To my son, Brian

THE
DOLLMAKER'S
DAUGHTERS

Prologue

At first nobody noticed the doll. A baby doll with one eye missing, it was swaddled in tattered black lace from which a chipped porcelain arm hung lifelessly. On Goblin Market's foggy patio the strange toy was obscured by salt-laden shadows and the folds of the girl's black satin dress. No one could see that the doll was chained to a leather cuff buckled to the girl's left wrist, or that another chain ran beneath the ebony beads of her blouse to a chrome-studded collar fastened about her neck. And at first nobody saw that her eyes were empty, as if she, too, had been fashioned from bisque and then cast aside before the addition of those delicate paint strokes which create the illusion of life.

Many in the crowd wore similar collars and wrist restraints, black leather corsets, jackets, and boots. As was the custom, most of the females and many of the males regarded each other courteously from eyes rimmed in dark kohl. Their lips were painted bluish red, the color of oxygen-depleted blood let from veins rather than arteries. Some displayed pairs of pointed acrylic teeth that made a clicking sound against the metal tankards in which Goblin Market served drinks and exotic coffee. All wore black. They were Goths, oddities even in the late-night underworld of a generation so

impossible to categorize that its elders referred to it simply as
"X."

"Good evening, Fianna," a boy of eighteen in lace cuffs and
a leather doublet called from the club's side doorway, "where's
Bran?"

When the girl failed to answer he turned back to the interior dance floor, where a handful of black-clad people moved
to chantlike music played in minor chords. Outside, the crash
of surf provided a slow, hypnotic pulse which guaranteed
Goblin Market enduring popularity among San Diego's Goth
watering holes.

In December the beach fog moved in ghostlike wisps across
the sand, creating by midnight a shifting netherworld in
which the Goths could imagine themselves lost in time. By
one in the morning when the club's weeknight crowd was at
its peak, nothing was visible beyond the doors of Goblin Market but a shroud of mist punctuated by hazy lights from the
street on its inland side. It was then that the boy in the doublet remembered the girl called Fianna and went outside to
the patio looking for her. Five seconds later his scream cut
through the fog like a glass knife.

She lay crumpled on a weathered bench beneath the papery
dead fronds of a date palm, her eyes wide and staring at nothing. But the boy in the doublet would swear later that when
he touched her shoulder, the doll moved in its blanket of lace.
He would swear that its head fell back like a real infant's, and
that its single eye was alive with pain.

Chapter 1

Bo Bradley woke in a cold sweat and tentatively extended one long leg six inches from its bent position. The leg slid comfortably between layers of soft fabric she was almost certain would turn out to be flannel sheets. Forest green with an all-over pattern of tiny red-nosed reindeer. She remembered buying the sheets two days earlier in a last-minute stab at Christmas decorating. The presence of her leg between them was, she thought, a strong indication that opening her eyes would probably be safe. She was in her own beach apartment, her own bed. That other place had been a dream. Or something.

Weird dreams were nothing unusual. She'd had them since childhood, a manageable aspect of the volatile brain chemistry bequeathed her by generations of mad Irish poets, musicians, artists, and lesser eccentrics. Manic-depressive illness. But the dreams were corralled by medication now, as well as by the long experience of their forty-one-year-old dreamer. So where, she pondered shakily, had this eerie horror come from?

The view from one cautiously opened eye confirmed the assessment performed by her leg. The familiar walls and furniture were there, solid beneath a scrim of darkness. From a lambswool bed on the floor Molly, Bo's dachshund puppy, snored softly. Everything was as expected. Except the dream.

It had been one of those Bo recognized as alien, not arising from the symbol system organized by her brain for its own amusement from the countless details of her experience. This dream, she acknowledged as she searched with her left foot on the floor for the armadillo house slippers she'd kicked off hours earlier, had come from somewhere else. It wasn't hers. Nothing about it felt familiar. Not even its near-maniacal sense of dread.

The dream had been of a cold, windowless room filled with breathy clicking sounds. Mechanical sounds. Repetitive and devoid of meaning. And the room was some kind of trap, or prison, or place of exile filled with grief and anger and a terrible sense of waiting. It felt like a long-abandoned subway station where no train has come in years, although one more is expected. And that train will be the last, and will carry nothing alive.

"In the Station of the Dead," Bo named a painting her brain was busily creating from the receding mental image. All gray angles with patches of fungus, an industrial sense, hopelessness. And across the bottom, empty tracks and a single red light feeble in shadows. She hoped she'd forget the painting by morning, when the urge to mix egg tempera might become irresistible.

In the apartment's miniature kitchen Bo shuddered at the dream-image and then focused on the coffee grinder atop a stack of catalogues on the counter. A wall of cottony vapor swirled against the window over the sink. Coffee would be good, she thought. Just the thing to take the edge off an unusually frightening psychic event that had drifted in on the fog. Except the grinder would wake Molly, and then it would be necessary to get dressed and take the little dog outside. A potty-run in dense December fog at two-thirty in the morning.

"No way," Bo whispered to the coffee grinder. "I'm not going out in that!"

From her purse on the countertop she grabbed a cigarette lighter and held its flame aloft in the darkened kitchen. "I know ye're out there, Cally," she announced in her grand-mother's brogue to a Celtic myth named Caillech Beara, the embodiment of death and madness. "It's your season we're havin', your feast that's a-comin', but here's light for me and the wee dog. It's far out you'll be stayin' now, Cally. And keepin' your dead dreams there in the fog, away!"

The ad-libbed exorcism was a compilation of facts learned from one Bridget Mairead O'Reilly, who brought satchels of peat to Cape Cod from Ireland every summer so that first one granddaughter and ten years later the next might know the meaning of light.

"Old Cally'll skitter from the flame," she told a wide-eyed four-year-old Bo. "It's to keep her moanin' far outside, the fire is, and to keep the livin' safe and warm. Always remember the flame's the heart of the livin', the light of it is, and Cally won't have none of it!"

Bo held the lighter aloft in her kitchen until her thumb began to burn, then watched as a violet oval with neon green edges floated across her retinas where the flame had etched its shape. The little ritual was reassuring, but did nothing to assuage the dream's hangover. The eerie painting, Bo under-stood with a sigh, was no distortion flung into consciousness *or* Scots-Irish bogeys. The image was simply real. She would never know what it was or where it had come from, but it was real.

"Shit!" she exhaled as the phone's abrupt ringing made her jump.

"What in hell?" she pronounced tersely into its beige plastic receiver.

"Bradley, you're up," the familiar, booming voice of Police Detective Dar Reinert informed her. "That's good. Got a favor to ask, and you people will get the case in the morning anyway, so you'll be ahead of the game, right?"

Bo groped for a way to define the complete absence of information in whatever he'd just said. Only the word, "favor," was clear, and she owed the burly child abuse detective several of those. He'd helped her on a number of the cases which landed on her desk at San Diego County's Child Protective Services where she worked as a child abuse investigator.

"Dar, what are you talking about?" she asked, scuffing the toe of one armadillo slipper against the tile floor. "Do you know it's two-thirty in the morning?" From her bedroom the flapping of hound ears signaled that Molly was shaking herself into wakefulness. Bo pondered for the thousandth time a canine evolution which precluded the use of litter boxes. She was going to have to get dressed and escort Molly through the fog to some carefully chosen patch of grass.

"Just got a call at home from the dispatcher," he said, yawning. "A couple of uniforms are down there, but they're spooked. The kid's going to St. Mary's in an ambulance, unless St. Mary's won't take her. Guess she'll have to go to County Psychiatric then. Friend said she was fifteen. Does a children's hospital take 'em when they're that old? And when they're psycho? The uniforms don't know what to do, and the vampire crap's freakin' 'em out. Thought you could boogie on over there and save me a trip across town since this thing's going to land over in Social Services an hour from now. Okay?"

Molly had waddled into the kitchen and was wagging her tail happily at Bo.

"Dar, I have to take the dog out, so tell me a few things in this order. The uniforms are down *where*, *what* kid is going to St. Mary's or County Psychiatric, *when* will you stop using the term 'psycho' to describe everything from drug addiction to hairstyles you don't like, and since when do you believe in vampires?"

His laugh reminded Bo of logs steaming in a roaring fire.

That sense of warmth and safety. "I don't," he said, "and what's happened is some kid who calls herself Fianna has gone catatonic at a club two blocks from your place. They thought she was dead. Manager called nine one one, uniforms were there in six minutes, but it's a mess. The club's called Goblin Market. It's a hangout for kids who think they're vampires or something. Dispatcher says we haven't had any calls from there before this. Uniforms say it doesn't look like drugs, and a kid in a Robin Hood suit told them this girl lives in a foster home. It's going to be CPS's baby, and the damn fog's so thick it'll take me an hour to get down there. How about it?"

"I've never seen a club called Goblin Market in Ocean Beach," Bo told him, puzzled. "Are you sure it's here and not Mission Beach or Pacific Beach or La Jolla?" The list of San Diego's beach communities, each with its own civic personality, routinely confused newcomers to the city. But Dar Reinert was no newcomer.

"Place is a restaurant called Delaney's, right on the beach. Delaney rents the space nights to this guy who runs the vampire club. You need to get out more at night."

"I'm going to," Bo agreed. "But only as a favor to you and the dog."

"Fax me your report from the office."

"Roger."

Five minutes later Bo tucked the wiggling dachshund under her left arm and opened the apartment door to a world made ominous by its lack of visual reference. Holding the stair rail, she edged her way down through swirling vapor to the street. Her corner. The terminus of both Naragansett Street and the continent of North America. The drama of the locale with its end-of-the-line geography had captured her imagination four years in the past, when she'd left St. Louis to take the job which continued to pay her rent. And which was about to draw her into a nest of vampires.

Grinning at the peach-colored globe of mist blooming around a streetlight, she acknowledged that she wouldn't have it any other way. Vampires would be interesting. They'd provide a diversion from the strange dream, she mused. The vampires would become allies in the daily battle with boredom her brain fought despite its harnessing medications. After a two-block stroll Molly tugged at her yellow leash, scampering toward the flashing red and blue lights of an SDPD patrol car parked in the public lot abutting the beach restaurant Bo knew only in its daylight persona. At night, she saw, it was something else entirely.

Over Delaney's sign a black plywood silhouette of castle turrets stretched toward the sky. Unlit, the prop looked real in the drifting fog. Bo crossed the parking lot beside the now-abandoned lifeguard station and felt Molly balk as they stepped onto the beach. The little dog had never liked sand. Bo picked her up and approached the eerily lit scene ahead with caution.

The uniformed officers Dar had mentioned stood in a partially enclosed patio attached to the small restaurant, illuminating with flashlights a pale girl dressed in black. She was sitting upright on a bench, her gaze transecting the posturing young cops as if they weren't there. Beside her a boy in a doublet and lacy shirt repeatedly offered a steaming metal tankard Bo presumed was coffee, but the girl didn't respond. Some forty other figures, all dressed in black, milled about, watching somberly. Bo had expected theatrics, but when a blond young man in a cape bowed and smiled at her, she instinctively pulled Molly closer and regretted an absence of pointed wooden stakes among the debris she carried in her purse. The fangs revealed by his smile weren't the peppermint-flavored paraffin variety Bo remembered from childhood Halloweens. They were real.

"I've misplaced my rope of garlic," she told him casually. "But trust me, my blood would taste like boiled tomato juice. Medication. You know how it is. By the way, does this run in your family?"

"A dentist in L.A. does them for seventy bucks," the caped figure explained, beaming. "They're a birthday present from my wife."

"Happy birthday," Bo smiled, nodding toward the scene on the patio. "Do you know anything about this?"

"Maybe she came to the end of the hunt," he suggested.

"The hunt for what?"

"Loneliness."

With that he swirled his cape, drew its hem with one hand across his chest, and retreated into the fog. Bo harbored a conviction that she'd just wandered into an avant-garde play understood by everyone except her. From inside she could hear a guitar strumming four chords over and over beneath electronic effects and a male voice intoning something in a British accent. It had to do with rust. Under Bo's arm, Molly began to howl tentatively.

"I'm Bo Bradley from Child Protective Services," she explained to the police, displaying the ID badge clipped to her sweatshirt. "Detective Reinert phoned me. I live near here, and he thinks this case will wind up with CPS in a matter of hours, anyway. What's going on?"

"Umm," the younger of the pair began, "is there something the matter with your dog?"

"She sings," Bo answered. "When she hears music, she sings. Now, what's happened to this girl?"

"Somebody's coming from County Psychiatric to get her. She's flipped out. Nuts. We have to stay here until they take her away. Creepy, huh?"

"What about St. Mary's? Dar said they were going to check that out first."

The crewcut young cop shrugged. "Dunno. The dispatcher just said County Psychiatric, and we're supposed to wait. Now that you're here maybe we can leave. I'll call in and see. God, this place is sick!"

Bo looked around. Nobody's eyes had pupils the size of quarters, nobody was staggering drunk, and despite their chalky makeup and black-ringed eyes, the denizens of Goblin Market appeared uniformly healthy. And possessed of sufficient disposable income to purchase expensive props for which there would be little workday use. Leather boots with silver skull buckles, capes and lace collars, studded armbands and wrist restraints, black vests and corsets and bustiers worn decorously over silk blouses.

"You don't know sick," she told the young cop. "You don't have a clue. Who runs this place?"

"Guy behind the bar with the hood over his head."

"Ah, the hangman," Bo noted. "What did he say happened to the girl?"

"He doesn't know anything, says she's been a regular, hangs with a guy named Bran who's some kind of computer geek and hasn't showed up tonight. Apparently she got here just before midnight, stood around on the patio for an hour or so, and then went mental. Nobody talked to her. Did you get a load of the doll?"

Bo looked at the seated girl. She was holding something, but it was obscured by folds of black lace.

"Doll?"

"Mega-creep shit." The cop sighed, heading for the patrol car. "Check it out."

Approaching slowly, Bo kept her eyes on the girl's feet. If this were a psychotic episode of some kind, Bo knew, an aggressive attitude and direct eye contact would only increase the girl's terror.

"Who're you?" asked the boy with the coffee.

"Bo Bradley. I work for Child Protective Services, the agency that handles foster care, among other things. I've been told that Fianna is in a foster care placement."

Looking up very slowly, Bo addressed the girl.

"Is that right, Fianna? Could you tell me the name of your foster parents?"

The girl called Fianna looked straight through Bo's forehead at a point lost in two hundred yards of fog. Her breathing, Bo noted, was fast and shallow, and she was trembling.

"I need to feel your pulse," Bo told her quietly. "I'm going to touch your left arm now, your wrist. If you'd rather I didn't touch you, I won't, but you'll have to let me know."

When there was no response, Bo set Molly on the bench beside the girl and reached for a pale arm hidden beneath wrinkled black lace. At its wrist was a black leather cuff from which a slender chain ran to an object in the girl's other hand. Bo tugged on the chain and then gasped as a small, chubby leg emerged from the wad of lace across the girl's lap. Discolored and locked in the characteristic bent-knee position of a young infant, the leg for a split second seemed real. And frozen in the transitory condition called rigor mortis.

Bo forced herself to breathe deeply and tugged the doll free of its covering. Although worn and missing an eye, the toy still bore evidence of the craftsmanship which had gone into its making. One blue glass eye gazed from beneath delicately painted lashes above a pug nose. Even the tiny upper lip protruded to a point over the recessive lower one in the typical embouchure of the newborn. The doll's painted hair had been dark before most of it wore away, Bo noticed. And its bisque arms and legs were still firmly stitched to a cloth body now covered in grime. Bo felt a wrenching sadness as she wrapped the toy in lace again and felt the girl's pulse. A sadness like that in the dream.

Running a hand through her shaggy silver and auburn curls, she shook her head to dispel the feeling. The pulse beneath her fingers was fast but strong enough. Fianna was clearly in trouble, but probably not from physical shock.

Her skin was cool but not clammy, her color within normal limits.

"She calls the doll Kimmy," said the boy in the doublet. "Lately she's had it with her all the time. Pretty weird, huh?"

"Do you know her?" Bo asked.

"Not really. She comes here sometimes. She goes with this guy named Bran. He's older. Works for some software company. I already told the cops all this. Bran never showed up tonight." The boy sighed and shrugged in embarrassment. "I was worried about her. That's when I came out here and found her whacked-out. I guess she's crazy, huh?"

In the question Bo heard an enormous distance taking shape between the staring girl and the boy, the crowd, the entire known world. It was a distance she knew very well, impossible to breach once in place.

"No!" she answered instinctively. "I don't think it's that. Something's happened, though, and she's in a kind of shock. She needs to be at home now. She needs to be taken care of. Do you know where she lives?"

"Bran told me once she has foster parents, but that's all I know."

The girl's left hand began to move slowly, as if she were searching for something only discernible to touch.

"How can I reach this Bran?" Bo asked.

"Dunno. That's, like, not his real name. People use different names here, old-fashioned names, y'know? Like, my real name's Mark Byfield, but everybody here knows me as Gunther. It's just something we do."

The girl's hand had found Molly on the bench beside her and hovered over the little dog as if testing a magnetic field.

"We?" Bo asked. "Who's 'we'?"

"Goths," the boy answered.

"Goths?"

"Yeah. It's a kind of a statement. It's a scene."

"Oh," Bo said, watching Fianna's slender, pale hand begin to stroke Molly's soft fur. In the girl's huge, dark eyes tears swam and finally spilled over the kohl and the white makeup on her cheeks. In her peripheral vision Bo saw an ambulance pull into the parking lot.

"The puppy's name is Molly," she told the girl softly, "and she's real and alive and so are you!" The words had come from Bo's heart, and Fianna seemed to nod slightly, as if they'd had an effect. "I want you to pet her while I make some arrangements for you to go to a hospital."

Holding her CPS ID badge over her head like a police officer's shield, Bo loped toward the ambulance attendants. "Take her to St. Mary's," she said as if the destination were a foregone conclusion.

"The dispatcher said County Psychiatric," a plump, cheerful young woman with rosy cheeks and strong arms answered. "We'd need some kind of authority, a doctor or something, to change it."

"Wait two minutes," Bo said, already running into the restaurant.

"Andy," she explained breathlessly on the phone to Dr. Andrew LaMarche, head of the Child Abuse Unit at St. Mary's Hospital and the only man whose extra toothbrush hung beside hers in a rack over her bathroom sink, "I know it's three in the morning, but I desperately need a favor."

Less than two minutes later she told the ambulance attendant, "Dr. LaMarche at St. Mary's has ordered the admission. They're expecting her."

"No problem," the young Brunhilde grinned, unlatching the gurney from its clamps on the ambulance floor. "Let's load 'er up!"

When the ambulance had vanished into fog, followed by the squad car, Bo carried a sleeping Molly back to her woolly bed in the oceanfront apartment. Everything looked the same, Bo thought, except different. Something had changed, not in the physical structure of the world but in her perception of it. A window had opened somewhere between the dream and the strange girl. It felt like a window in time through which something unfinished wept in silence. And, Bo realized, whatever it was bore a strange connection to her.

Chapter 2

In the morning Bo dropped Molly with the same elderly neighbor who'd cared for her fox terrier, Mildred, until the old dog's death months earlier. Then she headed inland on I-8 forty-five minutes earlier than usual. Probably forty-five minutes earlier than *ever*, Bo thought. It wasn't seven-fifteen yet. Unquestionably a record.

"Bo! Are you sick? What's the matter?" Madge Aldenhoven yelled through the still-locked side door of CPS's Levant Street offices in the heart of San Diego. "Don't you have your key? What are you doing here?" The supervisor's impossibly violet eyes revealed surprise tinged with something else. Fear. And Bo knew why.

"I ate my key last night in a psychotic episode," she smiled, tilting her head far to one side and allowing her jaw to hang slack. "I think it was right before I blew up the church, although it may have been just after I imprisoned the entire City Council in a frozen food locker and forced them at gunpoint to read the Yellow Pages aloud until they denounced capitalism. Anyway, I wanted to get here early so I could murder you and mail your body in pieces to remote desert military installations before everyone else arrives. Open up."

"That's disgusting, Bo," Madge said into a pile of paper on her desk after pushing the door only far enough for its lock to release, then scuttling into her office.

Bo leaned on her supervisor's office doorjamb and sighed.

"It's what you were thinking, Madge. Only for a second, but in that second you imagined that because I have a psychiatric illness I'm dangerous. You're alone here. When you saw me, you were afraid."

The older woman adjusted a pearl earring and patted the snowy bun at the nape of her neck. "I was stunned," she said briskly, turning to regard Bo through violet-tinted contact lenses. "You've never understood that getting to work on time is the mark of a professional."

The speech, Bo thought, sounded as if it had been written on a tea bag. Earl Grey.

"Madge, haven't you ever screwed anything up, made a mistake, broken the rules?"

"Not at work," the supervisor answered. "In dealing with children's lives it's essential to follow the rules."

Bo noticed that the woman's hand had come to rest reverently on a copy of the *San Diego County Department of Social Services Procedures Manual*. It was tempting to drop to one knee and mutter something in Latin, but Bo curbed the impulse, partially.

"*Caveat emptor,*" she whispered. "But *ubi est insula?*"

Since her high school Latin class in Boston she'd waited for an opportunity to ask, "Where is the island?" in a dead language. This chance, she thought, might well be the last.

"What?"

"I said we'll be getting a new case as soon as the hotline switches over from the night number," Bo answered. "I did the immediate response last night. It was in Ocean Beach. Dar Reinert called. He couldn't get down there in the fog."

The sun was finally burning off the haze. Bo could see light swimming through Madge's office window, turning the paper-strewn room a pale gold.

"What happened?" the supervisor asked.

"A fifteen-year-old with an old doll chained to her wrist and neck collapsed at a club frequented by vampires. She wasn't drunk or on drugs, but she wasn't talking. I called Dr. LaMarche, and he admitted her to St. Mary's."

The morning light painted green highlights in the folds of the older woman's blue silk blouse, then fell in a dusty pool on the carpet. Bo watched the light as if it were a friend.

"You know we don't have sufficient staff to deal with adolescents, Bo. Our resources must be devoted to the protection of younger children who are the most vulnerable. You had no business getting involved in this. It's not a CPS case!"

"The girl is in foster care," Bo mentioned, tossing a curling wisp of hair out of her eye.

"Then why on earth didn't you just call the foster parents?"

Madge had grabbed a Bic pen and jabbed it into the hair over her ear. The day, Bo thought, was beginning to feel manageable.

"She wasn't talking, so there was no way to get the names of the foster parents, much less a phone number. But she's our responsibility, Madge. She's already in the system."

"I'll phone the supervisor in Foster Care Placement and give her the girl's name. It won't be hard to trace the placement."

"I don't know her name," Bo replied. "She calls herself Fianna, but the kids who frequent this club all use these romantic pseudonyms. The cops interviewed everybody in the place. Nobody knew her real name or the real name of her boyfriend, who calls himself Bran."

"What's romantic about Bran? It sounds like cereal."

Bo saw Celtic designs in the light and floating motes of dust.

"The Fianna were the warriors of Erin," she said softly,

"long, long ago. And the bravest among them was Finn Mac Cool, who slew the Goblin of Flaming Breath whose name was Aillen, and saved Tara."

"Tara from *Gone with the Wind?*" Madge asked, pulling the pen from her hair and tapping it against her teeth.

"Tara is a hill near Dublin," Bo explained, disturbing the dust patterns with a movement of her right hand. "It was the ancestral seat of Irish kings."

"And Bran?"

"In his pack of hounds, Finn Mac Cool loved two best. Sgeolaun and Bran. People say that ghosts of these hounds are sometimes seen roaming among the fallen stones of Finn's castle in County Kildare, whining and impatient for the hunt."

"Oh," Madge Aldenhoven said, nodding. "This girl's boyfriend is named for a dog."

"A ghost dog, Madge. I think that's the point."

"What point?"

Bo recognized the impasse and gave up. Madge might enjoy a story, but symbolism was beyond her.

"What was your maiden name?" Bo asked, backing into the hall.

"Rasmussen. Why?"

"And your mother's?"

"Schramm."

"And *her* mother's?"

"I think it was Thompson, but don't ask me to go back any further," the older woman smiled. "Why are you asking?"

"I didn't think any Irish names would turn up," Bo answered. "Just checking."

"My father's mother's name was Quinn," Madge offered, triumphant.

"Then you *have* to understand about the ghost dog!"

"You're crazy, Bo."

"Yeah."

After flipping on the light in the cramped office she shared with another investigator, Bo sat at her desk and listened as the quiet office building gradually came to life. The conversation with Madge had been oddly pleasant, as if the long animosity between them were simply gone. Bo filed the impression for later reference, but didn't trust it. Madge had tried unsuccessfully for over three years to oust Bo from her job. One noncombative encounter did not, she noted, necessarily constitute genuine warmth. Still, it was strange to think of Madge Aldenhoven as a child. With a paternal grandmother named Quinn. Almost as if Madge might actually have at one time been human.

This is what comes of getting to work early, Bradley. Bureaucrats appear to have qualities of the living. It's an illusion. Don't let it happen again.

After leaving a note for Estrella Benedict, her office-mate and enormously pregnant best friend, Bo collected the multiplicity of forms necessary if Fianna's case had to be petitioned, and phoned the hospital for the girl's room number. Then she ambled back out to the four-wheel-drive Nissan Pathfinder she'd bought at a police auction, and exited the CPS parking lot as another hundred social workers and clerical staff were trying to get in. The feelings associated with being early were interesting, she thought. Arrogant and superior to those who were merely on time. Fortunately, she was in no danger of having the experience twice.

At St. Mary's Hospital she parked in a space marked POLICE and showed her ID badge to the eleven-to-seven graveyard shift guard just going off duty.

"You here for that teenager?" the man asked. "The one they brought in last night from the beach?"

"Well, she wasn't exactly on the beach—" Bo began.

"They called me to help hold her down," he went on sadly, fingering a pack of Camels showing above the top of his uniform shirt. "Had to put her in restraints and the orderlies were all in the ER with a bus full of Cub Scouts. Wrecked in the fog on their way home from Disneyland. Bad night."

Bo looked at the wiry, aging man and thought of Greek choruses. The news of the night handed over to the day, which would reconstruct from the narrative its own version of reality.

"Were any of the scouts badly hurt?" she asked.

"No, thank God," the guard answered, glancing dramatically at the ceiling through smudged bifocals. "Guess I'll go on now and get some breakfast."

"Good idea," Bo said from the elevator as its doors whooshed shut.

Restraints. Bad news. And hell to pay when Andrew LaMarche would quite reasonably demand an explanation for her insistence that the girl be admitted here, when she obviously needed to be in a psychiatric facility. Bo felt little transparent things tumbling around in her head. Just bits of things nobody could see. A puzzle. She was certain that the girl called Fianna wasn't psychotic last night, merely upset and in some kind of shock. So what had happened that would require restraints?

The girl was awake when Bo knocked politely on her open hospital-room door. On a tray beside the bed a full breakfast, including coffee, sat untouched. The doll was nowhere in sight, apparently stored with the girl's clothes by the hospital staff. Bo pretended not to notice the fabric restraint vest across the girl's chest or the sheepskin-lined leather wrist cuffs belted loosely to the bed frame. She knew what they felt like. It wasn't good.

"You might not remember me, but I saw you last night at Goblin Market," Bo began. "I work for Child Protective Services, and—"

"Kimmy's gone," the girl said, her voice whispery and too high. "Kimmy isn't here anymore."

In the pitch and childlike delivery of this news Bo recognized the flutter of hysteria. If the desperate train of thought, whatever it was, were not derailed, the girl's anxiety might escalate beyond her control, carrying her body with it. The predictable thrashing about for which restraints had been invented.

"I like the name you chose—Fianna," Bo said clearly and with no emotion. "The Fianna were brave and strong, long, long ago. Let me tell you a story about the Fianna. About the battle the Fianna waged against Murf, the Norse king, and his fleet of big ships with iron shields on their sides."

"Murf" had come from nowhere, and the battle Bo described as monotonously as possible had never happened. The point was to bore the girl down from hysteria with a flat, sequential, and impersonal narrative. Like most of the female gender, Bo guessed, Fianna would find descriptions of men throwing spears at each other a total yawn. But tracking the boring story might have a calming effect.

"And that's how the Fianna saved Ulster," she finished without noticeable punctuation, "and I want you to tell me your real name."

"Janny," the girl answered sleepily. "Or Janet or Janice. I don't know. I think it's always been Janny, though."

"And your last name?"

"Malcolm. Like Malcolm X. You know."

"Yes," Bo droned on, "a black political leader who was raised in foster homes in three different states before going to prison for robbery. I'm going to make a phone call right now, and then I'm going to come back and teach you how to stay calm. While I'm gone you're to repeat to yourself the story of the Fianna and King Murf, okay?"

"I don't believe his name was Murf."

"Might've been Wurf. Just do it."

"Wurf?"

"Just do it," Bo insisted from the hall. "It will help you keep it together until I get back."

The girl wasn't psychotic. Bo felt a certain pride in having been right all along. Something was wrong, something so frightening that Janny Malcolm had no resources for coping with it. But with help she could follow a distracting story, regain control of herself, answer questions.

"Madge," Bo said from the phone at the nurses' station, "I've got the girl's name. You can track her through the foster care office and call the foster parents. Something's happened to this kid, but right now what she needs most is security and familiarity. And I'll need to talk with her caseworker about getting her in to work with a psychologist. She's messed up, but I think it's situational rather than a real psychiatric problem."

"Good work, Bo," the supervisor answered. "What's the name?"

"Malcolm. Janny Malcolm."

Bo heard a sharp intake of breath, followed by silence.

"Madge?" she said. "What's the matter?"

"I . . . I just tore a nail on the edge of my desk," Madge said, her voice shrill. "And it won't be necessary for you to stay on this case any longer. It can be closed now that the foster parents are available. I want you to come back to the office immediately. Estrella just got a case I feel is too dangerous for her in her condition. I want you to go out with her on the preliminary investigation."

"Sure," Bo said. "It'll just take me a few minutes to document the reasons for releasing the hospital hold." Then she replaced the phone thoughtfully in its cradle.

There wasn't any hospital hold, Bo knew. Janny Malcolm's paper workup at St. Mary's had never been done because the staff had assumed the girl would be transferred to another hospital after the shift change. And there would have been no reason for a legal hold in any event, since the whereabouts of the minor's parents or guardian were unknown at the time of her admission. The hospital would have procured a judge's permission to treat the child, if any treatment had been necessary. As it was, Janny had merely spent the night in a clean bed, restrained from harming herself, but given no medication or other treatment. St. Mary's needed no hold to do that, and Madge Aldenhoven knew it.

Bo leaned against the nurses' station counter and pictured her supervisor's hands. The polished nails, filed smooth below the fingertips. A typist's hands, even though Madge never typed. Short, short fingernails. Impossible to snag on anything, especially the edge of a Formica-topped desk. Madge hadn't torn a nail, Bo realized, puzzled. It was the girl's name that made her gasp.

And in her three and a half years with Child Protective Services, Bo had never known investigators to work in pairs. It wasn't done. There were too many cases. If a case were dangerous because the adults involved were on drugs or made threats, then CPS turned the investigation over to the police. The guidelines were in the *Procedures Manual*. Madge, unaccountably, was breaking the rules.

"Something's rotten in Denmark," Bo whispered to a picture of a pink woolly mammoth on the wall. "Several things, actually."

Janny Malcolm was staring at the restraint cuff on her right wrist when Bo came back into her room. In the morning light she looked especially fragile, Bo thought. Like an old-fashioned doll meant for pink taffeta and lace mitts, but made up as an eighteenth century laudanum addict instead. The hollow eyes were especially informative, betraying too much worldly exhaustion for even an aging child to bear.

"I haven't got much time, Janny," Bo said, "but I want to help you."

"Okay," the girl sighed, trying unsuccessfully to sit upright against the pull of the body restraint. "I don't . . . really know what happened."

"You went to Goblin Market last night. A boy you know as Gunther said you just stood on the patio for an hour or so, and when he went to look for you, you'd collapsed on a bench. Do you know why you collapsed? Were you sick? Did you drink anything or use any drugs? Did something upset you before you went there?"

"I don't do that shit," Janny answered. "Goths, well, most of the really cool ones, they don't do drugs or get drunk or anything like that. It's not cool."

"What do Goths do?"

The wan face with its halo of dark, fine hair became animated. Bo saw a weak smile tug at the edges of the girl's mouth where the night's dark lipstick had crusted in blood-like flakes.

"Oh, it's really neat!" she began. "It's a scene. You just, well, you just get to wear these great clothes like in the old days, only sexy, y'know, and dance and listen to music. Some of them get a little carried away, I think. I mean, there's this girl who wears a bustier over just this *mesh* T-shirt, and you can see her breasts and everything. I mean, that's not really Goth. It's like, you're *supposed* to look like you're into kinky sex and everything, but really be nice underneath and have this, like, secret code where you have really nice manners and nobody outside knows the dirty stuff is just to fake them out so they won't find out the truth."

"What truth?" Bo asked, feeling herself spiral into the barely remembered confusion of adolescence.

"That you're really nice. Like, *nicer* than the real world. You know. Nicer than the way things are."

Bo nodded, gazing pointedly at the girl's wrists. "Fancy black cuffs with chrome studs and little chains really are nicer than real wrist restraints, even with the lambswool padding," she acknowledged. "Do you know why they put those on you?"

"I keep freaking out," Janny admitted. "Something keeps, like, coming into my mind. I don't want it . . . I don't want to think about it."

"Is it like somebody talking?" Bo asked casually. "Like a background noise or radio static that sounds like words?"

"Nooo! I'm not hearing voices or anything. I'm not crazy!"

"Some people who hear voices—religious mystics, for example—aren't crazy. And some people who don't hear voices are. But I don't think you're crazy at all. What I think is that something's really upset you, and you need to be safe and quiet at home for a while until we can get you some counseling. Would you like for your foster parents to come and take you home now?"

Bo watched for the girl's reaction. If there were a problem with the foster parents, if they were involved in whatever had traumatized Janny Malcolm, their culpability would broadcast itself from her body. Maybe just a twitch, a swift compression of the lips, a wild, roaming glance that avoids the question.

"I guess," Janny said with a nervous sigh Bo couldn't interpret. "I'd like to go back there, but what if . . . I mean, it sort of started happening when I was there."

The dark eyes regarded Bo warily.

"They don't know. Bev and Howard. I've been with them for two years now. They're okay. Bev even drives me down to the Goblin, y'know, like last night. She lets me go once or twice a week if I get my homework done. And she lets Bran, that's my boyfriend, she lets him drive me home. But I didn't tell them about this thing that started happening a couple of weeks ago. It's so scary. I was afraid, you know, I was crazy and they wouldn't keep me anymore."

Impulsively Bo leaned over and wrapped an arm under the restraint ties, hugging the girl close. What must it be like, she wondered, to fear both madness and the certainty of abandonment among strangers because of it? No wonder the kid was a wreck.

"Let's try an experiment," she suggested after Janny's sobbing had subsided. "I'm going to unbuckle your wrists and hold your hands while we talk about this thing that's happening to you. Can you manage it?"

"I'm scared," Janny answered, rubbing her wrists after Bo pulled off the cuffs.

"So am I, but let's see what happens. Now . . . a while ago you said, 'Kimmy's gone.' What does that mean?"

"I don't know," the girl answered, shaking her head. "But it's got something to do with this doll, this old doll I've had since I was little. I think the doll must be Kimmy, and it's dead or something. Except I always called my doll Lateesha because that was my friend's name in this one foster home a long time ago. She was black and older than me, and she was really nice. We used to play all the time. She showed me how to make doll clothes with cut-up pieces of cloth and tape. I guess she went back with her mother or something. One day she just left and I never saw her again."

Janny was regressing again, Bo noted. Talking about childhood interests in that high, breathy voice. Talking about a childhood only a foster child knows, in which other people appear and then vanish for inexplicable reasons. A childhood in which nothing may be trusted to remain the same. Bo held the girl's hands firmly and wished orphanages didn't get such bad press. At least in an orphanage a kid could develop a sense of place, a notion of identity.

"So maybe Kimmy's just a new name for Lateesha," she suggested. "Maybe you're growing up a little now, having a boyfriend and dressing up, being a Goth. Maybe calling the doll Kimmy is a way of beginning to stop being a little girl."

The analysis was both shallow and beyond Janny's comprehension, Bo realized, damning herself for indulging in instant psychology.

"No!" Janny wept, shaking. "There wasn't a Kimmy at all until a little while ago, and then all of a sudden there was, and then she was gone. Last night. Last night she wasn't there anymore. And I was supposed to go with her, but I couldn't, and it was like I wasn't anywhere because I couldn't. And it's not Lateesha, it's Kimmy. And I have to keep the doll. I have to keep Kimmy or she'll be like . . . like she was *always* gone, and she wasn't. So I have to . . . I have to . . ."

"Okay," Bo pronounced evenly as Janny clung to her hands, "this is what happens to you, this thing about Kimmy. And it's happening now, and you're still right here in this hospital, in this bed, holding on to me. You're okay. It's weird, but you're okay. And it's scary, but you're still okay. Now, tell me who the Fianna were."

"B-brave Irish warriors. Long, long time ago," Janny answered, relaxing a little.

"And who was the Norse king they fought?"

"Murf-wurf in the big boats."

"How many battles?"

"Lots. They all sound alike."

"They are all alike," Bo grinned as the slender hands loosened their grip. "You know, when I get scared I recite the names of shipwrecks. It works."

"Can I learn something to recite besides these stupid warriors?" Janny smiled shakily, letting go of Bo's hands.

"How about state capitals?"

"Oh, gag! I want 'Famous Vampires.' "

"No way. Too scary. When you're scared you have to have something really dull to calm you down."

"Shipwrecks aren't dull."

"They are if you just say the names and dates."

"Okay. State capitals."

"Excellent!" Bo exhaled, grubbing in her briefcase for a business card. "Here's my number at the office and at home. Call me as soon as you're ready and I'll drill you."

"I'm not so scared now," the girl said thoughtfully. "But I still don't know who Kimmy is, or where she went. You're one of the social workers, right? Then you've seen all kinds of kids. Have you ever seen another kid with something like this happening?"

"I don't know," Bo answered. "But I'm going to think about it. The important thing right now is for you not to be so scared. We'll let Kimmy be a mystery until you can recite *all* the state capitals, okay?"

"I'll try," Janny Malcolm agreed, "but will you, like, ever come to see me or anything? You're, you know, pretty good with this scary, crazy stuff."

"I ought to be," Bo grinned from the door. "And I'll tell you what. If your foster parents agree, you and I will have lunch this weekend, maybe do a little shopping afterward. Today's Thursday. How about Sunday afternoon if you feel up to it?"

"For real?"

"For real."

In the bustling hallway Bo confronted the several rules she had just broken, and didn't care. Something about this case, this terrified girl, felt strangely close in a way she couldn't define. Too close to walk away from.

Near the elevator a small a capella group in Edwardian costume was singing "Rudolph, the Red-Nosed Reindeer" as children in wheelchairs and casts peeked from the doors of their rooms. The song reminded Bo of her new flannel sheets and seemed to suggest a mystical connection to the events of the night before, when the strange dream had frightened her as badly as Janny was frightened of her doll. Bo stopped to listen, to let the symbolism of tiny reindeer flood her consciousness. There was some connection. She could feel it.

"Oh, shit!" she whispered suddenly, jabbing the down button.

Reindeer symbols. Mystical messages. The trappings of mania. She'd lost too much sleep last night, she remembered. And she was under stress because she hadn't sent a single Christmas card or begun her gift-shopping. And Estrella would have her baby within weeks, and Bo was worried about that. Besides, the holidays were hard on everybody. And even under medication just about anything could tip her volatile brain in directions best left unexplored. Like this teenager's delusional experience, which still seemed to hang tauntingly just beyond her reach.

"I'll call my shrink as soon as I get back to the office," she promised the elevator's padded wall. "I see what's happening here."

In the Pathfinder she jammed a tape of Bach's Brandenburg Concerto Number Three in G Major into the tape deck and matched her breathing to the music.

"The *Kate Harding*, 1892," she recited. "The British schooner *Lily*, 1901."

Something was scaring her. But she wasn't sure whether it was an encroaching mania or something else. Something empty and waiting for one last train in a station where no one ever goes.

Chapter 3

On the way back to the office Bo considered the calming exercise she'd given Janny Malcolm. What was the capital of Nevada? Las Vegas? Surely not. Then what about Wyoming? Idaho? Arizona? Blanks everywhere.

You couldn't pass an eighth-grade civics class, Bradley. You're pathetic.

"Es, what's the capital of Arizona?" she asked as she opened her office door. "Also the rest of the western states and Rhode Island."

Estrella Benedict turned her desk chair slowly, even radiantly, Bo thought, toward the door. Always attractive, the younger woman's clear skin had become translucent and glowing in the final months of her pregnancy. And the slower movements demanded by her unaccustomed bulk seemed less awkward than thoughtful.

"We've shared this office for three years and I should be prepared." Estrella grinned, shaking her dark hair recently cut in a sophisticated Sassoon bob. "But I never am. There is simply no way to prepare. You could come through that door and say anything. And it's got to be Phoenix. Why?"

"You'd think I would know that," Bo answered, biting a hangnail as she glanced at the case file on her desk. The cream-colored file folder with its red-orange stripe was new, she noticed. Brand-new. "Malcolm, Janny" had been penned across the stripe.

"Madge is so worried that I'm going to have the baby in my car on the freeway that she's sending you out on a case with me, can you believe it?"

"No," Bo answered, "I can't."

"At least it's close," Estrella went on. "In fact, we can walk."

"You're kidding."

The nation's sixth largest city, San Diego covered hundreds of miles, and as an agency of the county rather than the city, Child Protective Services spread its jurisdictional net hundreds of miles beyond that. In her work Bo had traveled north to the Orange County line, east over mountains into the ancient Sonoran desert, and south to the Mexican border without leaving San Diego County. But despite the marginal nature of the old central San Diego community in which her office building sat behind high chain-link fences, she'd never heard of anybody getting a case there. Probably, she thought, because the neighborhood's predominantly Southeast Asian immigrants hadn't yet acculturated sufficiently to view their children as property.

"It's an apartment on Linda Vista Road across from that Asian supermarket, only four blocks or so. The walk will be fun."

"You only get the Latino cases. How can there be a Spanish-speaking case in this neighborhood?" Bo asked, noticing for the twentieth time that the plaid wool lining of her black trench coat sagged indecorously from a rip along the front placket. She'd bought the coat during her college days in Massachusetts, when black ripstop nylon outerwear had somehow been a profound statement about the absence of basic human rights in countries with no alphabets. Now people born in those countries purchased octopus and strawberry-flavored rice milk at a supermarket three blocks from her office, their rights intact.

"I don't know, but you look like a vagrant in that coat," Estrella added.

Bo knit her brows at the case file on her desk. The case file for a child with a CPS history, a child in foster care. It should be fat, dog-eared, greasy with fingerprints of the many caseworkers and file clerks who would have crammed paperwork into it. It shouldn't be slim and new. Flipping it open with one hand, she saw that it contained nothing but a face sheet. Odd.

"I'm going to get an appropriate, California-type coat during the after-Christmas sales," she reassured her friend. "Don't worry, I'll look smashing at the christening."

The day had already lost its morning chill, but Bo kept her coat buttoned at the chest so that its ripped lining wouldn't show as she and Estrella strolled the neighborhood of prefab military housing built during World War II and later sold to private owners. Each two-apartment wood-frame duplex had been identical to every other when they were built, but over the years porches, carports, awnings, and cement-slab patios had been added to the dilapidated buildings, and native sagebrush grew wild in the tiny yards. An original tidiness had surrendered to the demands of time. Beyond a low fence matted with half-dead geraniums, Bo heard a ratchety, aggressive squawk.

"What in hell?" she blurted, lurching against Estrella, who shook her head.

"El pollo," Estrella laughed, pointing to a large chicken-wire cage hidden behind some towels drying on a low clothesline. Atop the cage was an animal with reddish brown feathers and a territorial attitude.

"Rooster," Bo pronounced. "And those things inside the cage are regular chickens."

"Very good, Bo. Next we identify moo-cows and horsies. Now, the way to tell the difference . . ."

Bo scowled at the rooster, who hopped to the ground and glared beadily from between two towels that said HOLIDAY INN.

"Es, we're in the middle of a city," she said. "There aren't supposed to be farm animals."

"A lot of these people were farmers in Vietnam, Cambodia, Laos. They like their chickens."

Bo imagined the rooster on a Styrofoam tray under shrink-wrap, and sighed as they rounded the corner onto Linda Vista Road, the main thoroughfare. Near a Jack-in-the-Box restaurant a smaller store announced itself with a sign saying HEO QUAY DAT TAT DAI NAAN CHO TOI NHA. For all she knew it could be saying "All hope abandon, ye who enter here." The proprietor, a tiny man in tiny Wrangler jeans and flip-flops, was scrubbing the security bars over the store's front window with soapy water and a hairbrush.

"You know, I've never actually walked around here," Bo observed. "I just drive through, in and out of the office. It's interesting."

"Little Saigon," Estella said. "It's been a neighborhood of immigrants since the military left. First it was Latinos, then people from Southeast Asia. But a few of the Mexican families just stayed. This case we're investigating is one of them. It's nothing serious, just a four-year-old girl who showed up at a daycare center with an odd burn on her back that she refuses to explain. The grandmother's at home with her now."

On the sidewalk ahead of them a Latino man in pressed black chinos and an elaborately patterned sweater talked on a cellular phone as he walked. The hand holding the phone displayed a huge gold ring set in flashing diamonds.

"Dealer or pimp?" Bo asked conversationally.

"Dealer."

"How can you tell?"

Estrella smiled at a young Chinese woman pushing twin baby boys in a double stroller. The man with the telephone, his conversation concluded, stopped and dropped to one knee to make cooing noises at the twins in Spanish.

"Pimps don't flash cellular phones on the street," Estrella answered, her gaze lingering on the plump baby boys in their quilted Chinese jackets. "But the pants are the giveaway."

"Pants?"

"Yeah. The black chinos with the knife-edge crease. Years ago those were part of the uniform of a Latino gang called *Los Brujos*, 'The Magicians.' As teenagers *Los Brujos* worked as drug runners for some small-time Mafia clones. Then they grew up, ousted the clones, and took over the business of supplying drugs to the children of their own people. Some of them still wear the black chinos."

"Like a school tie," Bo observed. "An old boys' network."

Estrella had wrapped both arms over her bulging abdomen. "More like a warning," she replied. "Those pants let other drug dealers know that a *Brujo* is working the territory. It isn't wise to mess with them. They kill their competition."

Bo admired the clearing sky through the bare limbs of a sycamore tree in the grassy median between Linda Vista Road and the fronting residential street called Morley.

"How do you know all these things, Es? You're a walking encyclopedia."

"I have a brother," Estrella answered, checking the face sheet in her case file for the address.

"So?"

"So it's that brown and yellow duplex over there, the one without a screen door. And my brother got involved with *Los Brujos* when he was only fourteen. He got in trouble with the police. My father was working as a foreman on a big avocado ranch up north, making good money, but he came home to handle 'Berto—Roberto, that's my brother's name. But the gang wouldn't let go of him, made threats, beat him up. Once they threw a brick through our living-room window with one of those glow-in-the-dark plastic skulls you can buy around Halloween taped to it. That meant Roberto was going to die. I was only eight at the time."

"My God, Es, what happened?"

"My father made arrangements for 'Berto to go and live with relatives in Mexico, in Zacatecas. They were very poor and even though my parents sent money, 'Berto had to work. Everybody works there; it's a hard life. He stayed for four years, dropped out of school, married a local girl who was pregnant with his child when he was eighteen. A year later he came back, but the girl and my niece whom I've never seen stayed there. She's seventeen now. She's going to graduate from high school this spring."

Bo watched as a city bus stopped to pick up a white-haired woman who looked like Lady Baden-Powell. Three years in the same office, she thought, and she didn't know Estrella Benedict, her best friend, at all.

"You never told me all this about your brother, Es. Why not? You know all about my sister's suicide, my manic depression, my scurrilous love life before Andy, everything. Why didn't you . . . ?"

Estrella steered Bo toward the brown and yellow duplex.

"It's not the same," she sighed. "You're white. You're from a nice family in Boston. Your mother played the *violin*. Nobody looks at you in restaurants and wonders if you're going to steal the ashtrays or skip out on the bill. I just didn't want you to know."

"Know what?" Bo said, unbuttoning her coat and angrily ripping off a two-foot swath of the loose lining. "That after all this time you don't trust me?"

Estrella took the wool plaid fabric from Bo's hand and stuffed it into her purse.

"Okay, my brother wears cowboy boots and a hairnet and thinks he's *muy macho*," she said, looking straight ahead. "He divorced the girl in Mexico, never went back to school, works occasionally at car washes and Mexican fast-food joints in Los Angeles, where he lives with a woman he's never married but with whom he's fathered five children he doesn't support. She and the kids live on welfare and money my sister and I send. He drinks too much and when he's feeling really *macho* he breaks her ribs. She throws him out and a month later he's back. It's been going on for years. He doesn't hit the kids, or I'd call CPS in Los Angeles and turn him in myself, and he knows it. My brother is a worthless, abusive loser and I'm ashamed of him. Now do you feel trusted?"

"I'm sorry, Es," Bo answered, feeling too tall, too pale, too fluent in English, and too privileged to be standing under a small coral tree in front of a shabby duplex with a child's construction-paper wreath taped to the door. "I just didn't want to be . . . left out."

"Well, now you're not," Estrella sighed and held Bo's arm for balance as they climbed three sagging wooden steps to the small porch of the duplex.

"Bueno?" said a round woman in red nylon stirrup pants and a pink sequined sweatshirt as she opened the door. Behind her Bo could see a little girl wearing a dress and sweater over green corduroy pants that were too big for her, playing on the floor with a grimy blond Barbie doll. Estrella and the woman conversed animatedly in Spanish as Bo settled into a fake fur beanbag chair that had once been purple but was now faded on top to a mottled gray. From her vantage point near the floor Bo had to look up to see the other two women seated on a couch and silhouetted against the window which faced the porch. The perspective, she thought, provided a comfortable distance from a conversation of which she couldn't comprehend a word.

"Sí, gracias," Estrella said after a while, and then said something to the little girl which caused her to remove her sweater and lean over her Barbie doll with her head touching the floor.

Bo watched as Estrella unbuttoned the back of the girl's dress and then took a Polaroid picture of the child's bare back. The faint marks visible there looked less like burns than scratches to Bo. Scratches that made a sort of design, like the branch of a tree laid vertically against the child's spine.

"Ask her if she and her friends have been playing tag with sticks," Bo said to Estrella.

The little girl sat up and eyed Bo with contempt. "She doesn't have to ask me that. I can understand English. What's tag?"

"It's where you catch somebody by chasing them and touching them. After you touch them, they're caught," Bo explained.

"I don't play that," the child said softly. "I play dolls. Lai has a doll just like this one, only her brother cut its hair off. Her brother is Chu. He's in first grade."

Lai and Chu. Bo shot Estrella a wide-eyed look of sudden comprehension and silently mouthed a single syllable. "Hmong." Pronounced "Mung," it was the name of an ancient people displaced from the mountains of Vietnam by a war that had nothing to do with them. As refugees many Hmong had come to the United States. A considerable number had wound up in San Diego and settled in this neighborhood near countrymen they would never have seen in their homeland. A Stone Age people, the Hmong had kept to themselves in the mountains of Southeast Asia. And had kept alive certain ancient traditions honoring the mystical connection between humankind and nature. One of these involved pressing a heated branch against the back of a child to mark that child's connection to natural forces and to bring the child luck. Madge had insisted that her entire unit attend a multicultural in-service on Hmong practices less than a month ago. For once, Bo acknowledged, Madge had been right.

"Are Lai and Chu your best friends?" Estrella asked, launching the gentle interrogation which would reveal an interesting dimension of the neighborhood's cultural mix.

"Lai is my friend," the girl answered wearily. "Chu is a *boy*." The blinding ignorance of adults to an immutable social reality filled her voice with scorn.

"Of course," Estrella grinned. "Sometimes I'm really dumb about things. But I'll bet you and Lai have lots of fun sharing secrets and playing, don't you?"

Bo accepted a glass of warm tea from the child's grandmother and settled back to await the end of the story, which would involve a child of an ancient Asian tribe scratching a secret tree design on the back of a Latina child "for luck." The scratches marked a friendship, not a crime. Bo wished that Janny Malcolm's case could be resolved as easily, whatever Janny Malcolm's case was.

What about the strange teenager had upset Madge Aldenhoven enough to prompt an unprecedented infraction of rules? Bo stifled a yawn as Estrella continued her interview. An electric space heater near the kitchen door switched on every four minutes, blowing warm air against the side of Bo's face. The heat was making her sleepy, and to avoid unprofessionally nodding off in the home of a client, Bo focused on details of Estrella's silhouette against the window. She was relieved when a man appeared on the porch and passed in front of the window. It was something to think about, a way to stay awake. The postman maybe, or a resident of the adjoining duplex. Except there was something familiar about him. His sweater. One of those intricately patterned sweaters invariably worn by men who also wore ostentatious gold jewelry. It was the *Brujo* they'd seen on the street!

Loud knocking on the adjacent door resulted in its opening, followed by angry words in Spanish and then an Asian dialect. The conversation was audible through the wall dividing the duplexes. Bo watched as alarm spread over the faces of Estrella, the girl, and the grandmother. Then in a practiced series of movements the older woman ran to lock the deadbolt on the front door, pulled the child to her feet, and dragged her through the kitchen into a bedroom, closing the door behind them. As the voices beyond the wall fell to lower, more menacing tones, Bo saw Estrella go pale and start to stand, then notice the window behind her and fling herself back onto the couch on her side. Her knees were pulled up, her whole body wrapped protectively around her abdomen. Suddenly it all made sense to Bo.

"The baby!" she yelled, scrambling out of the beanbag chair and flinging herself across Estrella as a deafening blast sent a cloud of wallboard and white dust against the ceiling. A second blast came from the porch, followed by a sickening thump. Then desperate movements from the adjoining duplex, the sound of someone running, silence. It had all happened, Bo calculated, in less than ten seconds. Estrella was sobbing.

"It's okay, Es," Bo said over the pounding of her own heart. "One of them's on the porch, probably shot. He's not moving. The other one ran."

"*Don't* go out there," Estrella whispered as Bo raised her head to peek out the window. "Just call the police and then stay away from the window until they take him away. There could be more shooting. Stay down and get to a phone."

As Bo dropped to the floor she noticed that the Barbie doll's hair was full of glass from the shattered TV screen, and that her own black coat was filmed in white dust. For a moment she felt ghostly, as if in fact she'd really been shot and was now dead but hadn't yet realized it. It could happen that way, she thought. Like a dream in which you believe you've gotten up and dressed and ready for work, only to waken to the fact that your mind has tricked you, you're still in bed, and you're going to be late. Maybe after you're dead your mind dreams the next moments you would have had, she thought. Maybe your mind stretches the illusion of your life until the last oxygen is exhausted from the last brain cell, and then the illusion fades into darkness.

"Es, am I dead?" she yelled from all fours, panic making her voice crack.

Estrella heard it and slid off the couch to the floor.

"No, but you're probably in mild shock," she said softly. "You must've been psychic or something right before it happened. You couldn't have understood the Spanish when the *Brujo* said 'If you shoot me you're a dead man,' but you seemed to know what was coming and you tried to protect me and the baby. We appreciate it, Bo, and we love you. So just relax until the shock wears off, okay? Somebody else will have called the police. Just relax."

"Es, if two gunshots can send me over the edge, what does a lifetime of this do to little kids? Little kids who live with it every day?"

"Maybe they think they're dead, too," Estrella replied through tears as a siren wailed and then stopped beyond the locked door.

"Call the medical examiner," a male voice announced noncommittally, "this guy's a goner."

Standing to look out the window, Bo and Estrella saw the *Brujo* crumpled on the steps, his sweater soaked with blood. The sound of the back door slamming indicated that the girl and her grandmother had left to avoid involvement with the police. It seemed like a good idea to Bo.

"Let's get out of here before it's too late," she suggested. "I'll call Dar from the office and tell him we were here. If the investigating officers need us, we'll talk to them later."

"You're on," Estrella agreed, wincing as she headed for the back door. "I'm really feeling funny, Bo. Maybe I'm just upset, but I'm having these twinges. . . ."

"Oh, my God!"

Grabbing her CPS ID badge from her pocket, Bo opened

the front door and held the badge before her. Just a plastic card on a clip, it lacked a certain verve, she thought.

"Bo Bradley, CPS," she growled authoritatively at the uniformed cop. "My partner and I were interviewing a client here when the shooting occurred next door. No one in this duplex was injured, but my partner is almost nine months pregnant and needs to be transported to a hospital now! The shock may have brought on—"

"Oh, jeez," the chunky, bespectacled cop murmured as his rosy cheeks turned pale. "This is a crime scene; witnesses have to remain for interrogation. But she's going to have a *baby?*"

"Well, she's not going to have a chrysanthemum," Bo replied, noticing that one of the cop's lug-soled boots stood in a pool of darkening blood. "And we walked here, so we'll need a squad car to transport her."

"Lady, I can't just order that. You'll have to call an ambulance. We're not running a taxi service here. We've got a homicide to investigate."

Bo looked at his name tag. WM. BEADER, it said. No rank. Meaning Bill Beader was a rookie working out of the storefront SDPD Community Relations Office across Linda Vista Road. That's how he'd gotten there so fast.

"Beader," Bo intoned, "you're looking at either a commendation for close cooperation with Child Protective Services or a write-up for failing to come to the aid of another law-enforcement officer in distress. Either one will stay in your record forever, but that second one will chain your career to a desk because no cop in the world will work on the streets with a guy who puts procedure before helping one of his own. You choose."

"Get her in the car," he sighed, gesturing to the black-and-white at the curb. "I'll drive her myself as soon as the homicide guys get here."

Bo cocked an ear at the sound of sirens howling up Linda Vista Road.

"They're here," she noted. "Es, what hospital?"

"Mercy," Estrella answered, her face pale. "Bo, I think this might be for real!"

"Oh, jeez," Bo and the young cop breathed in unison, then helped Estrella down the steps and through the crowd to the squad car.

"Lights and sirens," Bo insisted from the steel-caged back seat.

"No kidding," Bill Beader replied, and took off as if vampires were at his back.

Chapter 4

On the tarmac at San Diego's Lindbergh Field, an American Airlines commuter flight from Los Angeles International Airport concluded its thirty-minute low-altitude cruise just off the California shoreline. The passengers, mostly tourists and businesspeople, exited the plane through the jetway. Within three minutes none could have described the color of the plane's upholstery or remembered the row in which they'd sat. None noticed how closely the flight crew watched them deboard. And none knew that the ground crew unloading baggage below was waiting for one of two coded messages: "Move before unloading cadaver" or "Wait fifteen minutes, unload cadaver at this gate." If procedures went smoothly, as they did at hundreds of airports every day, the passengers would never know that they had flown in the company of a dead body.

Optimally, the plane would be moved to another gate for the unloading of the unobtrusive but carefully secured cardboard box. That way if a passenger from the flight remained in the gate area and happened to glimpse the unloading through a window, he or she would assume the body had been on a different plane. Nothing the airlines industry tried had succeeded in persuading baggage handlers to treat these necessary shipments as they would treat any other parcel. Something in the strong, young people employed at this vigorous work seemed to insist on respectful ritual. They would shoulder the box as if it were actually a coffin, go to extraordinary lengths to pad and brace it on the transport trailer, remove their caps, make religious gestures, even pray over it. And if these behaviors were witnessed by a passenger who'd just flown on that plane, there could be trouble. Because even the most rational people, the industry had learned, are made uncomfortable by confinement in an enclosed space with the dead. And this discomfort may find expression retroactively in diminished ticket sales. It was a long-standing industry rule that passengers must never know the nature of certain cargo with which they might be traveling.

Today the plane was not moved. The box from a Los Angeles mortician was unloaded and transported without notice to the unmarked van of a San Diego mortician, parked at an assigned space inside the baggage area. The baggage crew, having waited uneasily the fifteen minutes presumed necessary to clear the gate area of deboarding passengers, were as usual relieved when the mortician's van joined the stream of outgoing airport traffic. A sad and vaguely scary responsibility was out of their hands.

Twenty minutes later the van's driver, also an embalmer and cosmetologist, pushed a remote control and backed into the garage of a mid-city mortuary. Then he quickly closed the garage door behind him. He'd worked for a number of these establishments in his sixty years. It was always important to keep the doors closed.

After sliding the box from the van onto a gurney, he wheeled it into the cold room without turning on the light, set the brake on the gurney, and went out back for a smoke. The body had been embalmed in Los Angeles, so there was nothing much to do except the clothes and makeup. And that had to wait until the family or whoever was responsible came over with clothes and a picture or description he could use. He enjoyed the work and knew he was good at it, even though it wasn't something people liked to hear about.

Reentering the garage through a side door, he checked the orders pinned to a cork bulletin board by the mortuary's owner/director, who only came in for the big funerals. Most of the time the owner played golf with a cellular phone on his belt for business calls.

Private service to be held tomorrow noon. Economy casket. No public announcements, no press of any kind. All inquiries must be referred to me. Do not confirm identity of deceased to press or any outside inquiry. Expenses to be covered by private individuals Aldenhoven and Mandeer. Burial immediately after service in Mt. Hope Cemetery. Aldenhoven will be by after five with clothes.

The driver grinned happily. Plenty of time to catch a matinee of that new sci-fi movie, the one about mutant insects from the future coming through computers. He'd be back well before five.

Twenty miles from the mortuary Daniel Man Deer stood in a narrow canyon on the south face of Fortuna Mountain, staring at the dried excrement of a large animal. The scat contained the usual mouse fur as well as the longer and more substantial fur of a mule deer. He knew that the deer carcass was probably somewhere north of Highway 52 on the vast expanse of land still owned by the military, off limits to human animals. But not, he judged from the segmented shape of the scat, to the feline variety. The scat had been left in the middle of a "corridor" he'd suspected was the path of a bobcat, and now he knew. The next task would be planning a method for keeping the cat alive.

Through prescription sunglasses Man Deer scanned the ground for the sheen of old metal that might indicate the presence of unexploded ordnance. The park had been used as a weapons training area during World War II, then neglected by the military for a half century. Now a fifty-three-hundred-acre regional park only eight miles from bustling downtown San Diego, the wild gorges rising from the San Diego River still held the threat of explosives manufactured to stop Hitler's Reich. Seeing nothing suspicious, he eased his muscular six-foot-two-inch frame to the ground and thought about death. About the dead.

In nature, he acknowledged, death demanded nothing beyond itself. The mule deer had undoubtedly been ill, injured, or old, and quickly killed, probably by coyotes. The presence of the deer's pelt in the bobcat's waste indicated that the cat had not been the first to feed on the carcass. The first predators invariably claimed the protein-rich liver and other internal organs, leaving the rest for latecomers. The deer had simply taken its place in the food chain without prolonged suffering or unnecessary trauma.

But human death was another matter entirely. Human death required honor and ritual and devices for the protection of the living from its unknowable realities. Realities which might transgress the boundary between living and dead if not controlled. Daniel Man Deer knew all about that from a shattering moment in his past. Nodding slightly, he sighed and accepted the fact that it might be happening again. He wasn't sure, but he had a feeling about what had wakened Mary last night. What had made her scream in terror and then cling to him in the dark.

It occurred to Daniel Man Deer that this crisis might be the reason for the changes that had come over him in the last two years. His early retirement at fifty-eight from a long and lucrative career in the mortgage industry. Reclaiming the old Kumeyaay spelling of his surname even though Mary thought it was ridiculous and refused to change *her* name from the anglicized "Mandeer" to the Indian "Man Deer." Maybe this crisis had necessitated his dogged research into the Indian life which had belonged to his grandfather, Jeremiah Man Deer, a San Diego dockworker who'd unloaded freighters for fifteen dollars a week until he was beaten to death by a gang of drunken young midshipmen in Navy whites.

Dan had never known his grandfather, but he did now. Beneath the forest-green polo shirt of the Mission Trails Regional Park volunteer, he wore a chipped stone on a leather cord. A stone from the river gorge below him where his ancestors had lived for over ten thousand years before the arrival of the Spanish. In his heart he felt he knew these vanished ones, and he would honor them by protecting the wild things still roaming with their spirits on the land. In exchange, they would show him the way to protect Mary from the unhappy spirit that might be reaching toward her from the land of the dead. They would help him. And he would be ready.

In a gray silence falling over the canyon he recognized the coming rain and smiled. Like the hundred-and-fifty-million-year-old Santiago peaks towering over the river gorge, he belonged there. A little rain couldn't change that.

Chapter 5

Pewter-colored clouds had gathered in cottony towers as Bo folded herself into Madge Aldenhoven's car in front of Mercy Hospital. Backlit by the sun through ragged patches of blue, the clouds seemed gilded. Bo would not have been surprised if Renaissance angels playing herald trumpets had appeared between them. The image was another reminder that she hadn't sent a single Christmas card.

"What's the status of Estrella's condition?" Madge asked with characteristic precision.

"Braxton Hicks contractions, not the real thing, so my godchild isn't likely to make a debut today," Bo answered. "But there's a problem with Es's blood pressure. Her doctor wants her to stay in the hospital until some tests are in. Then she wants her to stay home until the baby's born. I'm afraid she went ballistic when we told her what happened today, the gunshots and all. Doctors can be so overbearing—"

"Estrella's doctor is quite right in advising her to stay home," Madge interrupted, tight-lipped. "This work is dangerous. I don't think you understand how dangerous it can be."

A large raindrop hit Madge's windshield, creating a shape in the surface dust that reminded Bo of a blood platelet. The supervisor's voice was tremulous with emotion. Anger, Bo thought. Or fear.

"What happened today was a fluke." She shrugged, running both hands through her graying auburn curls. "Too many men running around with guns. People get shot in shopping centers, parks, their own cars stopped at traffic lights. What I can't figure is how you knew Es would run into trouble, how you knew to send me out with her. Let's face it, two investigators on one case is a bit irregular."

"I didn't know," Madge said, carefully steering the car onto the old Cabrillo Highway which transected the heart of San Diego from north to south. "I was simply worried about Estrella's vulnerability. She should have taken a leave of absence months ago."

"Umm," Bo replied neutrally as they drove beneath the ornate Laurel Street Bridge in Balboa Park. During the holidays the bridge was strung with amber lights, creating a dreamlike atmosphere Bo associated with Venice, even though she'd never seen Venice. The glowing bridge reminded her again that time for shopping was diminishing by the minute. As yet she had no gift for Andy, nothing for Estrella and Henry or Eva Broussard, her shrink. No thoughtful little tokens for coworkers or the neighbor who cared for Molly every day.

"The truth is," she sighed dramatically over the swoosh-thump of Madge's windshield wipers, "I'm feeling a little shaky myself, now that the excitement's over. Maybe it would be best if I took the afternoon off, got away from things for a few hours."

"Of course," Madge agreed without adding the usual lecture on professional commitment. "I'll close Estrella's case and transfer the Malcolm girl over to foster care. Perhaps you should call your psychiatrist, too. I'm sure a violent experience like this can be, er, can present difficulties for someone with your, um, problem."

Wow, Madge, well put! Any more delicacy and even I wouldn't have known what you were talking about.

"That's thoughtful of you, Madge," Bo said sweetly. "But you know, I just don't feel comfortable closing the Malcolm case until I've at least had a chance to talk with the foster parents. The girl was pretty decompensated last night; they put her in restraints. In the event that this case goes back to juvenile court for a placement change or something in the future, the record isn't going to look very good if it doesn't show a thorough investigation of the situation."

Against the black steering wheel Madge's knuckles showed bone.

"I assume by 'decompensated' you mean hysterical," she said.

"'Hysteria' actually means 'wandering womb,'" Bo grinned, sinking into her coat collar. "Until recently the male medical establishment was sure that moodiness in women was caused by unmoored uteruses floating around like empty potato-chip bags in a park pond. Now they're embarrassed and don't use the term much. And 'decompensated' means psychiatrically fragile, having trouble assessing reality. Janny Malcolm was frightened of something, thrashing around, at times not able to assess quite where she was or what was going on. But I don't think—"

"What was she frightened of?" Madge interrupted, the planes of her face oddly prominent beneath pale, papery skin.

"It's hard to say," Bo hedged instinctively. "That's why I want to talk to the foster parents. You know how the press has been lately, claiming CPS just transfers kids around in the system without really checking on them. I think we should cover our tail on this one."

"In case the girl has a problem which will require a more secure environment, more professional care," Madge said, completing some thought of her own. "I agree, but have that file on my desk before the end of the day tomorrow. It will be

Friday. I don't want the case to remain open over the weekend, beyond the forty-eight-hour investigatory period. Any longer than that and it automatically goes back to court. Let's avoid that."

"Roger," Bo answered, feigning interest in two ragged men searching in the rain for recyclable trash in the ice plant bordering the freeway off-ramp. "Do you have any idea how long Janny's been in foster care? I haven't looked at the file yet, but it's pretty thin. Is she new?"

Madge floored the accelerator and made the left turn off Genesee Avenue onto Linda Vista Road as the yellow traffic-light arrow turned red. In the rainswept gloom Bo was sure she saw tears swimming in the supervisor's violet eyes.

"The name sounds familiar," Madge said tersely. "But I don't know the details."

Bo had been lied to by child molesters, drug addicts, and sadists in the course of her job with Child Protective Services. And she'd known each time. She could pinpoint a lie at the moment it was spoken. When Estrella had asked how she did it, how she knew, Bo had only been able to explain it in her own terms.

"This is going to sound crazy," she'd told Estrella, "but it's this feeling. A feeling that smells *blue*. It's like a flash of blue that I feel behind my nose."

This one, she thought, had been a sort of aquamarine. But why was Madge lying about Janny Malcolm?

"I appreciate your coming over to Mercy to get me," she said politely as Madge swerved into the CPS parking lot.

"I do the best I can," Madge answered with a tremolo of emotion Bo sensed had nothing to do with Mercy Hospital, Estrella, herself, or anything else in the immediate frame of reference.

"Of course," she smiled supportively, trying not to recall the several times Madge had urged the Department of Social

Services to free Bo Bradley from its employ. "I'll see you to-morrow."

Hurrying into the building, Bo grabbed Janny Malcolm's case file from her desk and ignored the pink phone memos stacked beside it. They were inevitably a snare from which responsibility would permit no escape. Best not to look at them.

Fifteen minutes later she was safely inside the ritziest department store in Fashion Valley, the central San Diego shopping mall closest to her office, admiring Christmas decorations so tasteful they barely condescended to be red and green. More like deep maroon coupled with a color that looked like moonlight on a lodgepole pine. Bo inhaled deeply and prepared to enjoy herself.

For Madge, the other workers in her unit, and the clerical staff she bought apples on painted sticks, covered in Belgian chocolate and crushed hazelnuts, wrapped in red cellophane and tied with little gingham napkins. Next she selected a washable wool couch throw in a MacAlister tartan she hoped wouldn't show Molly's red dachshund hairs, for the little dog's elderly caretaker. Estrella and Henry, she decided, would soon need reminders of the romance that had brought a noisy and demanding newcomer into their home. Embroidered silk sheets in a creamy ecru against which Estrella's dark hair and skin tones would show to advantage. Grinning impishly, she handed the clerk her credit card. Es would never buy anything this extravagant for her own home. It was perfect.

"I'm sorry, but there seems to be a problem with your card," the clerk said cheerfully. "Would you mind waiting while I check on it?"

"Um, it may be maxed out," Bo said, chagrined. She'd just mailed in a sizable payment against her balance, but the transaction probably hadn't been processed yet. The previous two purchases had pushed her available credit to its unimpressive limit. "I'll just write a check."

Time for Plan B, Bradley. Let's face it, that last little manicky spending spree involving the custom-upholstered recliner wiped you out. SAY NO TO SHOPPING!

A month ago she'd gone with Estrella and Henry to a furniture store to help them pick out a comfortable rocker for the anticipated cuddling and three A.M. feedings. But their selection had fit Bo so perfectly, its reclining back and lumbar support felt so good, that she'd ordered one for herself. And she'd been mesmerized by the selection of custom fabric selections displayed for her by a salesman in, she remembered, a bolo tie. The chair's delivery had caused a row with Andy, who regarded it as evidence that she would never move in with him rather than what it was—a typically manicky overindulgence. Now it was near Christmas and she had no extra money for gifts. The chair clearly represented everything about her that needed work, she thought, but so what? It was the most comfortable piece of furniture she'd ever owned, and she loved it.

"A check will be fine," the clerk said, "as long as it's from a local bank and you can show a California driver's license."

"Do you know the capital of Montana?" Bo countered, showing her CPS ID instead of her driver's license just to rattle the woman.

"Helena. And thank you so much, Ms. Bradley. Merry Christmas."

Clerks in ritzy department stores, she realized, could not be rattled.

The sky was already clearing as she strolled past a towering tree of poinsettias in the center of the outdoor mall. A haggard mother in a belted trench coat was trying to photograph the tree as a little girl pulled on the hem of the coat.

"I want to see the dolls," the child whined, pointing to a specialty shop Bo hadn't noticed before. "Puh-lease. You *said . . .*"

The shop's facade recalled elegant, old-fashioned stores in which Dickens might have shopped. A paned window with fake frost. Coachlights beside the door. Polished brass doorknob and kickplate. From hidden speakers the strains of "God

Rest Ye, Merry Gentlemen" could be heard, played by a brass choir. Enchanted, Bo wandered closer to admire the window display where animated elves moved about in a miniature workshop. Sharing the window with the elves was a profusion of dolls.

Bo identified Raggedy Ann and Andy, Howdy Doody, the cast of *Little Women,* and the Pillsbury Doughboy before her attention was captured by a splendid baby doll in a white basket tucked under a twinkling Christmas tree. Made of bisque porcelain, the doll's detailing was remarkable. And its pug nose oddly familiar. Bo shouldered her way into the crowded shop with a sudden sense of foreboding.

"The baby doll in the window," she said when a harried clerk approached, "the one in the basket. Is this some kind of special doll? It's so beautifully made."

"That's Johanna," the clerk replied as if the name explained everything. "A collectible. Would you like to see her?"

"Yes," Bo said, feeling dizzy.

She hadn't played with dolls even as a child because they'd scared her. Something about their stillness had made her feel uncomfortable, as if they masked another dimension that existed only when she turned her back. Now she felt the glassy stares of a thousand eyes as the baby doll was placed in her hands.

"She's one of a numbered edition," the clerk went on. "Only two thousand are made for Christmas each year and then the mold is broken. You can see the edition number stamped on the back of the neck. Why don't you let me put your packages behind the counter so you can look at her closely. But be careful. We only get one each year, and she's quite valuable."

"How valuable?" Bo asked as her bulky packages were whisked to safety.

"Five hundred and ninety-five dollars, excluding tax."

Bo whistled softly and tightened her grip on the doll's torso, soft beneath a smocked white pinafore over pink pantaloons. On the doll's feet were lace-edged white socks and pink satin booties. In the wispy dark hair was a pink satin ribbon.

"The wig's synthetic," the clerk explained. "The less expensive collectibles use the synthetic hair."

"*Less* expensive?"

"Oh, some of the European collectibles range into the thousands, use human hair individually set in wax, real baby teeth, all sorts of things. Doll collecting is as old as the human race, you know. There's always a market, especially for the really lifelike ones."

Turning the doll over, Bo tugged at the pinafore's ruffled collar and saw "293" stamped in the porcelain of its neck. In an arc above the number were the words "Palm Valley, CA." Beneath the number were the initials "J.M." She could feel the doll's bright glass eyes looking at her shoes. It didn't particularly like her shoes.

"Thank you so much," Bo said breathlessly, her eyes roving the store for something less threatening than the object in her hands. At the end of an aisle she saw a display of Barbies, their identically vapid smiles strangely comforting. "Oh, there are the Barbies!"

"Of course you've heard of the Palm Valley Doll Works," the clerk mentioned as she placed Johanna back in her basket. "One of the oldest California factories."

Bo had scurried to the aisle display, which included a bearded Ken doll that could be shaved, as well as a convertible, doll house with pool, and beauty salon.

"Um, no," she said over her shoulder. "Hey, is this a Latina Barbie?"

"That's Barbie's friend, Theresa," the clerk explained. "And she is a Latina. Such a shame, isn't it, that these dolls are so popular when there's workmanship like this one from Palm Valley?"

Bo grabbed the dark-haired Theresa doll and quickly

picked out horseback riding and nurse costumes from a selection including, she noted with distaste, cheerleader and exotic dancer outfits as well. A little girl whose neighbors shot holes in her life was going to get a new doll.

"I'll take these," she told the clerk. "Gift-wrapped, please."

"I probably shouldn't tell you this," the clerk said confidentially as she ran Bo's credit card without incident, "but Johanna may become very valuable if the dollmaker retires this year. He's quite elderly now, and this is his signature doll. This one may be the last."

Bo couldn't tell if the trembling in her shoulders was the result of relief at safely exceeding her credit limit or a foreboding that seemed to resonate from the clerk's words. A sense of old and terrible drama racing toward her like a train in a subterranean tunnel. The clerk was taking forever to wrap Bo's purchases in peppermint-striped paper.

"He still lives here, you know," the woman went on. "He has a studio in his home and designs the prototype there, although the dolls are made at the factory in Palm Valley. They buy the design from him."

The porcelain doll watched Bo from its basket on the counter, its legs bent at the knee in perfect imitation of a very young baby. Its upper lip, even though smiling, projected over the lower one, and its brows and lashes were painted with a feathery realism that made Bo's heart pound.

"Those initials, J.M.?" the clerk concluded as if she were party to an insider stock trade, "that's Jasper Malcolm, one of the last master dollmakers in this country. Not very many people know he's right here in San Diego."

Malcolm. Bo stared as a breeze from the opening door ruffled the doll's hair, creating the illusion of movement. It almost seemed as if the doll had nodded, and then abruptly returned to its inanimate state. Abruptly become nothing more than a doll in a crowded and too brightly lit shop. The lights were giving Bo a headache.

It was always just a doll, Bradley. You're tired. Go home, take your meds, call your shrink. Don't think about the name Malcolm. Don't think about Janny's doll. Just take your Barbie and run!

Safely inside her car, Bo turned the radio to a Country and Western station and sang "Desperado" at the top of her lungs until she reached the little duplex where there was now a hole in the living room wall.

"*Feliz Navidad,*" she said to the grandmother, extending the brightly wrapped package and then leaving quickly.

There was nothing more she could do for that child, nothing more she could do for any of them. Like every child abuse worker, she knew better than to try. But Janny Malcolm's case was different. Janny Malcolm's case was unlike anything she'd seen before.

Heading west into the sun toward home, Bo decided to call Eva and then spend the rest of the afternoon making her own Christmas cards as an economy measure. It would be fun, she thought. If only she could get the image of an empty, waiting subway station out of her mind.

Chapter 6

At home Bo gathered Molly from her caretaker and took the little dog for a walk along the beach. Then she curled comfortably around Molly atop her rumpled bed and drifted near sleep. The sound of canine teeth gnawing on a rawhide pretzel was comforting, she thought. The soft crunching provided a barrier against eerie dreams.

Two hours later she awoke refreshed and took stock of her life. It appeared to be working. As long as she could have stretches of time like this, time absolutely alone, her life would work. As long as she could take naps or stay up until three A.M. painting, as long as people weren't standing around expecting her to be polite or even to talk, as long as she didn't have to conform to any reality but her own, she could make it through anything. On the beige Formica kitchen counter her answering machine flashed the usual threat to her composure. Its tiny red light was blinking furiously, a record of the calls Bo hadn't heard because she'd turned the ringer and voice monitor off. Carefully folding a terrycloth dishtowel into a thick square, she placed it over the blinking light. Then she took a carrot from the refrigerator and rummaged through her utility closet for art supplies. The card stock was a little bent, but it would do. And the carrot's shape was perfect.

In minutes she'd cut the heavy white paper into postcard-sized rectangles with an X-Acto knife. After painting each card in swirls of blue acrylic with a band of black at the top, she sliced the carrot in half lengthwise and cut a raised design into it using a single-edge razor blade broken into pieces. The design was of a rough pier, its perspective stretched to the artist's "vanishing point" by the shape of the vegetable. After rubbing white acrylic on the design with her thumb, she pressed the carrot diagonally against each painted card. What emerged was a white pier stretching from an invisible shore to a night horizon obscured in darkness. A style somewhere between Munch and de Chirico, she decided. The only light seemed to emanate from the pier itself.

"Joy in your journey," she penned in white ink across the lower right expanse of blue. "Bo."

Fifty hand-painted Christmas cards for the price of a carrot. And she could send them at postcard rate. Feeling righteously frugal, Bo dried the cards briefly in the oven and then sprayed them with a clear varnish that would keep the paint from chipping in the mail. She wasn't sure she actually knew fifty people, but the cards were too interesting not to send. Maybe she'd just go through the phone book and mail the extras out at random, she thought. Total strangers would spend the rest of their lives wondering who "Bo" was. The thought was intriguing. She wasn't absolutely sure who Bo was, either.

"Eva," she said without preamble when the psychiatrist answered Bo's call on the second ring, "I had a dream last night that wasn't mine. And I'm afraid it's got something to do with a new case involving a teenager who carries a doll. Her name's Janny Malcolm, and apparently there's a famous dollmaker in San Diego who's also named Malcolm. And I'm sure Madge is hiding something about the case. Are you busy?"

"In a broad sense, yes," Eva Broussard answered, her Canadian French accent lending a sense of drama to the ordinary words. "There are some developments in my research that are rather exciting, but nothing imminent. I'm glad you called. Mrs. Aldenhoven contacted me earlier. She seemed to feel that you were under a great deal of stress due to a shooting incident this morning. You didn't mention that."

Bo knit her reddish eyebrows into a rumpled line she could feel at the top of her nose. Any contact with other people invariably brought this exhausting web of complexity and manipulation, she acknowledged. Being a hermit was so much easier.

"Eva, Madge hasn't cared if I lived or died since I took that job. Now suddenly she's calling my shrink to express her *concern*? Give me a break. She's setting it up to get me off this case by documenting a call to my psychiatrist about my job-related stress."

"I suspected it was something like that," Eva Broussard noted dismissively. "Of course I told her I wasn't at liberty to discuss any of my clients or, indeed, to verify my professional relationship with any individual. But I am interested in your dream and the doll, not to mention the shooting. Are you feeling all right?"

"I took a nap," Bo nodded at the phone. "Then I made Christmas cards. I feel fine, except there's something about that dream. . . ."

"How about dinner?" the psychiatrist suggested. "We could meet at a little Italian restaurant down the hill from here in La Mesa. It's in a shopping center off Avocado. Donato's. My treat."

"Let me check something," Bo said, stretching the phone cord to grab Janny Malcolm's case file from the recliner in the apartment's small living room. The foster parents' address was in Lemon Grove, a community west of Eva's high desert compound in Jamul and adjacent to La Mesa. "I'll meet you there at six-thirty," she agreed.

The foster mother, Beverly Schroder, answered the phone immediately and said she'd welcome a visit from Bo. Janny, she said, had been crying for no apparent reason since they'd brought her home from the hospital. It had something to do with an old doll the girl brought with her when she arrived from another foster home two years ago.

"I thought when she dug out that doll that it was, you know, part of her Goth costume," the woman told Bo. "The kids like to look bizarre, and the doll definitely helped with that. But it's more. It's become sick. She's obsessed with the thing, keeps carrying it around the house and laying it down on the couch or in a bookcase. A while ago I found it in the oven. I should never have allowed her to go to that Goblin place."

"Is the oven gas or electric?" Bo asked before she could stop herself.

"Electric. Why?"

Bo chose not to share her thoughts about why a disturbed and terrified youngster might place a symbolic object in a gas chamber.

"Um, it's just so unusual to find homes with gas stoves in San Diego," she dithered. "I've been thinking of moving and I was curious. Do you happen to have the name and phone number of Janny's friend Bran? I may need to speak with him as well."

Beverly Schroder's tone was hesitant.

"His name is Scott Bierbrauer and he still lives with his parents three blocks from here. We've known Scott and his family for years. We go to the same church, St. Olaf's Lutheran. That's why we let Janny go out with him even though he's five years older than she is. He's a nice kid, has a good job with a computer company even though he dropped out of college after a year. I'm sure Scott doesn't have anything to do with whatever is bothering Janny."

We'll see about that, Mrs. Schroder.

"Perhaps you could give me his work and home phone

numbers while I'm there," Bo insisted. "And in the meantime try asking Janny to recite the state capitals."

"What?"

"I told Janny at the hospital to try reciting something boring when she's feeling scared and nervous," Bo explained.

"My husband will be home in about an hour," Bev Schroder stated in a voice that suggested she would not welcome Bo until then.

"I look forward to meeting him," Bo answered. "I'll be there in an hour."

The Schroders were going to be humorless and defensive. Bo rummaged through her closet for something which might reassure Lutherans, who in her view could be forgiven anything because in 1700 their denominational ancestors had admitted to the chorus of the Lüneberg, Germany, church a fifteen-year-old apprentice named Johann Sebastian Bach. A world without the Brandenburg Concertos was a world Bo did not care to contemplate.

"Yes!" she said to a gray silk dress Estrella's sister had given Bo after wearing it once to a funeral. Under a black wool blazer the dress would whisper things about common sense and sane living. From a rack of earrings on her dresser Bo chose filigreed silver teardrops which had belonged to her mother. There was nothing to be done about her hair, which was already growing out in curly wisps from a short style chosen only three months ago. In subdued lighting, Bo decided, she'd look like an Irish farm girl on her way to enter a convent.

"Come on, Molly," she called. "We're going to have Italian!"

The Schroders' house was a two-story Craftsman, its stucco painted a fading pink. The street-level garage had been converted to a flat, probably for rental income. Bo sat with a sleeping Molly for a while in the Pathfinder as a damp wind blew through the yellowing sycamores and liquidambars of the old neighborhood. If the family needed income enough to rent out the ground floor of their home, she pondered, then what was their motivation for taking in a foster child? The county paid about $450 a month for the care of a child Janny's age. Were the Schroders fostering just for the income? And even if they were, did it matter as long as they were doing a good job?

Bev Schroder met Bo at the door in crisp black slacks and a sweater knit in Christmas designs. She was almost as tall as Bo and her thick ash-blond hair was short and swept back over earrings shaped like holly leaves.

"Thank you for coming," she said, showing Bo into a living room furnished predominantly in maple with an artificial Christmas tree in the front window. "This is my husband, Howard."

Bo shook hands with a slightly paunchy middle-aged man in jeans and a red cotton crewneck sweater over a starched plaid shirt. His brown hair was gray at the temples and thinning over a pink scalp, but his blue eyes seemed young. Acutely aware that things are never what they seem, Bo was surprised when she discerned no hidden blips or distortions concerning the Schroders on her personal radar. Here, apparently, things actually were what they seemed. A nice middle-aged couple who liked "Early American" furniture and took in foster children. With a rush of gratitude she noticed that their Christmas tree lights didn't blink.

"How is Janny?" she asked after settling into a ruffled navy gingham couch.

"We let her go out for a hamburger with the Bierbrauer boy," Howard Schroder said as Bev went to get coffee. "That way we could talk to you alone. They'll be back in fifteen minutes or so."

"Okay," Bo agreed, watching as he straightened a cuff of his immaculately pressed jeans. Then he traced the edge of his chair's armrest with the little finger of his right hand. The blue eyes had stopped meeting Bo's.

"We're, ah, pretty sure it's not a good idea for Janny to stay here any longer," he said to the beige shag carpet at his feet. "Bev didn't know how bad off Janny was when she brought her home from the hospital. And it's getting worse. Frankly, I'm afraid she might hurt somebody."

The last statement was punctuated by the arrival of Bev, burdened with an aluminum tray of coffee in cups shaped like the head of Santa Claus. The sugar cubes were red, and the cream pitcher was a cow with a red bow at its neck. Bo dropped red sugar cubes into the open skull of a Santa Claus and wondered at the exquisite choreography of married couples. Had they rehearsed this, or was their timing merely natural?

"Your husband has just explained that you have some concerns about Janny," she recapped Howard's announcement. Then she waited.

"Um," Bev replied, pouring cream from the cow's mouth with a trembling hand, "there's really something the matter with her. I mean, ah, well, we don't know anything about this child's background, about her parents. But I've heard it can happen like this. That one day somebody can be just fine, and the next day they're not . . . right. And they can become violent, you know?"

Bo felt an invisible hurricane envelop her in the warm, coffee-scented room.

Breathe from the diaphragm, Bradley, you idiot. You should have known this was coming. Don't overreact and don't tell them you're one of the "they" they're talking about.

"I can certainly understand your concern," Bo exhaled. "Has Janny exhibited violent behavior in the past?"

"Oh, no," Howard answered. "She likes to get herself up in these creepy old-fashioned clothes, and the music these kids listen to is pretty awful, but Janny's never even raised her voice around here, has she, Bev?"

"Of course not," his wife agreed. "But now it seems like she's, well, mentally ill."

The woman had whispered the words "mentally ill" as though the neighbors might be listening. Bo merely nodded expectantly, as though she were awaiting the conclusion of their train of thought.

"I mean, you read about these things in the papers every day," Bev went on. "Things where some mentally ill person just goes berserk and kills everybody in a restaurant. We just can't take the chance. So would you take care of the arrangements?"

"Foster parents can take a child to the receiving home at any time," Bo answered quietly. "But of course you know that from your training. If you feel that Janny represents a danger to you, then it would be appropriate for you to take her there. I have the phone number—"

"We thought you'd be able to take care of it," Howard said, again to the rug.

"I'm not a foster care worker, and I have another appointment after I leave here," Bo said. "But perhaps I can help you work out an alternate solution. Did the hospital staff offer any suggestions when you went to get Janny?"

"They gave me some pills for her," Bev answered. "I think they're tranquilizers. They said to give her one every four hours if she got upset again, and to make an appointment for her to see a psychologist."

"That seems reasonable," Bo said softly as black amoebas of anger exploded in ugly colors behind her eyes. "Has Janny had one of the pills yet?"

"Well, no," Bev answered. "It just seemed like buying into this silly behavior she's doing, giving her tranquilizers. We didn't want to encourage her. We've never had tranquilizers in this house. We feel that people should learn to control themselves instead of taking pills. That is, unless they actually have a disease of some kind. Don't you agree?"

Bo smiled thoughtfully at her purse atop Janny's case file on the maple coffee table. Inside were three plastic cylinders containing her twice-daily mood stabilizer, a mild sedative for emergencies, and an antispasmodic to control the intestinal cramps she sometimes got as a side effect of the first one. It was tempting to explain to the Schroders what would happen to her, sooner or later, without those medications. It was also tempting to pick up the coffee table and throw it through the window, followed by the Christmas tree. A satisfying fantasy.

"Oh, I think we all can be helped by medications at various times," she said in the voice with which she imagined Mother Teresa might speak to dying lepers. "And it certainly presents a solution for all of you tonight. Janny will sleep. And then tomorrow you can discuss her future with your foster care worker. In the meantime I just need to ask if you know of anything which may have upset or frightened Janny. Something in the last day or two."

"I never should have allowed her to go to that Goth club," Beverly Schroder answered. "But it was a reward for getting good grades. Janny's been there four or five times. Scott goes, you see, and he reassured us it was safe. But I'm sure that's what's done this to her. Nonsense about vampires and 'the dark side.' I'm never going to let her go there again."

Bo didn't press the obvious discrepancy between ejecting the girl from their home and resolving to curb her activities in the future. But the ambivalence was a good sign. Maybe Janny Malcolm wouldn't lose her home after all.

"I think time will help us solve the puzzle of what's happened to Janny," she said in the nun voice. "It's clear that you've provided an excellent home for her."

Both Schroders smiled weakly as a car door slammed outside, followed by the entrance of Janny Malcolm and a blond boy with long hair and a sparse goatee.

Seeing Bo, Janny smiled and said, "New York?"

"Albany," Bo replied. "I'm from Boston. The East Coast ones are easy. How about Michigan?"

"Lansing."

"Wow. Does it help?"

"A little," the girl answered. "But I can't get this thing about the doll out of my head. I'm afraid of the dark. It's like something's after me. Can Bran stay with me tonight, Bev? I feel safer with a friend around, and it's not like we're, you know, going to have sex or anything."

Howard Schroder rose to the moment majestically, Bo thought.

"How about one of those pills from the hospital tonight?" he suggested. "And you can sleep out here on the couch so I can stay with you right here in this chair. You're not going to be alone tonight. I'll be right here. Scott can come by tomorrow."

"Okay," Janny said, relieved. "I'm really scared."

Bo noticed the battered doll tucked under the girl's arm, but said nothing. Questions about Jasper Malcom and his expensive creations could wait.

"I'll walk out with you," she said, smiling at the boy named Bierbrauer.

The chilly air outside reminded Bo that she'd been sweating profusely in her successful attempt to impersonate a social worker. The gray silk dress was drenched beneath her blazer.

"By the way, who lives in the Schroders' downstairs flat?" she asked the boy.

"Nobody now," he answered. "They fixed it up years ago for Mr. Schroder's mother to live in. But then she got Alzheimer's and they had to put her in a home. She died three or four years ago, before Janny came. The flat's like a rec room now. My dad and Mr. Schroder play pool down there, that kind of stuff."

"Oh," Bo said.

The experience with Alzheimer's could account for the

Schroders' fear of even minor dementia. Undoubtedly the couple had been through some exhausting and painful times before making the difficult decision to find twenty-four-hour care for Howard's mother. They would wish to avoid any similar experience.

"So what's wrong with Janny?" Scott Bierbrauer asked as Bo scooped Molly from the Pathfinder and set her on the ground in a swirl of fallen sycamore leaves.

"I don't know, but you may be able to help. Tell me a little about this Goth business. I assume you picked Janny's name, Fianna. And what are the vampire teeth, the skull jewelry, and black leather wrist cuffs all about?"

"Gothic is about what a joke the whole middle-class scene is, you know? Everything's a lie. The politicians lie, the corporations lie, and religions are the biggest lie of all. It's like, there's nothing. They tell you to go to school and then get some job all day every day, and then you get old and you're dead and that's it. It's like everything they tell you is just this big commercial for something that doesn't exist, you know?"

They were walking slowly in the leaves near Bo's car. Christmas in San Diego felt more like Halloween in Boston, she reflected. And Scott Bierbrauer's remarks were both typically adolescent and impenetrably philosophical.

"So what does exist?" she asked, going along. Generations of philosophers had fallen short of an adequate answer to that question, but she was sure the boy would nail it with ease.

"Nothing," he said, smiling at Molly's wagging tail. "That's pretty Gothic, that nothing exists. And death is nothing, so we dress like vampires and people you see in old pictures. People who are dead. The whole Goth scene is like just saying screw it to the lies and accepting the truth."

As Molly sniffed the base of a cement-block ledge bordering somebody's yard, Bo congratulated herself on her choice of jobs. Commodities trading would have provided vastly more income, but not the opportunity to stand in leaves under a streetlight discussing existentialism with this bright, serious boy who had undoubtedly never heard of existentialism.

"And Janny understands all this?" she went on.

"Nah, she just likes the clothes. For a lot of them it's pretty superficial. You know, just someplace to hang out and feel accepted. A lot of Goths work in computers like I do. I guess you could say we aren't exactly truly wild. And we like the manners, the rules. A Goth won't just go up and hit on some girl. You have to be introduced."

"What about the doll Janny carries? Is that a statement about nothingness, too?"

"Well, yeah, in a way. I mean, Janny's past is kind of nothing, isn't it? She doesn't even know who her parents are, all those foster homes since she was really little. She said she's always had the doll. And she's always had nothing. See?"

"Bran," Bo said, rolling her *r*'s in the thickest brogue she could manage, "it's a deep thinker ye are with the heart of a poet."

"Hey, you do that pretty well," he grinned. "Do you really think so?"

"Aye," she answered, steering Molly back toward the Pathfinder. "Now go home and look up Jean-Paul Sartre in an encyclopedia. It's S-A-R-T-R-E, okay?"

"Who's that?"

"An early Goth."

"Wow."

Driving to her dinner appointment with Eva, Bo realized that she knew no more about Janny Malcolm than she had sixteen hours earlier at Goblin Market. It was as if a thick curtain hung in folds between the teenager and whatever was endangering her fragile security, even her mental stability. Only one thing had slipped through that curtain to provide a clue. A chipped porcelain doll.

Bo thought she could feel its single blue glass eye watching her. Certainly *something* was watching her. A sense of secretive and totally malign attention drifted in from the darkness behind her taillights. But when she turned to look over her shoulder, the leaf-strewn street was empty.

Chapter 7

By eleven forty-five the following morning Bo's enthusiasm for her job had turned, she realized, to a state more closely resembling entropy. Everything was wrong. Not only wrong, but perilously close to lunacy. Why else, she asked herself, would she be hiding in the excessively clean garage of a mortuary while Madge Aldenhoven and another woman attended a funeral? A strange funeral at which they appeared to be the only mourners.

Leaning against the whitewashed cement-block wall, she mentally reconstructed the series of events which had compelled her to follow her supervisor to this beige stucco building on a residential street just behind a shopping center. HEIDEGGER MORTUARY, read a small plaque beside the double front doors. Without the plaque, the building might have been anything from a dental complex to a private elementary school. A tribute to the Southern Californian's renowned distaste for reality.

The day had begun reasonably enough, she remembered as the recorded sound of a guitar and Indian flute floated through a closed door leading to one of the mortuary's three "chapels." Discounting, that is, Andrew LaMarche's dismayed early-morning announcement of a surprise visit by a young relative from Louisiana. The sixteen-year-old daughter of a cousin the dashing pediatrician hadn't seen in over thirty years.

"Her name is Teless and she says her *nannan* gave her bus fare for the trip as a Christmas present in exchange for promising not to marry a boyfriend who's apparently on his way to prison," Andrew explained raggedly over the phone. "I don't know what to do."

"What's a nannan?" Bo had asked.

"Cajun for godmother. Her godmother gave her the money. But no one contacted me and now she's here. She keeps reassuring me that she's not pregnant and asking me where the movie stars live. I've called my sister, Elizabeth, in Lafayette to see if she knows anything about this, but no one's home."

"It'll be nice to have a kid around for Christmas," Bo offered. "Don't worry. I'm sure she'll be lots of fun, remind you of those idyllic childhood visits to the bayou, all that."

"*Mon dieu*," Andrew LaMarche had sighed and then hung up.

Bo filed her lover's predicament for later contemplation and focused instead on the impact of Madge's costume that morning. A black faille suit, pencil-slim and so well cut that Madge looked like the widowed mother of an international fashion designer. But the black satin cloche hat with the quarter veil resting atop a stack of case files had really been the clue, Bo thought. When she'd said "Did somebody die?" Madge had blanched and muttered something about meeting her husband and his business partner for lunch. The lie had felt dark, Bo remembered. Navy blue, at least.

If it hadn't been for the hat, she might have overlooked the significance of a discussion in the hall between Madge and the CPS Police Liaison, Bo realized. The liaison was scrounging volunteers for the police department's Christmas toy distribution, and enjoying little success. Many of the donated toys, Bo knew, were still stacked in the CPS lunchroom.

"Is there anything left that's appropriate for an older child?" Madge had asked. "A teenager?"

"Not really," the other woman had answered, distracted. "Nobody ever knows what to donate for teenagers. I think we've got a couple of those clip-on sports radios, but the speakers are terrible."

"That won't matter," Madge had answered with a catch in her voice. "The gift is symbolic."

Later Bo had overheard Madge on the phone, saying, "I know it's silly, Mary, but I wanted something that would be like a real Christmas gift from Janny, a last gift because they never . . ."

Janny. Bo had heard the name before Madge turned from her office door, obscuring whatever else was said. Something about a gift from Janny. A plastic radio from the police toy drive? For whom? Why would Madge take a gift, ostensibly from Janny, to someone? And was this the engagement for which Madge had surpassed even her own sartorial standards? She looked as though she'd been summoned to the White House for a summit meeting. Black tie.

There would be no lunch with a husband, Bo already knew. That had been a lie. So where was Madge going with a flawed gift, supposedly from Janny? Maybe all the secrecy involved relatives. Wealthy relatives, from the care Madge had taken in preparation for this meeting. Bo had decided at that moment to follow Madge, see what this was about. It was the least she could do for Janny.

Now in the gloom she slowly turned the brushed chrome knob between the mortuary garage and the room beyond. Then she nudged it to a hair-fine opening she hoped no one would notice. A scent of carnations and metal fell across her face in the thin shaft of air from the other side. The door, she realized, was covered by a filmy drapery along the interior wall and situated immediately behind the gray steel casket.

Pressing her right ear to the narrow opening, she tried to hear what was being said.

A woman's voice, reading something. Poetry, Bo thought. It wasn't Madge, it was the other woman. The voice much deeper than Madge's, less controlled. And the poem was by Louise Bogan, Bo was sure. The poet was a favorite of hers, a kindred spirit.

" 'What is forsaken will rest,' " the woman's voice announced through tears. " 'But her heel is lifted,—she would flee,—the whistle of the birds/ Fails on her breast.' "

Bo knew the poem. It was about a statue, a girl carved in marble. For a moment the haunting Indian flute seemed, in fact, a "whistle of birds." And the sound would certainly fail to stir the heart of whoever lay just beyond the curtain. That heart, Bo acknowledged somberly, would not stir again. But who was it? From her position behind the casket she could see nothing. Why had Madge gone to such elaborate lengths all that morning to deny the fact that she was going to a funeral? And why was no one else present?

Bo had seen no option but to tail her supervisor. And an unlocked side door to the mortuary garage provided surreptitious entrance. But now what?

Through the knife-thin opening between the door and the frame, she saw a man approach the casket and lower the open half of its lid. The most wrenching moment in any funeral, she knew. The moment in which a singular, never-to-be-seen-again human face is removed from sight forever. Also the moment after which the mourners file out and the casket is removed to the hearse for its trip to a cemetery.

There were two hearses in the garage, as well as a beige van. The smaller hearse had been backed in, its rear door facing the door to the room now occupied by Madge Aldenhoven, a mortician, and two others, one of them dead. Bo scuttled to the shadows at the far side of the van, taking care to crouch close to the front tire. Blocked by its bulk she would be less likely to cast a noticeable shadow when the wide garage door was opened for the exit of the hearse. In minutes the taped music stopped and she heard the mechanical sound of draperies moving on a rod. Then a bump as something on wheels hit the door and rolled into the garage. A smell of cigarette smoke.

Bo held her breath as a pair of black-clad legs visible beyond the van's underside walked beside a heavy object being rolled from a gurney into the open hearse. Then the man neatly folded the gurney's legs inward and lifted it out of Bo's sight. A thunk announced the closing of the hearse door, and the feet moved quickly to the front of the black vehicle. A lit cigarette dropped to the concrete and was ground out by one of the feet, then picked up by a medium-sized male hand wearing a white glove. Bo could see the black cuff of the man's coat sleeve, the three buttons sewn there, an edge of white shirt. In the silence it was like a pantomime, she thought. Or a painting.

When the hearse was gone and the garage safely closed, Bo stood and looked around. The place appeared to be empty. There were no sounds from the interior of the building. Opening the door beyond which the brief service had been held, she stepped into an empty room carpeted deeply in mauve. A white satin skirt which would have disguised the gurney supporting the casket was flung over a vaguely art deco floor lamp, one of two which flanked a bare space marked deeply by the impression of small wheels. Bo could hear herself breathing through her nose. The sound seemed loud and inappropriate.

"As the cradle asks 'Whence?', the coffin asks 'Whither?'" she quoted her grandmother softly. It seemed necessary to say something.

Bradley, this isn't a wake, just an empty room. Save the Gaelic rhapsodizing over death until you at least know who's dead!

Moving soundlessly across the thick carpet, Bo edged into the hall. Silence. Apparently the mortician had handled the service alone and now was supervising the burial. To the right of the entry Bo saw another plaque affixed to the door of a front room. OFFICE. She knocked softly and, when there was no response, opened the door.

As she expected, there was a neat stack of papers atop a large desk. There was always a neat stack of papers. There had been papers at the Boston mortuary from which her sister Laurie had been buried after deliberately breathing the exhaust from her own car through a garden hose. And there had been a larger stack after the accidental deaths of both her parents in Mexico. Pushing aside a thousand dust motes swimming in the light from two side windows, she stepped closer and then heard the sharp intake of her own breath.

Beside the word "Deceased" on the death certificate facing her was the name "Malcolm, Kimberly."

"Kimmy," Bo whispered. "Kimmy Malcolm."

The death had occurred in the City and County of Los Angeles, California, the document told her, at 12:03 A.M. on the previous day. Bo memorized the address from which death had claimed someone with a doll's name. Then she realized that her palms were damp and her eyes felt too small. The air in the closed room seemed suddenly eggshell-colored and judgmental. It wanted her to leave.

"No problem," she pronounced through her nose, backing into the hall and then dashing through the garage door to the street. The Pathfinder was parked in the shopping center lot facing the mortuary, but Bo instinctively ducked into the first store she came to, just to decompress. It was a Target, one of the nationwide chain of variety stores that sold everything from cosmetics to pesticides. Now bustling with Christmas shoppers, it offered near-perfect anonymity as Bo confronted the fact that she was scared.

Not scared of dolls or caskets or death, but of California. Of having no past. Of being left out by virtue of never having been let in. Whatever had just happened in that bland funeral

home, she acknowledged as she examined a display of Christmas socks, was rooted in some past drama to which she was
not privy. Something involving Madge Aldenhoven and another woman. And something involving Janny Malcolm.

Kimberly Malcolm might be Janny's mother, Bo thought.
A drug addict, maybe, or a prostitute who'd left her daughter
in foster homes for years and now had died. Perhaps Madge
had handled the original case. It happened that way sometimes. A CPS worker might know the whereabouts of a missing parent for years, even maintain contact with that parent,
but never reveal those facts to anyone. It happened when the
parent, almost always the mother, was too damaged or strung
out or criminal ever to regain custody of her child, but too
desperately alone to release that child for adoption. In those
cases the social worker might become a sporadic link to the
child, a source of news or an occasional snapshot. Some of the
CPS workers took pity on these mothers. Bo was puzzled at
the thought of Madge in that role, but what else could account for her secrecy and her presence at the brief little funeral?

Turning at the end of the sock aisle, Bo sadly perused the
half city block devoted to hair care items. Estrella had phoned
to say she'd be going home from the hospital at noon to await
the birth of her baby comfortably ensconced in the recliner Bo
had helped her and Henry select. Overnight, Estrella had
drifted outside their shared office and was gone. Flipping open
the cap of a pearlized gray plastic bottle of conditioner, Bo
sniffed the contents and felt a surge of nausea that brought
tears to her eyes. Coconut. A smell like cheap suntan lotion, a
summer beach smell. It embodied California. Where Bo
Bradley didn't belong.

Even Andy had a family, she thought. A sister in Louisiana,
nieces and nephews, teenage second cousins who showed up
unexpectedly for Christmas. Even Eva Broussard had made a
new life for herself in her high desert compound, surrounded

by a handful of people from New York State who believed they'd seen extraterrestrials on a mountain in the Adirondacks. The recent discovery of several new planets believed to be capable of supporting life had inspired these people, Eva explained during last night's dinner, to create a computer screen saver featuring the new planets as they stood in relation to earth. In their spinning white galaxies, the new planets blinked fuchsia, electric blue, neon green. The screen savers were selling briskly, Eva said, and the renewed enthusiasm of the "Seekers," as the group had named themselves back in New York, would provide a finale to her research documenting their response to having seen almond-eyed aliens with silver skin in the Adirondack dark.

"I have concluded," the half-Iroquois psychiatrist told Bo over freshly baked Italian bread, "that the nature of experience is so ephemeral it doesn't feel 'real' unless validated by others. Thus human beings expend inordinate percentages of available energy in attempts to enlist others as support for their own experience. I doubt that any of the Seekers will see another 'space alien,' but they've established cohesion based on an enterprise which will encourage others to validate their experience."

"What?" Bo had asked. The shrink's French accent made her words sound like the voice-over for a lingerie commercial despite their academic content.

"The Seekers are marketing their version of reality, which includes an awareness of life on other planets," Eva simplified the theory. "And people are buying their product, begging for more. It validates the Seekers' experience."

"Mental health through capitalism?"

"I'm afraid so," Eva had smiled.

In the store's music section Bo stopped to listen to the Mannheim Steamroller Christmas CD playing from speakers inside a gated area containing electronic equipment. A solo flute soared over the shopping noise in the simple French folk melody called "The Holly and the Ivy." Bo knew the tune from a past in which her mother played it on the little violino piccolo she'd bought in Italy. The sound meant Boston and snow and the scent of pipe tobacco as her father strung lights on a tree placed in the bay window overlooking a streetlight. It meant her little sister Laurie at five, pantomiming the music she couldn't hear by dancing in time to the movement of their mother's arm across the wooden soundboard. Laurie's huge green eyes had *seen* the music, Bo remembered as strings swelled beneath the trill of the recorded flute.

"Ma'am, are you all right?" a tall boy in owlish glasses and a red vest asked Bo. "Is there something I can do to help you?"

"No, I'm just looking," Bo answered, wiping her eyes on the cuff of the bulky russet-brown sweater she'd worn to work in lieu of her disreputable winter coat. She hadn't realized that she was crying.

A new low, Bradley. All you need is a tin cup to complete the look. And a sign saying, PITIABLE NUT-CASE. PLEASE GIVE.

Striding with feigned purpose into the housewares section, Bo studied the price tag on a round white appliance with ten interchangeable blades. Its packaging featured color pictures of salads. Food processor. So far, so good. Identifying arcane objects could provide a path out of the mood that had descended on little flute-paws, she thought ruefully. But what in hell was the matter with her?

"Lo, How a Rose E'er Blooming" sang a brass choir from the same CD as she moved into Automotive Accessories to escape the music. The mood had come from nowhere, she thought. Or had it? Manic depression was characterized by mood swings, but they didn't swing quite this frivolously. Besides, she was taking her meds. This mood had its origins elsewhere, she was sure. This mood was, in fact, epidemic.

"It's the longest night we're approachin'," Bridget Mairead O'Reilly had told her granddaughter years ago at Christmas. "Old Cally's feast it is, when there's no escapin' the darkness nor the emptiness nor the cold. That's why folks long ago brought in a tree all green to remind them spring would come again, and put candles in its branches like little suns. And all the while Caillech Beara's out there a howlin' to birth the new year. All alone she is, Gormfhlaith." The old woman had paused, using Bo's Gaelic name for emphasis. "And it's in every one of us to know we're alone, too, when Cally's time is upon us. A natural thing it is, but frightnin' to the heart."

She'd held Bo close then, and rocked her beside the twinkling tree in a house sold twenty years later to a young doctor from Pakistan on the staff at Mass General.

"It's all gone," Bo told a shelf of car wax. "The house in Boston, the cottage on Cape Cod, my grandmother, my parents, my sister. It's Old Cally's feast, the season of death and madness. And I am alone."

Saying the words out loud to an oblivious collection of plastic containers felt good. It put boundaries on the epic loneliness and opened a way out. Everyone was alone, which was why everyone clustered together like magnets for the Midwinter Solstice. A way of putting up a fight. Bo's Irish soul understood the need for fighting very well. Quickly she located a pay phone and a quarter.

"Andy," she said into Andrew LaMarche's answering machine, "we've got to have a Christmas party! I'm not at the office right now, I'm at Target. I've just been to a funeral, or in the garage of a funeral, actually, which is what made me think of having a party. Sunday evening will be good, don't you think? Call me."

Then she placed a second call to Dar Reinert's voice mail at San Diego Police Department Headquarters.

"Two things, Dar," she announced. "First, I'm having a little get-together at my place on Sunday evening and I'd like for you and Deb to come. About seven o'clock. A tree-trimming party. And the other thing is, can you check out a Kimberly Malcolm who's just been buried from the Heidegger Mortuary? I think she might be the mother of Janny Malcolm, the kid who freaked out at the Goth club two nights ago. And, uh, Dar . . . don't give the information to the message center, okay? I don't want Madge Aldenhoven to know I'm investigating this case any further, and the switchboard automatically routes all my messages to her desk before I see them. This is just between you and me."

On the way back to the office Bo stopped for a rolled taco plate at a Mexican restaurant where only last year she'd fed a deaf four-year-old boy before fleeing with the child into a desert more dangerous than the mania electrifying her brain. At least the job wasn't boring, she told herself. For now, the job would do.

Chapter 8

Daniel Man Deer squinted into the gray sky above Oak Canyon and again raised the small binoculars to his eyes. A red-tailed hawk swooped over the sage scrub and chaparral of Fortuna Mountain, hunting. The hawk's presence so close to the bobcat corridor was a good indication that the cat wasn't around. Shouldering his heavy canvas pack, Man Deer began the rocky ascent toward the area where he guessed the cat usually crossed Highway 52 into the park from the relatively safer military property. The pack contained two new pump-spray canisters he'd bought at a home supply warehouse. Each canister was filled to the load line with watered-down urine, and their combined weight made the pack straps dig into his shoulders.

The urine had been an educated guess. He wasn't sure if his own species chemistry was quite right, but it was worth a try. The bobcat might read the territorial marking and not cross into an area already claimed by another animal. Man Deer laughed at the thought of what Mary would say if she caught him peeing into bug-spray cans in the garage. She'd think he was crazy. She wouldn't understand that he was doing it for her as well as the cat. Mary would never understand how one thing connected to another, how saving the cat might free her from the spirit invading her dreams, her life. It wouldn't end after the funeral today; he was sure of that. What he wasn't sure of was what to do about it.

Last night he'd awakened in the dark, aware that the bed was unnaturally cool. He didn't need to open his eyes to know that Mary wasn't beside him. The flesh of his chest, his arms and feet had sensed her absence even as he slept. The night before, when the first dream came, she'd screamed in her sleep and then clung to him, shaking. Now, on the second night, she wasn't sleeping at all. Pulling her pink quilted robe over his bulky shoulders, he'd gone downstairs looking for her. A thread of light beneath the utility room door told him she was in the garage. When he pushed open the door he found her sitting on the floor beside a faded storage box, her hands clutching a small red T-shirt to her face.

"Oh, Mary," he said, taking the robe from his shoulders and wrapping it around hers, "don't."

In the yellow garage light his wife's reddish brown hair appeared gunmetal gray. Artificial. Like a wig. And the pale flesh of her arms felt cold to his touch.

"Danny, I can't even smell him anymore," she wept. "I used to be able to smell him, a little. You know, that little boy smell? It was like leaves, Danny. Leaves and chewing gum. It was, wasn't it?"

Her hazel eyes were red-rimmed, and in the harsh light he could see the loose fold of flesh beneath her chin that she hated so much and disguised with a wardrobe of pretty scarves. She talked about having a "necklift" by one of the cosmetic surgeons patronized by the wives of his former business associates, and he'd told her that was fine, he could well afford it. But she never made the appointment. She'd learned there was no way to alter the truth, just as he had. They had both learned twenty-eight years ago. When the child they'd named David went to sleep atop his new bunk bed, a surprise for his fifth birthday, and never woke up.

"Intracerebral hemorrhage," a neurologist told Daniel later, after the autopsy. "An aneurysm in a large left-hemisphere blood vessel. There's no way anyone could have known, but the vessel wall was defective from birth, paper thin at a point deep in the brain. A time bomb. This would have happened sooner or later. I'm sorry. There's nothing that could have been done to save David. I'm so very damn sorry."

Dan didn't like to remember the time after David's death, the months and then years when he and Mary stopped loving each other and tried to make another baby anyway, and failed. He'd thrown himself into work and a series of affairs with women who told him he looked like Geronimo, or Cochise, or Sitting Bull. Women who played guitars and bought him silver concho belts he never wore. When Mary finally told him she wanted a divorce, he didn't argue but moved into an apartment near his office in La Jolla and stocked the cabinets with Johnnie Walker Black. On weekends he drank straight through from Friday night to Sunday night. He forgot David.

But one Sunday afternoon Mary came to him with an eerie light in her eyes. He was drunk, he thought, but she was insane. She had looked insane. He thought it might happen.

"I wanted to see you" was all she said.

In his blurred vision her eyes looked strange, not Mary's eyes at all but someone else's. Someone small and frightened and brave. And over the sound of a televised football game in the next apartment he heard a single word pronounced in a voice that could not be. A voice that was gone. The only voice ever possessed of the right to call him by that name, that single syllable.

"Dad."

Mary had not said it. The word had simply been there in the air between them, heard not with his ears but with his heart. And he could not hide from what it told him.

That he was a dead thing, infinitely more dead than the bright little soul who was merely gone. That he had crawled away from life like a coward, abandoning not only Mary in her grief but abandoning his own spirit as well. It was David, he knew, who had come with heroic courage across unspeakable boundaries to give him back his name. David, riding the strength of his mother's love for his father, looking at him through Mary's eyes, who had spoken the syllable that broke open his heart and saved his life.

He had wept in Mary's arms then, bent double on the floor, his shame like fire roiling in his veins. Later he'd crawled to the apartment's filthy bathroom and vomited until he emptied himself of the fire and was dry and frail as the pressed violet he'd once found in a library book. They went home then. He locked the apartment, kicked the key back under the door, and went home with the only woman he would ever love. The woman who had mothered the only child who would ever call him "dad." He had never stopped being grateful for the gift.

"Come on in," he now urged in the yellow glare of the garage light, enfolding her in muscular arms that dwarfed her small frame. "It's cold out here. I'll make some coffee and we'll talk. It's because it's Christmas, isn't it?" he suggested, offering a way out, hoping she'd accept the lie. "If he'd lived we might have grandkids now. We'd be out buying trail bikes and computer games to put under the tree. God, we would've loved that, wouldn't we?"

But her arms remained stiff and tight against her sides, her fists knotted in the red shirt.

"No. It's not Christmas. We've been through a thousand holidays since he died. It's not that," she answered in a voice cold with rage. "It's just . . . I don't understand, I will never *understand* . . . how a mother could . . . how she could . . ."

"Come inside," he repeated as she began to rock, the little shirt against her face and her bare knees white against the cement floor. "I don't know what—"

"How a mother could deliberately *kill*," his wife sobbed, "her own child."

"Well, they say that sometimes in this post-partum depression—" he began, pretending something she'd read in the paper or seen on television had raked up the old anguish.

"No, Danny, nothing like that." She lowered the red shirt to her lap and turned to him. "That's horrible, but it can be understood. This cannot, and you know it. Quit pretending you don't have any idea what's upset me. That I would have given my very *life* for David, and couldn't, and yet another woman took another child in her hands and—"

"Mary, what's happened? Please tell me what's happened."

But he knew then. Knew the name of the spirit that had affixed itself to his wife. And knew why.

"Kimmy Malcolm finally died last night, Dan. It's over."

In the yellow silence of the garage Daniel Man Deer felt something in his brain snap and then relax, like an old rope tied too long to a terrible weight. A memory. It had been waiting.

"Thank God," he whispered. "Oh, Mary, thank God."

What he hadn't said was that it wasn't over. He hadn't said that after thirteen years of secrecy and silence, it had just begun.

Two hundred yards away, the hawk plummeted behind a split boulder and rose again with a whiptail lizard wiggling in its beak. Dan watched the bird climb the gray sky and vanish between two low hills. Nothing had changed for thousands of years, he thought. A sprawling city had grown up thanks to the old dam constructed here by Indian labor under the heel of the padres, but eventually the dam had crumbled and the city had never come closer than it was now. The rocky hills and twisting valley that once harbored a Kumeyaay village were as they had always been. And the spirits here were undisturbed. Free.

A scent of sage on the breeze alerted Dan to the place where the lizard had scampered its last. In the damp earth beneath a coastal sage bush were the marks of a scuffle. The hawk's beating wings would have bruised the sage enough to release its characteristic odor into the air. Breathing deeply, Dan knew the moment for what it was—a sign that he was on the right path, the path which would lead him to the Old Ones and a way to free Mary from the burden now haunting her. The sage smell made him light-headed for a moment, as if he were walking just above the surface of the ground. That was good. A good sign.

Nearing the highway, he dropped the pack, removed one of the canisters, and pumped it. Then he began spraying the rocks, the dusty path he believed was part of the bobcat's territory, all the way to the edge of the pavement. Then he walked a half mile in both directions beside the road, spraying the ground. Later he'd drive east on 52, park the car somewhere, and spray the eastbound shoulder.

"Kill them weeds, Injun!" a man in a western shirt yelled from a pickup truck, and threw a half-empty can of beer in Dan's general direction. The can bounced and spewed yellow foam on the road before coming to rest in the ditch. Dan thought of rattlesnake venom and then forced himself to stop thinking altogether. He could allow nothing to break his concentration. He had to be there for the cat entirely. That was how he would contact the Old Ones, by saving the cat and earning their respect. And they would find a way to tell him things never recorded because there was no written language when they lived here. They would find a way to tell him how the angry dead may be silenced, how the living may be allowed to forget.

But it was going to take time. And there might not be very much time now. Something terrible had been released at last, and he was sure a long-awaited chain of events had already begun. A chain of events that would almost certainly involve more pain. And almost certainly involve more death.

Chapter 9

Mary Mandeer stood in ankle-high grass and thought about the construction of her shoes. They were ordinary black pumps with ordinary two-inch heels. But because of the way they were made, she couldn't shift her weight to the balls of her feet, couldn't stand on her toes. The shoes forced an even distribution of her weight, which meant that her heels sank into the damp ground with every step. She could actually feel the tearing of roots as her heels punctured the earth's surface. She could feel the occasional pebble, the rotting twig. It was good to have something to think about as they watched the gray casket being lowered into the ground.

There was no graveside service. She and Madge had agreed that a few words at the funeral home would suffice. Now the only sound was the creaking of a small winch attached to some sort of tractor. The winch was lowering Kimberly Malcolm's body into what Mary hoped would be a final peace. God knew, the child deserved an eternity of peace. A billow of exhaust from the tractor scented the air unpleasantly.

"I think that will do," Madge Aldenhoven said as a breeze moved the black net veil covering the inch of thick silver hair visible between her forehead and the edge of a small hat. "I think we can go now."

Mary felt her heels digging again as she took five steps to the yellow-orange mound of earth and reached for a handful. It felt sandy and wet.

"It's over now, Kimmy," she whispered. "Be at peace."

The dirt made a scratchy thunk on the casket lid when she threw it into the grave, but brought no sense of finality or closure. Mary hadn't really expected it to.

"I'm ready," she said then, and punctured a wavering line of small holes in the earth leading from Kimmy Malcolm's grave to Madge Aldenhoven's car. It was the kind of thing Dan would notice, she thought. The kind of thing Dan would say meant something.

As Madge started the car Mary waved to the mortician standing beside the hearse. That the man knew absolutely nothing about what now lay six feet beneath San Diego's rocky soil made her feel grounded in reality. *Not knowing* was reality, she decided in that moment. Not knowing was healthy, was comfortable, was necessary. Some things shouldn't be known. So from now on, she wouldn't know them. The man nodded politely and raised three fingers of his white-gloved right hand in a small farewell. The gesture was a perfect dismissal, Mary thought. Good-bye. The end. *Finis.*

"How is Dan doing, now that he's retired?" Madge asked.

There had been no conversation about Kimmy Malcolm, no discussion of the case so many years ago that only now would close. Mary remembered when she'd taken the job with the Welfare Department after David's death, after Dan moved out. She'd thought she was going to be on her own and would need a job. But after she and Dan got back together she found she liked having somewhere to go every day, something to do. So she stayed on, and stayed up with the endless paperwork, kept her caseload clean. The cheaters couldn't get by Mary Mandeer, but she wasn't beyond stretching things a payment or two for the ones who really needed help. And then, years later, the department had asked her to move into a new division

called Child Protective Services. It would involve not only
adoptions and foster care, but the investigation of child abuse
as well. Mary had thought it over and finally agreed to the
new job, where she was assigned to a supervisor only slightly
older than herself named Madge Aldenhoven. The two had become friends, Mary remembered, almost immediately. And remained friends, until the Malcolm case. Almost fourteen years
ago now. It felt like yesterday.

"Dan's reclaiming his Indian heritage, working as a volunteer at Mission Trails Regional Park," she answered Madge's
question. "He spells 'Man Deer' as two words now, and spends
half his life at libraries researching Kumeyaay history. It's
quite interesting. How about Tom and the boys?"

"Tom's opened a fancy plumbing fixtures mail-order business with a friend of his," Madge said brightly after a pause in
which her neck flushed in streaks above the black fabric of her
suit. "The business is sort of a retirement thing. And both
Tom, Jr., and Randall live outside California now. Tom, Jr.'s
career Navy, moves around a lot, and Randall married a nice
girl from Virginia he met at a youth hostel in Austria, of all
things. He has a good job with her father's company. They
have two children, seem happy."

They weren't even out of the cemetery, Mary Mandeer realized, and there was nothing left to say. Nothing, that is, unless the forbidden topic was broached. The topic which had
brought them together again after thirteen years of silence.

"Do you really think all the secrecy was necessary?" she
asked Madge. "Do the police know? Do you think there will
be any follow-up?"

Madge guided the small car through a patch of dry leaves as
though she were being judged on the maneuver. In the rearview
mirror Mary saw the mortician push his cap to the back of his
head and light a cigarette. Then a curve in the cemetery road
obscured what lay behind them.

"There was no announcement in the paper, Mary, so there's

no way the press could have learned about this easily. I don't know if the Kelton Institute informed the police when Kimberly died. As far as I can ascertain, they would have had no reason to. We have been legally responsible for Kimberly since . . . since before it happened. When she died they phoned the hotline and asked for me. The hotline gave them my home number, they called, I called you. All of these communications have been discreet. There's only one potential source of trouble."

"What's that?" Mary Mandeer asked as they exited the cemetery. The hum of cars on the street was pleasant, she thought. It was pleasant to have this old obligation completed, to be leaving it behind.

"Janny," Madge said.

"Oh, my God, is she still—"

"She's still here, still in the foster care system. There was no way, well, you know there was just no way for . . . for anybody to claim her. But two nights ago, the night Kim died, Janny had some kind of seizure at a nightclub. They thought she was dead and called the police, who phoned one of my workers to investigate since it was quite foggy and she lives near the club. Janny was hospitalized and still isn't doing very well. It's quite possible that she's mentally ill, which wouldn't be surprising under the circumstances. The worker, Bo Bradley, is something of a troublemaker, but she isn't stupid and she's likely to develop an attachment for the girl."

"Just take her off the case, Madge. What's the point in letting somebody dig all this up now? And by the way," Mary said, pretending interest in a used car lot out the passenger's side window, "did you let, um, *him* know that Kim was gone at last?"

"Yes," Madge answered softly. "I phoned him before I phoned you."

"Good."

"Mary, there's something else about Janny," Madge went

on, biting her lower lip. "She carries an old doll around with her. And she calls it Kimmy."

Mary Mandeer felt something cold catch in the back of her throat.

"She was only two! She can't possibly remember."

"No, she can't," Madge Aldenhoven sighed, "but apparently she does. Probably just the name, which she's connected to the doll. It's dangerous, Mary. I'm worried."

"It was a long time ago, Madge. And we didn't really do anything wrong."

"*You* didn't really do anything wrong," Madge replied through clenched teeth. "But I did and now it's come back to haunt me."

Mary said nothing more. Not talking, she thought, might be the gateway to not knowing. It was worth a try.

Chapter 10

"Murder," Dar Reinert said for the second time as Bo stood in her empty office staring into an equally empty hall. He'd called as soon as she got back. "It's officially a murder now."

"What do you mean, 'now'?" she asked, cradling the phone against her shoulder as she tried to extricate herself from the bulky sweater. "Do you mean Kimberly Malcolm was murdered? When? Where? And who *was* Kimberly Malcolm?"

A familiar rattle of keys at the side door presaged Madge's return. Bo stretched a leg to the edge of her office door, trying to nudge it closed. No dice. Whatever Dar was saying could not be heard over the purposeful entrance of the supervisor, clasping a new case file firmly in her right hand.

"I think I've got a new case, Es," Bo told the detective as if he were Estrella. "Let me call you later, okay?"

"The history on this thing'll make you puke," Reinert went on. "I'm gonna run a copy of the file and bring it over. Leave your truck unlocked. I'll put it on the front seat."

"It's not a truck," Bo answered. "But no problem. Talk to you later."

In the shadows cast by the desk lamp Madge looked like something out of Dickens, Bo thought. The Ghost of Christmas Future, maybe. That sepulchral darkness. It occurred to her that in four years of daily, usually hostile contact with the older woman, she'd never actually been afraid of Madge Aldenhoven. Until now.

"We'll close the Malcolm case and transfer it over to foster care," Madge said. "Here's a new case I want you to begin immediately. It's pretty messy. You may need police backup." Something in her voice suggested that argument would be pointless.

"Sure," Bo replied, "but I haven't done the closing summary yet."

"I'll do the summary for you. It's important that you get out on the new case. It's a sibling petition on a three-year-old who's been living on potato chips and sleeping on a pool table in a bar. She's already been brought in, but apparently there's a baby brother still in the care of the mother, who has an extensive drug and alcohol history. You'll need to pick up the baby."

There was no point in hanging on to Janny Malcolm's case file. It contained no information. Bo took the orange-banded manila folder from her briefcase and handed it to Madge, aware that in saying nothing about Kimberly Malcolm she was allowing Madge the illusion of secrecy, and of closure. Saying nothing, Bo knew, could be as reprehensible as lying.

"How was the lunch with your husband and his business partner?" she asked, pretending to read the new case file.

"Very nice," Madge answered too quickly. "I had a continental salad with raspberry vinaigrette."

"Mmm."

How many times, Bo wondered, had momentous decisions, irrevocable rifts, deadly conflicts been established in just such banal exchanges of untruth? But there was no going back. For a split second Bo felt something like pity for the woman standing in her office. She was sure what lay ahead wasn't going to be pretty.

"I'll have the cops meet me to grab this baby," she said. "It's a rotten neighborhood even in broad daylight."

"Yes," Madge agreed, looking across Estrella's empty desk and out the window. "But we don't say, 'Grab this baby.' "

"I do," Bo insisted, but the older woman was already out the door, gone.

"Dar, meet me at Tenth and Market," Bo whispered into the phone seconds later. "I need backup for a baby-snatch at a wino hotel. You can tell me about the Malcolm case then."

"Are you kidding?" the deep voice growled. "Call some uniforms for backup. I wouldn't send my worst enemy into that place, not without body armor and a gas mask. Trust me, you'll have to burn your shoes once you get out of that sewer. That is, *if* you get out. Why don't I just meet you at the curb with the Malcolm file?"

"Dar, I don't believe this. What happened to 'protect and serve'?"

"I'm a detective, Bradley. One of the perks is I don't have to wade through wino shit and infected needles. Is there really a kid in there?"

"I'm not going down there for cocktails, Dar. There were two kids. The three-year-old girl was picked up from a bar after the owner called the hotline. At the receiving home she said her baby brother was in a room up there with her mother. Nobody's seen mom or the baby for over twenty-four hours."

"Shit, Bradley. You know what this is gonna be."

"Probably," Bo answered.

"A *baby*?"

"I'm going to get the car seat now. Meet you there in fifteen minutes."

"Uniforms. I'm bringing uniforms. You know I can't stand to see this stuff close up, Bradley. I've got kids, you know."

"Dar, how did you wind up in the child abuse division?"

"I like to nail the SOBs," he answered with characteristic gruffness, "throw their sorry asses in prison where they'll find out what it's like to be defenseless. What I don't like is this neglect stuff. It's messy, not real police work. It's your thing, Bradley."

"Which is why I'll see you in a few minutes."

"You win." He sighed. "But you owe me one."

"Agreed." Bo smiled and hung up.

The infant car seat she'd grabbed from the supply room was old and dotted with a sticky residue that had once been chocolate. Heading south on 163 toward San Diego's downtown, she wondered how many babies had been fastened into it over the years. Wondered where those babies were now.

Most of the CPS workers kept pictures of babies on their walls, Bo remembered. Not snapshots but commercially done posters and ad artwork featuring babies. The most popular was a narrow, three-foot-long poster of about thirty multiethnic babies in pastel terrycloth sleepers. Several of the workers had that one on their walls, but when Bo had asked why, they'd just looked at her as if she'd asked what the American flag was for. There was something about babies, she admitted to herself, that caused other people to dissolve in dewy-eyed inanity. "Aww," they crooned, "that's what it's all about, isn't it?"

Bo had routinely stopped short of asking what *what* was all about. She thought of babies as simply very immature people with distinctive habits and personalities. There were some she liked and others she didn't, just as she would undoubtedly like or dislike them when they had teeth and political opinions. There was nothing about babies that made her feel gushy. And nothing that would endear her to expensive replicas of them, either.

The old urban highway became Eleventh Street as it drained into downtown San Diego, and Bo slowed the Pathfinder to accommodate traffic signals and pedestrians. She was on her way to seize a real baby, but a different one drifted across her mind. An old porcelain baby with a missing eye.

Where had Janny Malcolm's doll come from? she wondered. And what did it have to do with the body Madge Aldenhoven had committed to the ground only hours ago?

Dar Reinert was standing in front of a corner liquor store as Bo parked illegally and got out. The Ruger revolver at his stocky chest ruined the lines of a new gray tweed sportcoat, Bo noticed. But not the stylish impression created by his blue and gray checked shirt and navy tie featuring tiny cartoon mice in handcuffs and leg-irons.

"Great tie," she grinned.

"My five-year-old picked it out, then couldn't wait for Christmas to give it to me. I think it gives a strong message, huh?" he bantered. "Look, let's just get this over with, okay? I've talked to Ahmed, the guy in the liquor store, who says there's four rooms-for-rent above the store. Only access is that door over there," he said, pointing to a wide steel door with flaking yellow paint and a new deadbolt lock. "A fire code violation. The door leads to a set of wooden stairs. Burn them and there's no way out except to dive through the second-story windows. Put that in your report."

"Can we get a key from Ahmed?"

"Got it. He won't go up there, though. Says he wouldn't *dream* of going up there without a sidearm, at least. And he said he's heard a baby crying, although not today. Let's do it."

Bo watched as the burly detective unlocked the door, opened it, and then pulled the Ruger from its shoulder holster under his jacket. "Police!" Reinert yelled in a voice Bo thought would unquestionably scare even the cockroaches into thoughts of relocation. A cascade of sour, musty air rolled across her face from the open door, but there was no response to the warning. Nothing moved on the floor above or on the unlit stairway. Not even, she noted as they stomped up the wooden steps, an emaciated black man in purple suspenders and a woman's pink velour house slippers who appeared to be sleeping upside down against the stairwell wall. Bo could see a trickle of congealing blood running from his nose.

"Dar?" she began.

"Forget it. He's not dead, he's drunk. Fell down the steps. He'll wake up. We're not here for him."

The closer they got to the upper hall, the worse the odor, Bo noticed. Mildew, vomit, urine. And something less obvious. A pervasive sickroom smell that announced the proximity of death. The hallway, she realized, was a last way station for those already dying, for whom the future was no longer an option. The hallway reminded her of the dream.

"Don't touch *anything*," Reinert growled, holding the Ruger in both hands as he glanced up and down the colorless hall. "Ahmed said the baby crying was right over the store, which would be down here."

As they turned right, a door opened revealing a filthy communal toilet and a pale young man with a shaved head and a large rose tattoo over his left nipple, which was pierced and threaded with dirty string. Blood ran down his right arm from a puncture in the brachial artery at the bend of his elbow. Bo could see a blackened spoon and a syringe lying on a greasy paper napkin beside the toilet.

"Just ease your butt back in there and close the door," Reinert told the boy softly. "Nobody saw you and you didn't see nobody. Stay in there until you hear us leave."

The shaved head nodded slowly and then the bathroom door closed again. Dar stood with his back to the streetside wall and motioned Bo toward a closed door. "Go on," he urged. "I can cover both the room and the hall from here. Knock first, then stand to the side of the door."

When there was no answer, Bo turned the knob and pushed the door ajar, then stood back. Nothing. Silence. In the dim light filtering through grimy windows she could see what appeared to be an ocean of clothing mounded in heaps on the floor, but no furniture, and no baby.

"Dar, this is weird," she said, wading in. "There's nothing in here but clothes. Wall-to-wall dirty clothes."

"Try the kitchen."

Bo glanced toward the old-fashioned sink and accompanying hot plate which comprised the room's cooking area. On the hot plate a baby bottle of greenish, curdling milk stood in a coffee can half full of water, flies rimming its edge. An empty Pampers box was overturned beneath it. Bo snapped a Polaroid of the scene for the court report and turned to leave, but something stopped her. There was somebody there. She could feel it.

Dar moved into the doorway and grimaced. "Place is empty, Bradley. Let's get outta here. Uniforms can come out later and grab the kid. Let's *go*!"

"Dar, there's somebody here," she said.

"There's nothing here but clothes. Don't go nutso on me, Bo. This scene isn't secured, isn't safe. Some fry-brain could come out of one of these doors at any minute, shooting, waving needles. The mother's taken off with the kid. She'll be back and we'll have a crew waiting. Now come on."

Bo caught her foot in a pair of women's shorts that had been ripped in half, and fought back a ringing nausea. The clothes were dragging her down, making her dizzy. But she couldn't leave. Not yet.

"Dar, shoot the gun," she said.

"Oh, God, you *are* crazy. I knew this was a mistake. Bradley, you can't handle the stress of this work, you really can't. And I can't discharge a firearm within the city limits unless I've got a damn good reason, which I don't. Am I gonna have to drag you outta here?"

Bo could feel her eyes burning from the insult. "Crazy." The minute you revealed a difference, just the smallest divergence in perception, they dragged out the c-word. But she was right. There was someone else in the quiet room. She could sense another presence that was there, but not conscious. And desperate. It could be an animal. But she'd bet her precarious sanity that it wasn't. Slogging back to the hot plate, she picked up the coffee can and held it high over her head.

"Go to hell, Dar," she yelled, and slammed the can down on the metal hot plate with all her strength. The resulting crash was precisely what she wanted. As Dar Reinert plunged angrily into the room, a thin wail rose from a wad of stained sheets on the floor beneath the window. A stringy, mewling cry, but not an animal.

On her hands and knees Bo grubbed through the sheets until she found him, gray and dehydrated, but alive. In the baby boy's sunken eyes Bo saw an old man, and the vision made her angry. He was only about three months old.

"Bradley, how in hell . . ."

"I'm crazy, remember?" Bo snarled as she ran some water from the sink over her fingers and allowed the baby to suck the moisture. Then she removed a diaper which hadn't been changed in at least two days, wrapped the baby in a blouse and two sweaters from the floor, and turned to the door.

"*Now* we'll go," she said, turning the full fury of her green eyes on the man who might or might not remain a friend after today. "And don't ever call me crazy again!"

The drunk in his pink house slippers didn't move as they stomped past his head, the baby crying his high-pitched cry like a mourner in the gloom. Bo hugged the little body close and said, "That's good, get it out, tell us all how sad it was in there. And then get ready for some good times, because your crazy social worker is going to make sure you never go back there. And I mean *never*!"

Back on the street Reinert holstered the revolver and laid a big hand on the baby's wispy brown hair. "Gotta hand it to you, Bradley," he said. "I didn't know this guy was in there. I would have left. He might have died. So whether you're crazy or not, I'll never call you crazy again, deal?"

"Deal," Bo answered. At least it was honest. "I've got to

take the baby to St. Mary's," she went on. "He needs emergency care and I need the documentation of his condition for court. But I still want to know about Kimberly Malcolm. When—"

"I'll escort you to St. Mary's, lights and sirens. It's the least I can do, right? So load him up and follow me. We'll be there in five minutes. And as soon as Buster gets taken care of, you and I can have a chat about what really happened to Kimberly Malcolm."

As Bo strapped the weak and wailing baby into the car seat she thought again of Janny Malcolm's doll. There was something about babies, about baby dolls, but it didn't scan, didn't go anywhere. And after a few minutes the tiny boy's piercing cry began to make her ears ring, give her a headache. He was moving about inside the sweaters, his little fists batting the air. He was angry, Bo decided. Well, he had good reason. But the sound of his anger was getting to her, combined with Dar's siren just ahead.

"I'll bet you've never even heard of Handel," she told the baby, "but you're going to love *The Messiah*." Jamming the tape in the tape deck, she ran it forward and pushed the play button. "This is called 'The Hallelujah Chorus,'" she grinned, turning up the volume. "Sing your heart out."

Chapter 11

The cafeteria of St. Mary's Hospital for Children had been decorated, Bo decided, by a committee savagely devoted to political correctness. Attached to the usual garlands of fake and fireproof greenery over the doors were colorful plastic Hanukkah dreidels, while a Styrofoam snow woman beside the cash register held a sign urging eaters to CELEBRATE KWANZA! There was no Christmas tree, but the bottlebrush trees surrounding the patio had been strung with tiny white lights.

"Let's sit by the patio so we can enjoy the lights," she told Dar Reinert, who was ambling behind her with a large coffee and a dish of rice pudding. She could smell the extra nutmeg he'd sprinkled on the pudding from a shaker by the coffee urns.

"I haven't had rice pudding since I was a kid," he grinned. "But when it's gone, so am I. Can't spend the whole damn day on a CPS case. So listen. I pulled an old file on this Kimberly Malcolm. Sucker goes back thirteen years. She was beaten, hit over the head with a flat object. Something with an edge. The medical report from this hospital said the injuries were consistent with a two-story fall onto the side of a cement block. Except the injury occurred in a one-story cottage with no cement blocks anywhere in the vicinity. The detective on the case, guy named Pete Cullen, ran down everybody who'd ever been near those kids but got *nada*. It was never solved. It never will be."

"Wait a minute," Bo said, breathing coffee steam, her elbows braced on the small table. "This Kimberly Malcolm was head-injured thirteen years ago and just died? I thought you said it was murder. That can't be murder, and who was Kimberly? I thought she might be Janny's mother. Why was she seen at a children's hospital?"

"Mother?" he scowled into the rapidly vanishing rice. "Kimberly and Janet Malcolm were sisters, Bo. Twins. Identical twins. They weren't quite two years old when it happened. The mother said somebody broke into her place down in Mission Beach and grabbed the little girls, and there was a scuffle in the dark. Both the kids sustained injuries, but Kimberly got the worst of it. Massive brain injury. The mom said she never saw the guy, that he threw the kids down and ran out. Nobody believed her, but nobody ever put the pieces together, either. Now that Kimberly's dead we could reopen the investigation as a murder, but it's a waste of time. Cullen had a reputation as one of the best. If he couldn't crack it, nobody could. The damn thing's cold now, stone cold."

Bo stared at the lights outside and tried not to think about stone cold. "Where is this Cullen now and where has Kimberly Malcolm been for the last thirteen years?" she asked. "There was no mention of a twin in Janny's case file."

"Impossible," Reinert boomed. "CPS was all over the case, made all the arrangements. I forget the social worker's name, but it's in the file. 'Reindeer' or something. I put a copy under your front seat while you were in the ER with the baby. Maybe it's somebody you know. And Pete Cullen retired a couple of years before Deb and I moved down here from L.A. He lives up in Julian, drops in downtown now and then. The guy's a legend, Bo. A real cop's cop. If he couldn't pop the Malcolm thing it couldn't be done."

Bo ran her hands through her hair and watched as the detective chased a final grain of rice with a plastic spoon. There had obviously been a comprehensive CPS file on this case, and that file had obviously been withheld. It wasn't difficult to guess who had simply run a copy of the current face sheet and fastened it into a new folder. But it was impossible to guess why.

"Gotta run," Reinert sighed, standing and eyeing his empty pudding dish with affection. "Tell the doc hello. Guess Deb and I will see him at your tree-trimming thing Sunday, huh?"

"Oh, yeah," Bo nodded. She'd forgotten about her impulsive decision to have a party. And hadn't she promised to take Janny Malcolm out for lunch and shopping on the same day? Janny apparently remembered nothing of the grisly past Dar had just outlined. Or did she? And where was this mother who said someone had broken in and attacked her toddlers thirteen years ago? Bo couldn't wait to get her hands on the police file.

"And Dar," she smiled as he left, "thanks for the back-up!"

"Just promise me you'll call uniforms next time, okay?"

Bo stared into her cooling coffee until a rustle of attention among the lunching hospital staff announced the arrival of Dr. Andrew LaMarche, director of the Child Abuse Unit and a celebrity at St. Mary's due to his often highly publicized expert testimony on criminal cases. At the moment he looked less expert than frazzled, Bo noted. Although the warmth that leaped to his gray eyes when he saw her suggested a reserve of energy set aside for concerns other than the professional.

"Alone at last," he whispered dramatically, taking the chair just vacated by Dar Reinert and leaning to kiss Bo's cheek. "I've missed you, Bo. Let's run away to Las Vegas and get married!"

"Andy, you promised to stop proposing," Bo chided.

"That was before my young cousin, Teless, arrived," he said, sighing. "You have to marry me now, rescue me from my own home, save me!"

"It can't be that bad."

"She plays rap music. Her favorite is by a group of women who yell things about food. I was awakened this morning by the sound of a woman chanting 'Artichoke hearts can't break' over and over. Then the workmen arrived to finish grouting the kitchen tile, and they *liked* the artichoke thing and she got one of them dancing—"

"Andy, she sounds relatively normal. You'll survive. Right now I need to know about the baby."

"He'll make it. He's dehydrated, malnourished, has three different skin diseases plus acute diaper rash, an eye infection that could have resulted in blindness if left untreated, and pinworms. I've ordered X rays, but it'll be a while before I can confirm healing fractures if there are any. He also has some chest congestion, so I ordered a TB test just to be sure, and of course HIV tests. I don't think he's ever had a bath and his nails have never been cut, resulting in infected scratches on his face, neck, and abdomen. This is one of the worst neglect cases I've seen. He was filthy. Where did you find him, Bo, in a sewer?"

"Essentially, yes," Bo answered. "I'll need a copy of your preliminary report so I can petition this one today. I don't want to take a chance on the mother showing up and taking him out of the hospital over the weekend."

"I already faxed the report to your office and put a hospital hold on the baby. He's not going anywhere. We work well together, Bo. Surely you can see the importance of saving me from a complete emotional collapse."

His graying chestnut-brown hair and mustache were as neatly trimmed as ever, Bo observed fondly. And the expensive tweed jacket over an oyster-gray French-cuffed shirt made him look like an English professor.

"I won't marry you, but I will rescue you from rap music

tonight if you promise to read Victorian poetry by candlelight in that jacket."

His answering smile stopped just short of excessive enthusiasm. "Browning?" he queried.

"No, Tennyson," Bo answered.

"Oh, dear."

"Tennyson's so *sleazy*," she went on, fanning herself with a napkin. "I can hardly wait."

"*Mon dieu*," Andrew LaMarche exhaled, blushing.

"Molly and I will come by tonight," Bo said as she stood to leave. "Maybe your cousin can help me plan the tree-trimming party. And I want to hear you play the harpsichord, now that it's finished."

"The sheet music that accompanied the kit is a selection of Beatles hits, Bo."

"I'll pick up some Bach and some Christmas carols this afternoon," she grimaced. "Take care of my baby for me, okay?"

A darkness flitted across his face at the remark. Bo pretended not to see it and bit her lip as she hit the cafeteria doors with both hands.

How long are you going to drag this out, Bradley? He's a lovely, wonderful man who wants marriage and a family. Neither of you is young and as long as you're around, he's not going to have that. The only honorable thing for you to do is to change your name and move to Czechoslovakia. Now!

The troubling train of thought was filed for later consideration when Bo saw the paperwork Dar had left for her in the Pathfinder. A thick file folder of Xeroxed police files dating back thirteen years, it would provide not only a view into Janny Malcolm's past but information which might explain Madge Aldenhoven's more recent behavior. Settling into the driver's seat, she turned on the radio to a pop station playing Christmas carols and began to read. In less than a minute her brow was knit in ridges. It was the most puzzling story she'd seen in a lifetime of social work.

"Answered call to home of TAMLIN LISETTE LAFFERTY, 720 Nantasket Street, Mission Beach, at 6:42 A.M.," the first officer on the scene had written.

Found LAFFERTY and three minors—JEFFREY LAF-FERTY, 5; KIMBERLY MALCOLM, 18 mos. and JANET MALCOLM, 18 mos.—in the house, which is owned by LAFFERTY's father-in-law, GEORGE LAF-FERTY. TAMLIN LAFFERTY stated that she awakened around 5:30 A.M. when she heard an intruder in the house. She further stated that she saw a "tall, skinny man in a light-colored nylon jacket" in the bedroom she shared with the twin girls holding one of them under his arm and grabbing into the crib for the other. LAFFERTY said that she screamed and fought with the man who then threw both minors down and fled. She then at-tempted to phone her estranged husband RICHARD ("RICK") LAFFERTY at the home of his father in El Cajon. When no one answered she gave the twin girls bottles and put them back in their cribs. She stated that an hour after the incident she found KIMBERLY rigid and with her eyes rolled back, at which time she phoned the SDPD. Response time: 22 minutes.

Bo stared out at St. Mary's parking lot and listened as the Mormon Tabernacle Choir sang "Oh Holy Night" through speakers mounted under her dashboard. The night docu-mented in the police report had been anything but holy, she mused. Something terrible had happened. And even from a thirteen-year vantage, the story told by Tamlin Lafferty sounded contrived, unlikely.

Why had she waited an hour after a break-in to call the po-lice? What was she doing in that hour? And where was the es-tranged husband? Bo had seen a sufficient number of unhealthy marital relationships in her work to predict from the one paragraph she'd read what the Lafferty marriage was probably like. "Codependent" was the current catchphrase, but "pathetic" more closely approximated Bo's assessment. Tamlin Lafferty had been unable to think of anything to do in an apparent emergency involving three very young children except to call her husband in a suburban area of San Diego from which it would take him at least a half hour to reach Mission Beach. Unless, of course, the unanswered and therefore unprovable phone call was a lie designed to mask the fact that the "intruder" was the estranged husband, Rick Lafferty. But what had happened? Who were these people, and where were they now? Why had they not been at Kimberly's strange funeral? Where had Kimberly been for thirteen years? And why had they abandoned Janny to a lifetime of anonymity in the foster care system? Bo felt a satisfying energy begin to throb softly inside her skull. It was like opening a new book or smoothing the first brush of paint on a blank canvas. Curiosity warming dormant synapses and creating light.

The bulk of the report had been written by Pete Cullen in an informal style not intended for official use. These were the notes from his investigation, Bo realized. As messy and yet as thorough as her own. When appropriate he'd attached copies of germane documents. Bo noticed Rick Lafferty's dishonorable discharge from the U.S. Army for "frequent unauthorized absence from duty, malingering and insubordination." A marriage license indicating that Tamlin Malcolm and Rick Lafferty had married at eighteen, some twelve years before the incident in which a baby girl had sustained a head injury that would take thirteen years to kill her. Bo added the years on her fingers, calculating that the parents of Janny and Kimberly Malcolm would be forty-three now. But where were they?

Cullen had also attached copies of forms legally changing the surname of Kimberly and Janet from "Lafferty" to "Malcolm," although further perusal of the file revealed no divorce papers. Bo drew a series of question marks on the dust filming her dashboard. Tamlin Lafferty had legally changed the names of her daughters to her own maiden name, but not her son's name. Estranged from her husband, she nonetheless lived in a house owned by her father-in-law while her thirty-year-old husband lived with his father. Bo shook her head and read on.

"Rick Lafferty works intermittently as a construction laborer, usually on jobs provided by his father, George Lafferty," Cullen wrote.

Both father and son are regarded as master bricklayers in the local construction community, but Rick is seen as a loose cannon who can't be relied on to finish projects on time or within budget. Some of the men who have worked with Rick say he has a drug or drinking problem, some say his wife drives him crazy with demands for things he can't afford to buy, and another bunch just says there's something wrong with the guy but they don't know what it is. He isn't disliked by co-workers, but he isn't friends with them either. Apparently he hangs out mostly with his father and keeps his business to himself. Both Rick and George Lafferty state that they were asleep in George Lafferty's home at the time of the attack on Kimberly Malcolm and that they did not hear the phone ring. Helen "Dizzy" Lafferty, wife of George and mother of Rick, also states that she was asleep with her husband at the time of the attack, and that their bedside phone did not ring.

"Okay, so the phone call thing was a lie," Bo told the Pathfinder's steering wheel. "Or at least Pete Cullen thought it was."

Flipping through the voluminous file, Bo found the section she was looking for. "Department of Social Services' Child Welfare Division has assigned the Malcolm case to Child Protective Services," Cullen noted. "The social worker, Mary Mandeer, has been cooperative but unable to provide any additional information which might help conclude this case successfully. See attached."

The DSS forms were thirteen years old, relics no longer used anywhere in the system. Still, they provided the answer to at least one question troubling Bo. Mary Mandeer's hand had been unsteady when she signed the last "change of placement" form for Kimberly Malcolm eighteen months after the intake forms and the original face sheet. Eighteen months after something that had been like a two-story fall onto the side of a cement block. Bo felt her own hand tremble as she read the disposition.

"Kimberly Malcolm will be transferred to the Kelton Institute where courtesy supervision will be provided by Child Protective Services of Los Angeles County," a clerk had typed. The inked letters looked strange, old-fashioned. The enclosed tops of the *e*'s were solid black. Bo tried to remember the last time she'd seen a typewriter, tried not to think about Kimberly Malcolm at three, caught in the shadows between life and death. Somehow the blackened *e*'s hinted at old secrets hidden between the lines, behind the words. Bo felt a chill that made her palms sting. This case was something worse than she'd imagined. This case involved the unthinkable.

Nobody talked about Kelton. Workers in the grisliest cases, the head-trauma cases, knew about it but never discussed it over lunch or even after a few drinks at a unit cocktail party. The name, if spoken at all, was whispered, after which all eyes looked away and the subject was quickly changed. There were rumors about Kelton. That the nearly dead there sometimes awakened immediately before death and insisted that no time had gone by, that they were as they had been.

A story drifted over from the Adult Protective Services workers, who routinely dealt with the elderly, that an eighty-six-year-old man profoundly brain-damaged by street thugs when he was seventy-nine had somehow managed to leave his bed (if indeed there were beds) at Kelton on the night of his death, and to board a city bus, where he terrified nine passengers by recognizing each of them and calling them by name before he fell in the aisle and was still. The passengers believed that the boundaries of their own lives were revealed in the way he pronounced their names. The passengers believed that death itself had crept onto the bus.

Estrella, Bo remembered, had told her the story years ago. And when Bo asked what the Kelton Institute was, Estrella had talked about a facility where the bodies of those whose brains exhibited almost no electrical activity were maintained until final, physical death occurred. Head injuries and massive strokes, mostly. A few whose families couldn't bring themselves to authorize the cessation of life-support systems and were willing to pay to keep the heart and lung machines and intravenous feedings going indefinitely. A place of stopped transition. Like an abandoned subway station.

The realization was like an icy breath inside Bo's shoulders and back. The dream. It was the dream. Shivering, Bo glanced at the authorizing signature below Mary Mandeer's.

"M. Aldenhoven," it said, "for the San Diego County Department of Social Services."

As she eased the Pathfinder out of St. Mary's parking lot Bo heard a train whistle slicing the air from someplace east, toward the desert. Its Doppler effect, the eerie two-note moan created by moving sound and stationary listener, brought tears to her eyes with its message of inevitable loss.

"Aye, Cally," she whispered, "it's your feast it is now, your time. But there's more to this than death. Something it is in this that's evil. Something rotten that never should have been."

In the distance the train howled softly and then was silent as Bo drove back to her office, drumming her fingers on the record of an old but exhaustive police investigation that had missed something. Something that was still there, still hidden. Still, she thought while snapping her teeth together just for the sound, waiting.

Chapter 12

Walking back into her office building under a glowering sky, Bo realized she had made no decision about the Malcolm case. There was really no decision to make, she thought in an attempt at rationality. While intriguing, the case was only a historical curiosity. One among thousands gathering dust on corridors of metal shelves in a windowless ground-floor storage room behind the word-processing office. Kimberly Malcolm was dead. Kimberly Malcolm had in significant ways been dead for many years.

Madge, Bo assumed, had been involved in the Malcolm case with the social worker Mary Mandeer. Mandeer was probably the other woman at the funeral, the one who recited Louise Bogan's poem about a girl who was a statue. The two women had arranged and participated in the closure of an old case for reasons belonging to the past. Bo knew she would read the rest of Pete Cullen's file. But maybe she would only read it out of curiosity. There were sufficient numbers of live children demanding her professional attention, like the baby boy she'd just found in a sea of dirty clothes. The Malcolm case, she decided vaguely, was best left in a past that had not included Bo Bradley. Besides, she didn't *want* to think about it. Not about the Kelton Institute and not about whatever realm lay be-

tween life and death. Not about an eighteen-month-old toddler trapped in that realm for over thirteen years. Thinking
about it pushed open a door Bo recognized as dangerous. A
door that could open into nothing but horror, grief, and madness.

Leaning against Madge's door frame with her hands jammed
into her denim skirt pockets, Bo felt herself sliding into "the
look." She hadn't meant to. It just happened organically sometimes. The heavy-lidded, medicated manic-depressive look that
made people feel transparent and exposed. Bo had experienced
it herself at a fund-raising dinner for San Diego's suicide hotline, which had at one point been nothing more than an answering machine. Seated with other psychiatric "consumers,"
she'd been uncomfortably aware of the steady, intrusive gaze of
a chubby, bespectacled young man across the table from her.
His look forced her to acknowledge that she was acting, that
all social interaction was essentially a sequence of exhausting
roles which existed only to obscure the flawed personalities
hiding inside them. His look made her nervous.

"Why are you staring at me?" she asked.

"Sorry. It's the meds. I've got manic depression, and sometimes—"

"Look, *I've* got manic depression and that's not the look we
cultivate. It's supposed to be, you know, wild and zany."

"Never could do wild and zany," he said with a slow smile,
continuing to stare at Bo as though she were covered in pages
that could be read.

"Duel, then," she challenged, matching her eyelid level to
his and staring hypnotically into his face. "Loser picks up the
parking tab for the whole table."

"You're on," he agreed, and then just sat there like a Bud-
dha with laser eyes. In less than four minutes he'd made Bo so
uncomfortable she conceded the challenge and forked over
twelve dollars in parking fees. After that she practiced. By
now it came naturally, sometimes unbidden. This time, she

thought, it was probably a response to the idea of the Kelton Institute and a toddler's body growing to young womanhood there without a brain, without awareness.

"What is it, Bo?" Madge asked, looking up from a stack of case files. "What are you staring at?"

For a split second Bo imagined being able to talk to her supervisor, imagined saying, "How have you survived all these years in a job which demands daily confrontation with the unspeakable? How do you keep the truth about what people do to helpless things from killing you?" But Madge was in one of her renowned snits, and the moment passed. The snits were legendary and occurred in response to nothing in particular. Everybody in the building knew there was no remedy but to stay out of Madge's way. She could be vicious.

"I got the baby on the sibling petition," Bo answered. "Took him to St. Mary's and I'll go over to court and file it right away. It was pretty bad."

"That's our job, Bo," Madge answered as if she, too, had just climbed a set of reeking stairs into a corridor of hell. "And I have to say I'm growing a little tired of your whining. With Estrella on leave everybody's going to have to shoulder the extra burden. Complaining about 'bad' cases is scarcely professional. Surely we can assume they're all 'bad.' Just do your job, Bo. I haven't got time to pamper you."

"Pamper?" Bo said as layers of possibility began to assume a pattern she could actually feel. "I don't recall asking to be pampered."

The older woman drummed her fingers softly against the side of her head. "Bo, I don't have time to play one of your pathetic, manipulative games. Get over to court and file the petition. I've already seen Dr. LaMarche's preliminary report. There will be no problem with the petition. What *are* you staring at?"

"Did you do the closing summary on the Malcolm case?" Bo asked, wondering if Madge actually knew or merely intuited that random changes in attitude routinely unnerved those under her supervision. Was this the same woman who had driven to Mercy Hospital to pick Bo up, the woman who said she had an Irish grandmother? Impossible.

"The Malcolm case is no longer any of your concern. I'm busy, Bo. Please stop harassing me or I'll have to call security. I really don't know why you insist on staying in this job when you can't conduct yourself appropriately."

Security? Bo felt the gratuitous insult like an acid mist permeating her body. It defined her, made manifest her status as leper. No matter what she did or didn't do, anyone could, at any time, cast her apart from the rest of humanity by pronouncing any of a thousand words meant to illuminate her essential, fearful deviance. And Madge had invoked that power for no reason Bo could ascertain except the need to establish a boundary. But Madge had gone too far. Way too far.

The pattern fell into place with finality. It had been sifting like sand in muddy water all along, finding its way to the bottom. The Malcolm case might belong to the past, but it also hid something Madge Aldenhoven did not want anyone to know. And she had just guaranteed that Bo Bradley would unearth whatever that was. Bo ground her teeth and experienced a rush of calculated vindictiveness. It wasn't particularly unpleasant, she noted. Neither was it pleasant. It was just necessary.

After filing the sibling petition at juvenile court, Bo phoned the office message center and left word for Madge that she was going to look for the baby's mother. Then she scanned Pete Cullen's notes on the Malcolm case. He had, as Dar Reinert said, investigated everybody connected to the little girls — the parents, a maternal aunt, the paternal grandparents, and the maternal grandfather, Jasper Malcolm. Bo wasn't surprised to see the dollmaker's name. It was part of the pattern; she could see that now. So was her impromptu visit to the toy store in Fashion Valley. Everything flowed into the pattern. There was no point in fighting it, although the momentary lapse into rationalism just before Madge's last outburst had been comfortable, Bo thought. No wonder people spoke about "behaving rationally" with such fondness. Behaving rationally really meant behaving comfortably. Not an option for Bo Bradley.

Checking Cullen's file, she chewed softly on her lower lip and headed east toward El Cajon and the last known address for Kimmy and Janny Malcolm's father, Rick Lafferty. Once there, she found that she was not surprised at what she saw despite the fact that anyone else probably would have been. It was part of the pattern; it made sense. Now all she had to do was figure out what that sense was.

One of several half-acre "estates" carved out of hilly chaparral in the late fifties, the Lafferty property looked less like Southern California than the set for an English Gothic. While the adjacent properties displayed identical watered lawns in which identical ranch-style houses were situated with unimaginative pride of place, the Lafferty house could not be seen from the street at all. The old subdivision had no sidewalks, Bo observed, so the eight-foot mortared stone wall fronting the Lafferty property was nearly flush with the street. Two arched gateways opened to a semicircular drive paved with bricks set in a basket-weave design. Bo parked and approached one of the ornamental iron gates, waving at a woman setting bulbs in the ground beneath a handsome live oak.

"Hi!" she called, improvising her approach from details of the landscaping. "I'm driving around getting ideas for ways to dress up a house we've just bought, and somebody told me this place had great stonework. Would you mind if I asked the name of your contractor?"

The woman pulled off her canvas gloves and stood, pushing a black bandana back against short ash-blond hair. In muddy jeans and an old sweatshirt she looked young, but her less-than-waspish waistline suggested a respectable maturity.

"Where's your house?" she asked, moving to the heavy gate.

"Del Mar," Bo improvised. Andy's new house in the San Diego seacoast village would do. "But I was visiting a friend up here and decided to drive around checking out ideas. Your driveway is lovely!"

"My husband Rick did it," the woman said. "But he doesn't contract out. You can find bricklayers at the sand-and-gravel companies, though. Just call a few of them and ask for names."

Rick. It had to be Rick Lafferty, Bo concluded. After all, how many master bricklayers named Rick could live at the same address sequentially? Especially in an area like San Diego where brickwork was uncommon, expensive, and actually undesirable because of the area's occasional minor earthquakes. There probably weren't enough bricklayers in San Diego County to fill a whole column in the Yellow Pages. So was this woman Tamlin, Rick Lafferty's wife? Bo smiled sweetly as she scanned the woman for hints of character or the lack thereof.

"It's my third marriage," she confided in what she hoped were girl-talk tones. "I really want to do it right this time, make a beautiful home for both of us. Before, I was always too busy with my job. You know how it is? You just never seem to have time for the little details that make a home special, like flowers and pretty draperies and plants in the yard."

Gag, Bradley! Why don't you just swing from the gate, beaming, and then burst into "Raindrops on roses and whiskers on kittens"?

The woman looked askance. "If you've got a husband like mine, he'll do all the work," she smiled dismissively. "We got married eight years ago and he's worked on this place every day since then. Walls, driveways, garden paths, fireplaces, even a stone gazebo in back overlooking the freeway. Keeps him busy. All I do is putter around. Listen, I wish you luck."

If they'd only been married eight years, this would be Lafferty's second wife, not Tamlin. But Bo had to know for sure.

"Thanks for the tip on bricklayers," she said. "Maybe if I mention that I've seen your husband's work they'll know the sort of thing I'm looking for. A brick driveway like this would be perfect in front of our house. It's sort of Tudor."

The woman was moving away. "His name's Rick Lafferty," she called over her shoulder. "Most of the masonry contractors around here know who he is. Just tell them you saw Rick Lafferty's driveway."

"Great. Thanks so much!" Bo replied, edging toward the Pathfinder while studying the house hidden behind a low rubblestone wall backed by thorny wintergreen barberry hedges. With two stone walls and a barrier hedge, the sprawling ranch-style house beyond seemed a prisoner of its own landscaping, although, Bo noted, there were no security bars at the windows. The protective walls and plantings were apparently symbolic rather than functional. But what had Rick Lafferty been trying to wall out, or in?

At a convenience store near the freeway on-ramp Bo stopped for a Coke and then pulled a frayed legal pad from under the passenger's seat. "Rick Lafferty," she wrote atop the page. "Still at father's address. Apparently remarried eight years ago. Has turned property into a fortress with brick and stonework. Check to see if his parents, George and 'Dizzy' Lafferty, are still alive. And where is first wife, Tamlin?" Then she opened the police file.

Cullen had named the location of Kimberly Malcolm's injury as a tiny Mission Beach street stretching only a few blocks across the strip of land between Mission Bay and the Pacific Ocean. Bo knew the area. Just north of her own beach community, it was small and comprised almost entirely of vacation properties. On the bay side were large modular housing resorts, and the short streets running from Mission Boulevard to the beachfront sidewalk were crammed with wooden cottages and more modern townhouses on tiny lots. While a few people lived in Mission Beach year-round, most of the beach and bay properties were rented to vacationers during summer and to college students at vastly reduced rates during winter.

Bo headed west on Interstate 8 all the way to the beach, navigated the maze of turns necessary to reach Mission Beach, and stopped a block from Nantasket. Some of the surf shops and streetside sandwich counters were closed for the winter, and the remaining businesses seemed eerily vacant without sun and flocks of bronzed teenagers. Bo locked the Pathfinder and walked slowly toward the corner of Nantasket and Mission Boulevard as a yellow haze broke through the cloud cover and was quickly swallowed again.

The cottage where somebody had harmed an eighteen-month-old child was on a block-long street ending at the sidewalk and seawall. Bo stood at the corner gazing down the length of the block and out to sea. Then she turned and walked swiftly to the address in Pete Cullen's file. There was nothing there.

Or rather there was too much there. The minuscule lot was dense with unkempt tropical plants moving ominously in the clammy sea wind. From beyond the scaling picket fence defining the lot, Bo counted four two-story feather palms, their dead lower fronds bent to the ground and moving with the wind. The sound made Bo think of huge moths trapped in brittle paper. Among the sagging palms a magnolia tree was covered with blueberry climber, and dead tangles of the vine matted clumps of unrecognizable shrubbery as well as the ground. Even in broad daylight the place lay in shadows.

Bo walked the length of the fence, trying to see through the overgrown plants. From the western corner of the lot she glimpsed the side of a cottage almost invisible amid the rampant green. It had shake shingles, although most were curled and rotted and many had fallen off. The windows were boarded over, but even that appeared to have been done years in the past and many of the graying boards had also fallen away. The patch of cement foundation she could see was coated in sickly green moss.

"May I help you?" a well-dressed man in his thirties asked from the deck of the modern dwelling next door. Bo noticed that a cellular phone was attached to his belt. At his left wrist a wide gold watchband caught the dim light. Yuppies and drug dealers, she thought, with their status-phones and gold jewelry.

"Is this property for sale?" she asked.

"Don't we wish!" the man answered. "Place is a blight. Drags down the value of the whole street. But it's not for sale. Tied up in an estate or something, I guess."

A nonvegetable rustle in the undergrowth made Bo jump.

"Tree rats," the man explained. "They love to nest in these palms. We were going to pay for an exterminator but then we realized the rats keep the vagrants from sleeping in there. My wife calls the place Hamlin."

Bo thought of children lost forever, children spirited into a mountain that closed around them and never opened again. It had happened to Kimberly Malcolm. The apt symbolism made Bo's hair stand on end. The pattern. She could feel it glowing inside her head. People, stories, random comments—all led back to a moment thirteen years in the past when something had happened here. Something that stopped time for one little girl and left another lost and alone.

"Well, Merry Christmas," she said, fighting a dizziness that shimmered in the tangled greenery. For a moment she thought she could see tiny red eyes watching from inside the shadows. Hundreds of them. "Gotta run."

After a quick drive home, Bo dashed up the steps to her apartment and phoned her shrink even before picking up Molly.

"Eva," she began, "I'm either getting manic or there's something, well, *magical* going on with this Malcolm case. I feel as though I'm just running on a track already in place, like a maze. Everything I turn up, everybody I talk to—it all seems to make some kind of huge sense even if I don't know why. It's a pattern, Eva. And that dream pulled me into it even before Dar called and asked me to—"

"Whoa, Bo," the shrink's deep voice warned. "Are you sleeping, eating right, taking your meds?"

"Yes. I'm really okay, I think. But Madge buried somebody today in secret, and the grandfather's this famous dollmaker. It happened years ago, Eva, in a cottage over in Mission Beach, and now the place is abandoned. There are rats—"

"I'd like to see you as soon as possible, Bo. Whatever you're talking about is obviously too complex for a phone conversation. What are your plans for this evening?"

Bo ran a hand through her short curls and scowled at the refrigerator across from her kitchen counter. "Dinner at Andy's," she said. "A teenage relative has turned up for the holidays. I'm going to meet her. And by the way, I'm having a tree-trimming party Sunday evening at about seven. Can you be here?"

"I'd love to come, and I'll bring something nourishing. But we need to talk before then. Breakfast tomorrow? Why don't I meet you in Del Mar near Andy's. I've been meaning to do some shopping up there and this will be perfect."

Bo pondered the ease with which her shrink made arrangements. "Thanks, Eva," she sighed. "I'll meet you at the bookstore around nine. We can pick a restaurant from there. And Eva?"

"What, Bo?"

"How much do you know about brain injuries, comas, that sort of thing?"

"You are not to think about this case anymore today," the psychiatrist intoned. "Is that understood?"

"Okay, okay," Bo grinned. "But I want to talk about brain death over breakfast."

"An enticing prospect," Eva noted dryly, and hung up.

Bo retrieved Molly from the neighbor's, then turned off the phone and enjoyed a leisurely bath before dressing in a forest-green sweater and long knit skirt that made her look wholesome and robust, she thought. With the addition of boots and a fur muff, she could pose beside a sleigh.

"Oh Tannenbaum, oh Tannenbaum," she sang as Molly howled gleefully from the floor, *"Wie grün sind deine Zweige."*

Over the din it was impossible to hear the message being taped on her answering machine. A terrified voice whispering, "She's coming to get me, oh, God, she's coming to get me, don't let her get me, please!" Then a click, and silence.

Chapter 13

"*Cher pacan!*" Teless Babineaux muttered, banging a skillet Andrew LaMarche had found perfectly adequate until now against his new cooktop. "Dis *moodee* thing give me *de chou rouge,* Nonk Andy. Ain't you got a iron pan?"

"I'm afraid not," he answered, studying the orange-mango salsa he was mixing in a white ceramic bowl. "And please try to speak English when Bo arrives, Teless. She tends to pick up speech patterns from people around her. It wouldn't do for her to latch on to some of your more colorful phrases."

"Now *you* givin' me *de chou rouge,*" the teenager grinned, stirring a mountain of shrimp, butter, and spices in the less-than-adequate skillet. The aroma reminded Andrew of childhood summers on the bayous of southwestern Louisiana with his aunt and uncle. Teless even looked a little like his aunt, or would in a few years. The same wide hips and thick, dark hair. The same blue eyes darting everywhere, amused by everything. He found himself delighted with her, with their shared family history and Cajun French.

"Young ladies don't say 'You're giving me a red butt' every time they're irritated," he smiled while inhaling the spicy smells.

"Sounds all wrong in English, don't it?" the girl agreed. "Promise I'll never say it in English around your old lady."

"I don't think the term 'old lady' is quite appropriate for Bo," Andrew replied, frowning. "I'm afraid she'll take exception to that."

"Not unless she's as uptight as you, *sha*," Teless said, leaning to kiss his cheek.

The term meant "dear," elided from the French *cher*. Andrew realized he was basking in the affectionate attention of his remarkable young relative. She had a gift, he observed, for incisive observation made palatable by a blanket, loving acceptance. She'd be fabulous with children. He wondered if she'd be interested in volunteering at St. Mary's, and then lost the train of thought as the doorbell announced Bo's arrival.

Teless got there first, her wooden spoon dripping roux on the flagstone entry floor which flowed from the door into both the dining room and kitchen. Bo had picked out the flooring, the most substantial change he'd imposed on the old seaside Tudor after gutting and adding a twenty-foot extension to the cramped and cabinet-heavy kitchen. He was sure the flagstone's grouting wasn't quite dry, and quickly dropped to his knees to mop at the buttery droplets with a tea towel.

"You must be Teless!" Bo said as Molly scampered to help lick up the roux. "I'm Bo, Andy's, um . . ."

"Old lady?" Teless suggested.

"Precisely," Bo giggled. The term, she thought, fit like a favorite sweatshirt. "Andy, why are you crawling around on the floor, which incidentally looks great?"

"Roux," he explained, standing to hug her. "But Molly's taking care of it. You look lovely tonight, Bo. Green's definitely your color."

Beneath the words was a sense of accomplishment, as if he, personally, were responsible for the affinity between redheads and the vernal color. Bo noted the hint of a surprise in his words, too. Probably something about her Christmas gift, she guessed. Something green. From deep in her personal history a treacherously female interest bubbled to the surface. Emeralds.

She'd always wanted an emerald ring. A wide gold band with chip diamonds and seed pearls spilling away from an emerald blazing green fire from its heart. She'd even made designs for the ring and then hidden them in old sketchbooks. Intelligent, socially aware people eschewed ostentation in favor of higher spiritual values; she knew that. These were her family's values, reinforced by her own experience in life. But everyone was entitled to one deplorable fantasy, she told herself. One unbecoming, self-serving, pointless capitulation to vanity. For her, it would always be the emerald ring.

Fortunately, there was no way Andy could know about it. Her gift would probably be a green silk blouse. More likely lingerie. She wished she felt comfortable enough to tell him what she really needed was a coat. After all, she'd promised Estrella she'd look presentable at the christening.

"Teless has made a sort of shrimp gumbo," he explained as the girl played with Molly. "Popcorn rice, yeast biscuits. My contribution is the appetizer and a chocolate raspberry torte for dessert."

"I can't tell you what this means to me," Bo grinned. "Just when I finally lost the last pound of the ten I've been battling for two months. And I love gumbo, but what's popcorn rice?"

"Louisiana special rice. Smells just like popcorn," Teless explained. "I brought five pounds for Nonk Andy. Would've brought crawdads, too, 'cept the bus man said they had to be froze with dry ice an' I didn't have no dry ice, me. This puppy like a boudin sausage on legs, Bo. T-Boudin!"

The teenager's speech was fascinating, Bo thought. And the girl herself was radiant with a natural beauty born more of spirit than of Madison Avenue. Molly adored her immediately, as, Bo was certain, did every Cajun boy in southwestern Louisiana. Including one, Andy had said, determined to marry her before he left for a stint in prison. Her godmother had been wise in sending Teless to California for the holidays, Bo mused. Brilliant, actually.

"In Cajun, 'T' before somebody's name means 'little,'" Andrew explained, taking Bo's coat. "Um, your lining's falling apart," he mentioned.

"Old coat," Bo concurred.

After a dinner in which Bo forced herself to forget the meaning of the word "calorie," Andrew proudly displayed the finished harpsichord which had prompted him to move from his condo into a house. Painstakingly crafted of cherrywood, it glowed softly in a spacious library-music room adjacent to the dining room. The flagstone floor had been laid here as well, but an Oriental carpet protected the harpsichord from contact with the stone. Bo pulled a package of rolled sheet music from her purse, smoothed it flat, and placed a sheet on the harpsichord's music brace.

"'Prelude and Fugue in G Sharp Minor,' from 'The Well-Tempered Clavier,'" she announced. "I also got the A minor and the A flat major, but the G sharp's my favorite. Could you start with that one, Andy?"

"My lady," he nodded, bowing and flipping imaginary tails over the edge of the harpsichord's tiny bench as he sat.

"*Ga!*" Teless exhaled. "Would you look at that!"

But Bo was lost in the music from the first plucked note. Sliding with it into a Bachian landscape she had learned to love as a child. The precision, the repetition, the theme announced and then hidden only to be heard again beneath another, or to be heard somehow vertically where before it had been horizontal. The music unfolding like a garden of roses in time-lapse photography, the imagery now blatant, now obscure, but always *rose*. The room with its bay window and shelves of books, its brilliant carpet and pewter lamps, might have been a starship navigating a universe of exquisite order. A universe made of music.

"Ah, Andy!" she sighed when he released the last keystroke, allowing the damper to silence its still-vibrating string. "How beautiful!"

"I made the springs from real boar bristle," he beamed. "And I told you about the crow's-quill plectra."

"Bach would be proud, Andy. And so would my mother. Where did you learn to play like that?"

"Our parents insisted that my sister and I have piano lessons when we were children. We both hated it, but we learned to play anyway. Later, during my residency at Tulane's Medical Center, I rented a room near the Quarter. There was a piano in the living room where the boarders hung out. I started playing just to get people to turn off the TV, and found that I enjoyed it. Plus, it took my mind off . . . things."

Bo knew the veiled reference was to the accidental death of his two-year-old daughter, Sylvie, in New Orleans while he was in Vietnam with the Marines. The child's mother, his high school girlfriend, had simply vanished after the little girl's death. More than twenty years had passed, and still he paid private investigators to search for her. The loss of the child, Bo realized, had opened a wound that would never entirely heal.

"Oh, *sha*," Teless said, touching his shoulder, "the whole family knows about your little girl that died, about Sylvie. Some even takes flowers to her grave there in New Orleans. I went once, with your sister Elizabeth and her husband Gaston, and my cousin Alcide and his wife MaryLou, and I think MaryLou's brother, Henri, but it might have been Alcide's friend, Norman —"

"I had no idea anyone remembered," Andrew said softly. "How nice to know about the flowers."

"Family's family," Teless said, shrugging. "You got any music here for singing?"

"I think I can manage 'Jolie Blonde,'" he smiled, banging out the opening bars of the Cajun classic on the harpsichord

which suddenly sounded, Bo thought, amazingly like an ac-
cordion. Teless sang the first verse in an enthusiastic alto, followed by Andrew on the chorus, teaching Bo the French
words as they went. Then Teless pulled Bo into a hearty two-
step around the harpsichord, oblivious to the museum-quality
carpet being stomped by their feet. Andrew, his head thrown
back, bellowed verse after verse until Bo was dizzy from
laughing.

"I got to go on now, call my old man, Robby," Teless giggled when the song was over. "Is that okay, Nonk Andy? Use
the long distance, I mean? Robby got sentenced today, but he
said they wouldn't take him off until Monday since his daddy
spoke for him. Prob'ly the last time me'n Robby'll talk for a
while, *oui*."

"Go ahead, but keep it under thirty minutes," Andrew
agreed. "And now, Bo, I want to show you my latest decorating tour de force.

"Okay," Bo answered, accustomed to nonstop decorating
crises beginning the day he'd taken possession of the house a
month ago. Her attention was on Teless in any event. The
teenager had been strangely cheerful about her boyfriend's im-
pending incarceration. No histrionics, no gnashing of teeth.
An epically unadolescent attitude. Something about this
boyfriend story, Bo thought to herself, was fishy.

"This way," Andrew said, leading her outside and across the
pine-littered lawn and driveway to the mock-Tudor garage
with its upstairs apartment. He'd offered her the apartment as
a compromise in their unending battle over the nature of their
relationship. She could live there, he said, or she could use the
space as a studio. It would be hers if she wanted it. Otherwise
he'd rent it to someone, a nice elderly couple maybe, who'd
live there and keep an eye on the property during his frequent
absences. "I think you'll be pleased with the look," he said,
unlocking a security gate at the base of the apartment's exter-
nal stairs, then a Dutch door opening into the apartment at

the top. The landing and stairs, Bo noticed, were fenced with redwood two-by-twos set three inches apart and secured below the landing floor and the base of each step. There was no way a small animal—a dachshund, for example—could wiggle through and fall.

"*Voila!*" he said, turning on the overhead light to reveal wide horizontal pine paneling bleached to a honey gray defining the small living room and dining nook adjacent to a sparkling new kitchen similar to the one in her apartment. Both the kitchen and dining area commanded a view of the sea through tall pines, and a brick-red freestanding fireplace on an island of flagstone pavers set off the inland-side wall, flanked by casement windows.

"The carpet's the tour de force, I think," he went on proudly. "Matte nylon indoor-outdoor in a Berber weave. Looks like wool, but it can't mildew and cleans with soap and water."

"Wow," Bo agreed, kneeling to inspect the dark green and blue plaid at her feet.

"It's a tartan called MacCallum. I assumed from your, um, plaid sheets that you liked tartans. Green tartans."

"I had no idea you'd noticed my sheets, Andy," Bo teased him. "What's in here?"

"Ah," he said. "Go look."

Bo opened a door in a bookcase wall and discovered a short hall, bathroom, small laundry room, bedroom, and a large, bare room with a skylight. The floor was covered in springy beige sheet vinyl. A granite pattern. Washable, easily replaceable. The south and west walls were glass and bordered by a widow's walk railed in the same close-set two-by-twos as the stairs and landing.

"Of course it's a little bare and empty at the moment," Andrew mentioned casually, "but with the right window coverings and . . . things, I think it will do nicely."

"Oh, Andy," Bo sighed, reaching for his hand, "it's my best

fantasy! A place that feels safe and warm with a view of the ocean and a studio where I can paint. But I can't . . . I can't take advantage of you. I can't let you keep giving when I give nothing. It's not right, and—"

"Bo," he interrupted, "you've given me my life. I don't know why, but from the beginning loving you somehow made it possible for me to be me. Just knowing that you exist, that you're in the world, makes me want to do things I've never done, try things I've never tried. You're like a window for me, Bo. A thousand windows. And all I have to give in return are things. Things I can buy, like a little carpentry work up here so you'll have a place to paint. I'm not trying to own you, Bo. I just want to be a window for you, too."

"Window," Bo repeated as they walked back into the empty living room. He was magnificent, honest, convincing. And he'd melted her heart.

"Window will do," she said as he pulled her to him with an urgency she shared, an urgency which quickly increased her familiarity with the new carpet. It smelled like nutmeg, she noticed peripherally as he wadded his shirt to pillow her head, and somewhat later, his.

"Mmph," she mumbled much later as they lay quietly in the moonlight pretending to be marble statuary, "I thought I heard something at the door."

"Impossible," Andrew said, snagging Bo's black lace bra from the floor with a toe and then swinging it above them. "What do they make these things with, flexible steel?"

"Just the underwiring," Bo replied. "Centuries from now archaeologists will find bra underwires while sifting through dump sites, and conclude that everyone had prosthetic knee replacements or something."

"Knee? This wouldn't fit anywhere in a knee, Bo. There's only one possible use—"

The knock at the door was completely audible this time.

"I'm really sorry to bother y'all," Teless yelled, "but there's a emergency call for Bo. Says he's a social worker an' you got to come talk right now."

"Be right there," Bo yelled back, grabbing her bra from Andrew's foot. "Damn."

It was Rombo Perry, a psychiatric social worker with whom Bo and Andrew had become friends after his help on an unusual case a year in the past.

"I *knew* I was interrupting something when it took so long for you to come to the phone, Bo," he apologized after Bo had sprinted to the phone in Andrew's kitchen, "but I'm working graveyard tonight and we just got an admission who says she knows you. Says she tried to call you earlier, that you were her social worker. Name's Malcolm. Janny Malcolm."

"Janny's in County Psychiatric? Why? What's happened?"

"I don't know. She seems terrified, says somebody's after her. Apparently her foster parents called the CPS hotline when she wouldn't stop screaming and hid in a closet. Hotline called the police to pick her up and bring her down here. She's oriented, knows where she is and what's going on, but she's got a doll chained to her wrist and goes stiff when anybody tries to take it from her, and—"

"Don't take the doll," Bo urged. "Let her hang on to it."

"It's got a bisque head, Bo. Breakable. You know the suicide precautions. The duty psychiatrist sedated her, but it doesn't seem to be having any effect. We need to get her calmed down. I thought it might help if you talked to her."

Janny Malcolm terrified and cowering in the back of a patrol car. Embarrassed by the uneasy attention of handsome young cops only a few years older than she. Humiliated by her own overwhelming fear. It was, Bo acknowledged, the reality implicit in Madge's threat earlier that day. Shameful, devastating.

"Yes, I'll talk to her," Bo said, and then waited as Rombo went to bring Janny into his office.

"Bo?" the girl's voice cracked, making two syllables. It was like the train whistle she'd heard the night she visited Janny's foster home, Bo thought. The pattern repeating itself.

"She came *after* me! She was looking in my window, Bo. I called you but you didn't answer, just the machine. And then I knew she was out there in the dark, and she'd find a way to get in and, and there were all these shadows everywhere and I couldn't stop screaming because they could be *her*, and I couldn't get away, and she was going to *kill* me, Bo."

"Janny, you're safe now," Bo said softly. "Nobody can get you in the hospital. Nobody can get in and get you. There are people there to protect you. You're safe. And I'm going to come see you. Tonight. I'll be there in about a half hour, okay?"

"Okay," Janny answered, her voice reedy with terror. "Come as quick as you can. She might be able to get in here. She's so big, she can *do* things, Bo. I'm so scared!"

"You're safe, Janny. I promise you're safe there. Mr. Perry is a friend of mine. He'll keep you safe tonight. See you soon."

After hanging up, Bo stood in Andrew's paneled den and thought about the girl's words. "She's so big, she can *do* things, Bo." Could this be a child's memory of someone "big," an adult, who had done something so terrible that Janny had buried the scene deep in her mind? What could an eighteen-month-old child remember? No one, Bo thought, remembered anything from infancy. A sense of security, maybe, of hunger quickly assuaged and the loving warmth of a mother's and father's touch. Or the opposite, hunger and a primordial sense of abandonment. But these were the underpinnings of social awareness and trust, not actual memories. Before the acquisition of language the human brain could not encode "memory," in the adult sense, and even adult memory was fragmented and inaccurate. And yet what if Janny were reacting to some mental image encoded long ago and then buried? And what if that image were of a twin sister, a darkened room, and the violent hands of someone "big"?

"I'm scheduled for surgery at seven tomorrow," Andrew mentioned from the hall door. "Molly and I will have a walk and head for bed. You go on and do whatever you need to do."

"Where are you going?" Teless asked Bo.

"To see a teenager who's been placed in a psychiatric hospital because she's so scared she can't stop screaming," Bo answered.

"Can I go?"

"No, that wouldn't be—" Bo began, and then stopped short of "appropriate." Teless was exhibiting no signs of morbid curiosity, just puzzlement and concern. And she was sixteen, just a year older than Janny Malcolm. A solid, good-hearted kid.

"Oh, why not," Bo altered her train of thought. "It's irregular and you may not be allowed in even with me, but I think you might be helpful. Have you ever been inside a psychiatric hospital?"

"Sure," Teless said. "At least if detox counts. My cousin Alcide used to go into detox at one of those hospitals for, you know, drinking. I've been to see him there, me. It was a lot better there than when he was at home, you know? And they finally got him to stop, too. Alcide's been sober for more'n a year now, goes to meetings and stuff. We're all real proud."

Bo wondered what topic would not elicit in-depth family histories from Teless. "Fine," she said, hoping to avert further documentation of Alcide's substance-abuse problems. "Let's go."

"Let me just get some big ole warm socks from Nonk Andy."

"Socks?"

"For the girl," Teless explained. "Them hospitals, always cold as ice. Alcide said the worst part was gettin' up in the night and puttin' his feet on them cold tile floors when he had to—"

"Great idea," Bo interrupted as Andrew bounded upstairs for the required items. Alcide, she noted, had been right. Cold floors were epidemic in hospitals of all kinds, even those created to protect their charges from ghosts no one else could see.

Chapter 14

Pete Cullen stretched his long legs under the old door mounted on sawhorses that served as his desk. Then he took off his glasses and rubbed his eyes even though only one of them felt the strain from staring into the damn computer monitor for the last four hours. The other eye, the left one, still moved in its socket and appeared normal even though it hadn't seen anything since Nixon was in office.

Not since a little shithead drifter named Donny Barsky found a wheelbarrow full of broken concrete behind the San Diego church where he'd just robbed the building maintenance committee of its cash and jewelry. He'd pulled off his shoe and sock, then filled the sock with jagged chunks of concrete before scuttling off to his favorite pawnshop. But the cops got there first, as he thought they might, and Barsky ducked into an alley to stash his take until later. When one of the cops came sniffing in the alley, Barskey hid in a Dumpster and then whomped the cop over the head with the concrete-stuffed sock from behind. The cop had been Pete Cullen. And the blow had sent three pieces of shattered optical lens from his glasses deep into his left eye.

Cullen hadn't thought about Donny Barsky in thirty years, but now he wished those days were back. The days when criminals performed simple, obvious crimes like robbery, battery, murder. Breaking and entering was nice, too, he thought. Forgery, embezzling, arson, even the old-fashioned ones like poaching. These crimes were comprehensible. These crimes could be solved and their perpetrators sent to prison where they belonged.

Donny Barsky had been murdered in San Quentin, Cullen remembered. Something about a cigarette scam he'd been running, and somebody wanted a piece of the action. But Barsky got greedy and held out, so the "somebody" arranged to have Barsky's throat cut with the edge of a spoon sharpened by hours of rubbing against cement floors. They were stupid. They killed each other. It all evened out. Not like now.

Now the crimes were weird and the criminals weirder. Cullen scowled at the stack of photos he'd just downloaded and printed off a Website called "Orthshu" accessible only through several time-consuming relays and created to eat so many megabytes of hard drive that nobody looky-looing out on the Web would touch it. Orthshu was listed, as the law demanded, with all the Webcrawler services as a forum for communication within the orthopedic shoe industry. The cover had been picked for its ability to repel the typical computer buff, a male between fourteen and thirty-five who would *not* be cruising the Web looking for pictures of orthopedic shoes. For the occasional foot fetishist bound to wander in, Orthshu's home page boasted an elaborate five-color cross-section of a shoe designed to lessen the pain of a foot condition called plantar fasciitis. There were byte-eating animated graphics with sound, highlighting marketing and sales information. All of it was accurate, updated weekly. Nobody bumbling on to Orthshu would know the site was bogus, a front for FBI communications with a handful of retired cops and MPs all over the country. The photographs on Cullen's desk, spooled in to his printer as pictures of shoes and then decoded by a rather simple software program, were of dolls.

"Shit," he said, loading the word with as much disgust as he could articulate, which wasn't much. At sixty-two, Pete Cullen had long since given up on language. He'd never trusted it to begin with. Before she left him for a personal injury lawyer with a ponytail, his wife Rae had spent eight years begging him to talk. But he couldn't. For the life of him, he could never think of a damn thing to say. At the end, when she was crying and packing to run off with the goddamn hairball, he'd looked at her hard and said, "This asshole, he talks?"

"Yes," she'd answered. "This asshole, he talks."

So he'd given her the divorce. No contest. Irreconcilable differences. For a long time after that there'd been some kind of jagged place in him, an aperture through which everything just blew. He felt insubstantial and sometimes had to press his big hands flat against the sides of his thighs or his rib cage or his skull just to reassure himself that he had form, that he looked like everybody else. And he was careful about his clothes, his detective's suits and ties. He looked good and he was good. The best, they said. And then one day he'd had enough, took an early retirement from the force and bought a cabin near the little mountain town of Julian, east of San Diego. He hadn't been there a month when somebody he'd worked with off and on for thirty years at the FBI called, and he was working again. When he felt like it. The photos stacked on his desk made him feel like it. A lot.

The first one out of the printer had been the usual—a legitimate ad for a collectible doll, placed in a few women's magazines with national circulation and a large number of local Sunday supplements. The list of newspaper ad sites, he noted with interest, included every state except Arizona and California.

The doll was called Honeybunch, and had been photographed in a lacy off-the-shoulder drape that failed to cover its pudgy chest. It had also been photographed nude to "reveal the attention to detail lavished on this adorable little lady."

The code words were in the text of the ad. "Realistic." "Life-like." "Poseable." The baby doll had been modeled on the body of a twelve-month-old child, but its makeup and flirta-tious over-the-shoulder gaze were those of an attractive, and eager, woman. Something about it, Cullen thought, looked fa-miliar. Something about the porcelain dimples, the cute pug nose, the sculpturing of the upper lip.

Pushing away from the computer in his state-of-the-art desk chair, he glided across the bare pine floors to a coffee table, grabbed the pack of unfiltered Luckies waiting there, and stood. Then he took the Sig Sauer from its shelf by the door, slid it under his belt, and grabbed a denim jacket from its peg. The fire in the Franklin stove was banked. Time for a walk. Ducking under the doorframe, he stretched to his full six feet four in the cold outdoor air and breathed deeply. He was happy, he realized. Deeply, incredibly happy. And it was because of the doll. Because of the doll he might just get the second chance every cop dreams of. The impossible second chance to bust the SOB who stepped on your dick and got away with it.

The deadbolt snapped with a satisfying thunk when he turned it. Then he activated the electronic security system which also protected the big Chevy truck in front of the cabin. If something were tampered with, he'd know it. First a beeper attached to his belt would signal that a field had been breached. Then the precise location of the breach would regis-ter on a battery-powered monitor hidden in one of the five mine shafts on his property, once the site of a working gold mine.

The system had only kicked in once, when a pack of booze-addled slobs in camo gear had missed closing time at the Julian liquor store and decided to raid the cabin for available alcohol when Cullen was out walking. They called themselves hunters and all carried sidearms as well as expensive rifles. Cullen had enjoyed blowing the hand-carved stock off a brand-new Remington before cuffing them to each other around the trunk of a huge live oak and leaving them there all night. It hadn't been necessary to say a single word until he phoned the sheriff the next morning.

Walking felt good, pumped up his brain. And the hills were crisscrossed by old gold mining roads, some so steep the wagons had dragged cut logs behind them to slow their descent. Overgrown trails now, the roads provided a palpable map for his legs. Sometimes he walked all night, thinking, like now.

The rest of the photos from FBI Headquarters in Virginia were grainy, far less professional than the slick magazine ad. And the rest of them demonstrated the real purpose for the doll, a purpose buried in coded language only a pervert would see in an ad for a toy. The rest of the shots were porn. Baby porn, mail-ordered to pusbags all over the world. Except there were no laws controlling the production and sale of doll pictures, even those featuring baby dolls so exquisitely fashioned that when shot through a scrim nobody could tell they weren't real. Doll porn, then, Cullen nodded to himself, glowering at the shadow of a Jeffrey pine. What the hell difference did it make? The idea, the very *thought* was the crime. And he was pretty sure he knew at least one of the criminals.

The dollmaker.

It had been years ago, just before Cullen's retirement. More than ten years, he calculated. More like twelve or thirteen. His hair had still been mostly sandy brown then, not stiff and gray. And he'd worn an intimidating black eye patch even on the firing range, where he continued to score at the marksman level despite having no depth perception. Somehow having only one eye suited him. He learned to see with his ears, his skin. Then or now he could drop anything from fifty yards, even in the dark. *Especially* in the dark, he thought, grinning. That was his magic, that his skin had become an eye. But it hadn't worked with the dollmaker named Jasper Malcolm. Nothing had worked.

The old man was lying. Cullen had sensed that from the first interview. Somebody had tried to kill a couple of babies, Malcolm's granddaughters, in a beach cottage. The mother said a stranger broke in. That was a lie. The father said he hadn't been near the place, and that was probably also a lie. But the mother's father, this simpering old fairy who spent his life making dolls, for chrissake, had looked Pete Cullen straight in his good eye and recited *poetry*!

Or at least it sounded like poetry. Something about doing what you weren't supposed to do and not doing what you were supposed to do, not being healthy. Stuff about God. The old creep had been crying, half crazy. Cullen had wanted to stomp him, just to shut him up. Not that he'd really said anything. That was the lie. Talking and talking, filling the air with noise, saying nothing. The old dollmaker knew who'd hurt those babies and covered it up with talk. Maybe he even did it himself. But Cullen had never been able to break him. Until now. Now he had something he could use to go back in. The doll in the porno shots had been created by Jasper Malcolm. Cullen was sure of it.

Ricky Jr., marketed in 1956 after Lucille Ball and Desi Arnaz made history by employing Lucy's pregnancy as a TV sitcom story line, was unimpressive. Made entirely of vinyl, it was indistinguishable from a hundred other inexpensive baby dolls mass-produced from the 1930s on. Jasper Malcolm smoothed his white goatee in a gesture immediately recognized by experienced collectors, even across the crowded floors of international doll shows. It meant that the doll before him failed to meet his standards. Still, the original packaging was intact and featured Lucy and Desi holding the worthless doll. The packaging alone would attract buyers. He placed it in a large carton labeled "American, 1950–1960." Then he turned to the next one.

Called Playmate, the 1955 Playco doll was completely unremarkable except for its molded vinyl head which boasted swept-under bangs and braids that fell to the doll's shoulders. An example of one of the early vinyl processes, it was valuable for the braids, which were difficult to mold. Subsequent vinyl head processing, he remembered, had abandoned braids, topknots, and ponytails because of frequent molding failures. He wrapped the doll carefully in acid-free paper and then bubble-wrap before boxing it and fitting the box inside the larger carton. Each box was labeled with pertinent information regarding the doll inside, the labels block-printed by hand. So far he'd packed over three hundred dolls, and he was tired.

"Bede, Compline!" he called to a large gray Persian cat batting at a catnip mouse among the dolls. Dutifully the animal moved to sit beside the old man now kneeling on a folded length of bubble-wrap, and licked a paw as the man read aloud from a frayed missal.

"I consider the days of old," Jasper Malcolm recited in a voice made tremulous by fatigue, "the years long past I remember. In the night I meditate in my heart; I ponder and my spirit broods . . ."

He had wanted to be a priest, had known after a while that he would love the priesthood with all his heart. Not Roman Catholic, of course. He was already married and a father when the realization struck him. Episcopalian, then. Dottie, bless her heart, had been so enthusiastic when he was accepted at the seminary.

There had been no way they could have known, then. No way to know of the evil that would shatter their lives. Afterward, after he'd fought it in every way he could and still failed, he accepted what had happened. He could never *be* a priest, but he could live as one. And so he recited the Divine Office of a contemplative religious every day—Matins at dawn, Lauds before breakfast, Vespers after dinner, and Compline in the dark of night. No one but his cat, the Venerable Bede, had ever shared this practice. It was quite proper, he had realized long ago, that he should live in solitude.

"Visit this house, O Lord; keep the devil's wily influence away from it," he prayed, and then stopped. The metaphoric dread embodied in the word "devil" could not be kept away, not any longer. Kimmy's death, so long awaited, would act as a catalyst now. Kimmy's death would activate a dormant series of catastrophes that only he would truly understand and that only he could ameliorate. Maybe. If only he had someone to help him. But there was no one. There had been no one since the accident almost thirty years ago. Since Dottie's death.

Well, there had almost been someone, he remembered with a familiar rush of emotion that made him feel both young and terribly old. There had been someone who loved him, believed in him, kissed and made love to him in the four-poster upstairs. But it had been wrong, and she'd gone away.

Still on his knees, he contemplated a large Shirley Temple "walker" doll with rooted saran curls and "sleep" eyes that clicked with age when they opened and closed. Maybe he could stay awake long enough to pack that one, too. It was important to get the dolls packed and shipped before it was too late. Half of them would go to St. Dymphna's, the other half to the trust he had established for Janny. They represented a fortune.

Coughing deeply, he wrapped a gnarled hand over the arm of a chair and pulled himself up. The cat stretched briefly against the sharp crease of his pin-striped trousers and then padded from the room. Just one more. He'd pack the Shirley Temple and then allow himself to rest until morning. If there were a morning.

Daniel Man Deer awoke suddenly, a faint chill rippling across his chest. Someone was standing near the foot of the bed, or had been. The image seemed to recede when he opened his eyes, but the certainty of its presence hung in the air for several seconds. It had been a dream. It had been a stocky Indian with a massive chest, dressed in stiff canvas pants and a strange, long jacket with narrow lapels and widely spaced buttons made of wood. He'd worn a faded scarf at his neck, and a top hat. It was a photograph, Daniel realized. It had to be. A studio photograph of an Indian made in the 1800s, probably one of several he'd seen while researching the Kumeyaay. But the face had been smiling, the dark eyes impish in the shadow of the incongruous hat. The face had been a message of encouragement and pride, he felt. And humor.

"Dan, what is it?" Mary grumbled from beneath the down comforter, reaching for him.

"A dream. I think the bobcat is safe," he answered. "I think the ancestors are pleased and will help us now."

"Dan, tomorrow I want us to talk about taking a trip, okay? I've been thinking about a cruise. Let's talk about it over breakfast."

"A cruise? I don't think now is the time, Mary. . . ."

But she was already snoring softly.

Chapter 15

By nine-thirty Saturday morning Bo was cross-legged in a yellow Adirondack chair eyeing quail-egg salad with radicchio and capers mounded atop pita crisps cut to resemble Christmas trees. The table was aqua-blue and Eva Broussard's chair was lavender. The coffee in Fiesta Ware cups was so delicious Bo had forced herself to restrain a moan of sheer animal pleasure at the first sip.

"It's true what they say about Southern California," she observed as they watched the Pacific turn from gray to blue-green in the morning sun.

"If you mean the fabulously pretentious cuisine, it can hold its own against ridicule from the Fatty-Acid Belt, Bo," Eva replied, sighing. "These salmon crepes surpass anything I tasted in Quebec, especially with the peach-ginger soup and braided kelp bread. I'm afraid I'm a convert."

"I was thinking of the fifties color scheme, the constant attempts to improve on the past by dressing it up and dragging it into the present."

"A result of proximity to Hollywood, the entertainment industry, don't you think? After all, what are motion pictures and television series but attempts to 'improve' things that have already happened by explaining them?"

Eva, dressed in a bulky red hand-knit sweater that emphasized her wiry, muscular frame, stretched her signature jeans
and moccasins to rest on an adjacent Adirondack chair and
pushed her dark glasses up to rest in stylishly cropped white
hair. Her coal black eyes turned to regard Bo.

"But then you're not really talking about California, are
you?" she said.

Bo ran a hand through her own thick curls and enjoyed the
cool sea breeze against her scalp. The quail-egg salad was actually good, she thought. And a red pepper sorbet sounded intriguing for dessert.

"Janny Malcolm's case, the dream I had, whatever happened
down there in Mission Beach thirteen years ago, it's all from
the past, Eva. Madge was involved in it, and another social
worker who's retired now, named Mary Mandeer. They signed
off the paperwork authorizing the transfer of Kimmy Malcolm
to the Kelton Institute. Then when she died last week they
arranged for her funeral, just the two of them. A secret funeral. Janny doesn't know any of this, doesn't even remember
she *had* a twin sister, and—"

"Twin?" Eva interrupted. "On the phone you said 'sister.'"

"Identical twin," Bo went on, signaling the waiter to bring
more coffee to their outdoor table. "Eva, I'm sure that dream,
that empty place I called 'The Station of the Dead' when I
thought about painting it—I'm sure it was some kind of
image of Kimmy Malcolm's world at Kelton. There were these
clicking sounds and an awful sense of waiting . . . for death."

Eva Broussard stared at the glassy, flat surface of the sea as
though it puzzled her.

"The dream troubles you, doesn't it?" she said, her Canadian French accent and deep voice giving the words a reso-
nance Bo had come to trust unconditionally. "How do you
plan to deal with this?"

Bo pushed up the sleeves of her black turtleneck sweatshirt
and propped her chin on her hands.

"I've read the medical file from the police report, Eva. Kimmy sustained a severe brain injury comparable to a two-story fall onto the edge of a cement block. She wasn't expected to live but somehow she did. Or at least she didn't quite die. The report said that she was blind and subject to constant seizures, that she could no longer swallow or make sounds. It said that she had lost all brain function above the cerebellum, the old, preconscious part of the brain that just regulates breathing, heartbeat, stuff like that. It said she would never regain consciousness, and that a medically induced coma was necessary to control the seizures."

"None of which answers my question, Bo."

"Was Kimmy Malcolm really alive?" Bo went on. "And how could she stay alive in that condition for thirteen years?"

"I assume this line of inquiry will eventually lead back to the condition of *my* patient," Eva sighed. "You know there is no simple answer to your first question. Definitions of life vary. As to the second, survival of a child for thirteen years with the massive brain deficit you describe would be extremely rare but not impossible in a clinical setting. What are you really asking, Bo?"

"I think something happened in Kimmy Malcolm's brain as death became imminent. There are stories about things like that at Kelton. I think she somehow sent psychic energy, maybe even imagery, out. And Janny picked up on it, which is what's causing her so much stress right now. And maybe that dream . . . maybe for some reason I did, too."

The psychiatrist sipped coffee and merely waited.

"I'm not manic, the meds are fine," Bo continued. "My sleep patterns are normal, there are no unusual stressors in my life."

"Unless you regard shots fired through a wall into a room where you and your closest friend are interviewing a child as stress-free," Eva interjected softly.

"The dream came before that, Eva. What I want to know is—am I crazy?"

"People are always asking me that," Eva smiled and then leaned to ruffle Bo's hair. "And you already know you aren't. What you want me to say is that I agree with your theory. I neither agree nor disagree, Bo. What you have described is a belief which cannot be proven, like the Seekers and their visits from extraterrestrials. You have every right to believe it if it makes sense to you. My only interest in this belief is in how it will affect the ways in which you deal with your life and problems, your feelings about the dream and about the case. What are you going to do?"

"Janny says something's coming after her trying to 'get' her," Bo said, pondering three artificial sweeteners, honey, and refined, brown, and raw sugar in individual packets. Brown, she decided. The molasses flavor would enhance the fresh Guatemalan coffee steaming in her cup.

"And you think this something is Kimmy's ghost?"

"I don't know," Bo answered. "Something like that. She calls her doll Kimmy. She says the doll was called something else until a few weeks ago. That may have been when her sister began to fail, began to . . . die. They were identical twins. I've read that identical twins sometimes have a kind of psychic connection, that when one dies, even in infancy, the surviving twin feels the presence of the other one throughout life."

"I'm familiar with such narratives," Eva said with, Bo thought, an exquisite neutrality.

"So do you think it's possible that Kimmy's spirit is trying to stay attached to Janny? Maybe make Janny remember who was there that night, the person that killed Kimmy?"

"How does Janny describe this entity attempting to 'get' her?"

"She said it was outside her window last night. It terrified her so badly she decompensated enough to get slapped into Country Psychiatric."

"And the foster parents have confirmed that there actually *wasn't* someone outside the window?"

Bo felt something like a thin wet sheet coming to rest lightly over her head and shoulders. Reality. She'd forgotten to check that, she realized with chagrin.

"I told you about my shrink years ago in St. Louis, Dr. Bittner?" Bo said, her cheeks flushed. "She always said there's nothing but reality."

"How I wish we could have worked together," Eva Broussard smiled broadly. "She of course recognized that beliefs can sometimes blind us to critical aspects of reality. And I'm sure she attempted to impress that fact upon the minds of *all* her manic-depressive patients, who would be so vulnerable to more fanciful, less boring interpretations of events."

"Touché," Bo said. "But I still think there's something creepy about this case."

"The empty shell of a child's body growing to maturity without the child herself pretty much sets the standard for 'creepy,'" Eva agreed. "But it's time for me to go and we still haven't talked about you. What *are* you going to do with all this, Bo?"

"I'm going to find out what happened thirteen years ago."

"Why?"

"Because Janny has a right to know. It will help her come to terms with herself, control her terror."

Bo heard the wavering whine beneath her voice that meant she was dissembling. Eva Broussard heard it as well.

"Your insurance company is not paying me to encourage haphazard thinking," Eva said evenly. "Janny's probable response to information about the *existence* of a twin is unknown, as is any assumption of benefit to her from information about her twin's murderer. Moreover, we're not talking about Janny, we're talking about you. What's going on, Bo?"

"I'm so sick of Madge with her arrogance and her insults,"

Bo admitted, her head bent over her coffee. "And she's hiding something about this case—"

"Ah," Eva interrupted, "you want to hurt Madge. The important thing is that you're aware of your motivation."

"My motivation is petty and vengeful, isn't it? But besides that, I'm just curious, Eva. Dar Reinert told me the best detective around back then couldn't crack this case. It's never been solved. Dar says it never will be. Two girls, one dead and one abandoned to the foster care system as if she had no family, but there's a grandfather, this famous dollmaker, who's still alive and lives in San Diego, and the police report said nothing about the parents being dead, so where are they? I don't get it."

"What will the cost be to you if you pursue this?" Eva asked while pulling a wallet from her purse in preparation for leaving.

"Maybe my job, maybe nothing." Bo grinned. "I just want to know what happened. I want to solve a case the best cop in San Diego couldn't crack."

"I can certainly understand that," Eva replied thoughtfully. "And telling you to be careful will be a waste of breath. I'm looking forward to your tree-trimming event tomorrow. See you then!"

Bo stood to hug her shrink good-bye and then flung herself back into the yellow Adirondack chair. It was time for red pepper sorbet and some thinking.

Eva had, as usual, been right. The strange dream might represent some connection to Kimmy Malcolm and it might not. Deep inside Bo knew that it did, but so what? Psychic phenomena were, she acknowledged, interesting. But they were also random, inexplicable, and woefully short on the sort of data necessary for solving thirteen-year-old mysteries. Better to focus on reality.

The police report on the Malcolm case had been thorough but lacked any documentation about CPS's investigation. Bo enjoyed her sorbet and its accompanying shortbread cookie while pondering the California laws which afforded more protection to CPS files than any other stockpile of information in the entire justice system. Even the cops could not access those files or obtain copies of them. The idea had been to protect the children involved. Its result was often to protect CPS.

And Madge had taken the information gap a step further in deleting the old file from the new, and nearly empty, folder she handed Bo. So what had Madge done with that thirteen-year-old file? She wouldn't have sent it back to storage, Bo thought, smiling into her sorbet dish. Because Bo or any other worker in the system could simply request it back out. No, Madge would have to keep that file away from the storage room for a while. At least until Janny Malcolm's case was back on routine maintenance status and the foster care worker assigned to Janny would not be likely to request it. Then, three years in the future when Janny was eighteen and no longer legally under the "care and custody" of San Diego County, the file would be microfiched and stored in another facility. Always it would enjoy the strictest legal protection.

"But not at the moment." Bo smiled to herself and found her keys.

Half an hour later she pulled into the nearly vacant parking lot of her office building, parked near the rear door, and then walked Molly among the sparse plants comprising CPS's landscaping. A few social workers were in the building, their cars parked in a clump as if for company. Madge's car was not among them.

"Hey, Bo!" a worker from another court unit greeted her as he exited the building. "Working Saturday again?"

People were in and out every weekend, trying to keep up with caseloads and the accompanying tons of paperwork. Before her involvement with Andrew LaMarche, Bo had done all her paperwork in the office on weekends when it was quiet. Nobody would bat an eye at her presence there now.

"Just have to authorize a stack of vouchers for Medi-Cal payments," she yelled back. "The doctors need money for Christmas!"

"They're out of luck, then." He grinned as he unlocked his car. "Medi-Cal takes six to nine months to pay."

"I didn't say *which* Christmas," Bo countered, and unlocked the door.

The hall was quiet and musty with the odor of old building, cheap paint, and paper. An institutional smell. Bo secured Molly in her own office and checked the other eight cubicles lining the hall. All empty. But any one of a hundred people could show up at any time. Bo ducked into Madge's office and closed the door.

As usual, every available surface was piled high with case files. An old picture of Madge, a man, and two boys peeked over the stack of three-ring binders in which Madge filed every shred of information disseminated to its employees by the County of San Diego. Dental insurance forms, revised parking regulations, announcements of cholesterol testing and stress-management programs—Madge kept them all. There was something *sentimental* about Madge's hoarding habits, Bo thought. Like the collecting of mementos characteristic of young teenage girls, their scrapbooks of ticket stubs and snapshots that would later be thrown out as embarrassingly juvenile trash. It occurred to Bo that Madge's identity was wrapped up in her job in the same way a thirteen-year-old's identity might be wrapped up in a horse or a cheerleading squad. An obsessive identity meant to be transitional, temporary. Except in Madge the temporary had become permanent. The glass over the photograph, Bo noticed, was smudged and filmed with dust. And the younger Madge staring out from it seemed as stiff and unreal as a middle-aged doll.

"Okay, where would you stash it?" Bo whispered to the photograph.

There wouldn't be time to go through every one of the hundreds of files littering every flat surface including the floor. She would have to think like Madge, get into a Madge-like frame of reference in order to find the old Malcolm file. But how did Madge think? Bo forced her mind to become a flat, reflective surface, envisioned her supervisor, and drew a blank. From every conceivable angle, Bo could imagine Madge doing nothing but following rules. Gleefully following rules. Being happy and even oddly intense about following rules, as if guidelines for every aspect of behavior were a blessing.

"Okay, then, what are the rules for old files?" Bo muttered, feeling suddenly like a voyeur. She hadn't intended this psychic intrusion on the older woman who was a co-worker as well as nemesis. Still, it was necessary. And Madge would have constructed a legitimate reason for keeping Janny Malcolm's file. Something defensible, procedural. But what? The file really belonged over in foster care with Janny's foster care worker.

"Except for a change in status!" Bo breathed. If Janny were to be transferred to relatives in another state, for example, or removed from foster care because she'd been sentenced to serve time in a juvenile correctional facility, then the case would be handled by the court unit. And there was nothing about Janny which might necessitate such a change except her medical condition. Bo scoured the room for files with the protruding light blue Post-its that indicated a child undergoing critical medical treatment, and saw a stack of them under a chair between a filing cabinet and the far wall. The Malcolm file was the fourth one down, thick as the phone book for a town of a hundred thousand people. Breathing fast, Bo grabbed it and scuttled back to her own office.

Mary Mandeer had done the entire investigation and had originally placed Janny with a maternal aunt named Beryl Malcolm shortly after the incident in which Kimmy had been injured. The home investigation on Beryl Malcolm documented Mandeer's opinion that the home was "adequate" and that the aunt's concern for her nieces seemed "distant, but appropriate," but that supplemental payments might be necessary for incidental expenses since the aunt didn't work and was apparently supported by her father. Madge Aldenhoven had signed the approval for additional foster care funds.

Bo scribbled Beryl Malcolm's address on a legal pad and then cocked her head in puzzlement at the next address on the old list. "Tamlin Malcolm Lafferty," it said, "Mother House, Sisters of Saint Dymphna, Julian, CA." Bo mentally surfed her Roman Catholic childhood for memory of a saint named Dymphna and came up with nothing. But the name sounded Greek. Maybe Dymphna was a Greek Orthodox saint. And why was Tamlin Malcolm, a married mother of three, in a convent?

Knitting her brows, Bo noted the information and read on. The father, Rick Lafferty, was listed at the same address he now occupied. The maternal grandfather, Jasper Malcolm, had an address in the old Victorian San Diego neighborhood called Golden Hill because of its exposure to the setting sun. Kimmy's older brother, Jeffrey, Bo read, had been placed with his paternal grandparents, George and "Dizzy" Lafferty. The elder Laffertys had moved to a small Connecticut town called Redding Ridge less than a year later, taking Jeffrey with them.

"Why did they agree to care for Jeffrey and not Janny?" Bo frowned. "Why did they abandon her?"

The slam of a car door in the parking lot roused Molly from a nap in Bo's lap, and an extended growl vibrated against Bo's stomach. In the silence she could hear a key turning the lock of the exterior door. Slamming the case file shut, she jammed it to the back of a bottom desk drawer and grabbed a handful of legal forms. The characteristic authority of the turning lock was familiar and brought a hot flush of guilt that bloomed from her neck to her scalp.

You'd make a rotten criminal, Bradley. Now what in hell are you going to do?

"Bo," Madge Aldenhoven pronounced with a tremor of alarm, "what are you doing here?"

Molly's juvenile barks and scramble to escape Bo's grasp provided a momentary distraction.

"Looking for that form we use to document parent searches," Bo lied. "The mother of that baby I picked up yesterday hasn't turned up and I want to have the report ready for the detention hearing."

"The detention hearing won't be until next Wednesday," the supervisor scowled.

In a rumpled khaki dress and tennis shoes Madge looked older, Bo thought. Frazzled. There were dark smudges beneath her eyes, and her usually gleaming silver hair hung dispiritedly from a rubber band at the base of her neck. Bo couldn't remember ever having seen Madge's hair fastened with anything short of a museum-quality clip.

"I'm running a little fever and I was afraid if I didn't get it done now I might be really sick by Monday and not feel like coming in to do it. By the way, somebody was down here looking for something in your office. You might want to check with the front desk—"

"Who?" Madge asked.

"I don't know. I think it was Diane something-or-other. Somebody from the other side."

Nice save, Bradley. Now if she'll just go check, you can get that damn file back in her office.

Fully a third of the female CPS social workers seemed to be named Diane, Bo remembered, so that had been a stroke of genius. And "the other side" was in-house parlance for the offices in the front of the building. Adoptions, foster care, the police liaison, and the public relations representative. That had been a stroke of idiocy, since none of them ever worked weekends. But Madge might feel compelled to check it out anyway.

"I'll see if anybody's over there," she nodded. "And go home, Bo. You look flushed."

Bo made noisy leave-taking movements near her office door until she saw Madge turn the corner at the end of the long CPS hallway. Then she grabbed the Malcolm file, her ears ringing with guilt, and stuffed it back into the stack of "medical crisis" files in Madge's office. She wasn't sure where, exactly, it had been. Fourth or fifth, she thought, and jammed it under four other files. Then she grabbed Molly and dashed to the waiting Pathfinder. There hadn't been time to read much of the file, but at least she had names and addresses. And a growing headache born of nefarious behavior.

Shaking it off, she drove two blocks away, locked Molly in, and walked back to stand in the open cement-block entry to the ladies' room at the pocket park across from the CPS parking lot. Shadowed by the building's overhang, she could see out but no one could see in.

Minutes later Madge left the office building through the rear door and walked toward her car. In her left hand was a thick case file flagged with a light blue Post-it.

"Under no circumstances may any county employee remove a case file from county property," Bo recited from the procedures manual. "The penalty for doing so is termination of county employment."

Bo felt as though she were watching a statue trying to commit suicide by jumping off a bridge. Impossible but nonetheless terrible and wrong. Madge Aldenhoven was removing the Malcolm file from county property. Bo couldn't see the name on the case file, but she didn't have to. Madge was going to take the file home, keep it, maybe destroy it. Later Madge could admit that the file had been lost while in her possession, and accept responsibility. There would be the predictable flap from the director's office. Madge would be called in and reprimanded, but nothing much would be done. A veteran supervisor with an impeccable twenty-year record of employment could be forgiven for one lost file.

"But *why?*" Bo breathed against a cement block. What could Madge possibly have done thirteen years in the past that would drive her to risk her job, her very identity, now? There was at least one person who knew, Bo remembered. Mary Mandeer, the other worker on the case, who'd recited a Louise Bogan poem at Kimmy's funeral. Hurrying to her car, Bo hoped Mandeer was listed in the phone book. And that she had the fatal flaw characteristic of many who work to clean up human messes—a belief that change can be imposed rather than merely engendered.

"You're going to work undercover," Bo told Molly minutes later. "Think of yourself as a voice for the voiceless."

Chapter 16

Daniel Man Deer had just finished editing a chronology of activities by a local Indian leader named Olegario in the late 1800s when the doorbell rang. He'd barely heard it over Carlos Nakai's Indian flute on the living-room stereo. Mary had gone shopping with a friend, so he irritably abandoned his computer and stomped to the door. He was working on a biography of Olegario and the chain of lies, broken treaties, and usurpation which characterized the leader's attempts to work with San Diego's white settlers. He did not want to be interrupted.

"Yes?" he said to a woman with green eyes and freckles who was holding a small dog in her arms. Something about her made him uneasy.

"I'm Becky Harrison from Animal Crackers," Bo smiled. "A member of our organization suggested that Mary Man Deer would want to know about our holiday effort in behalf of the local no-kill shelter. Is she here?"

The only "Mandeer" Bo had located in the phone directory had been spelled "Man Deer," so she'd pronounced the name that way. The broad-shouldered man standing before her was obviously an Indian and was looking at her as though she'd just stolen his horse. Clearly, this wasn't the right address.

"Who told you Mary would be interested in this group?" Dan asked, reversing her assessment. He wasn't surprised. Mary either joined or contributed money to at least a hundred organizations determined to right various social evils. This one obviously had something to do with animals.

"Um, Diane." Bo pulled the common name out of thin air for the second time that day as Molly's throat began to vibrate in response to music drifting from the open door. "Diane Singer. She's a social worker, and—"

"My wife isn't here, but I'm sure she'd want to give something. If you'll wait I'll get my wallet—"

"Oh, no, we're not fund-raising, we're trying to organize a lobbying effort. Our goal is to introduce legislation prohibiting intrastate shipments of very young animals into California from unscrupulous 'puppy farms' where—"

"Why don't you just leave your card, Ms. Harrison? My wife can call you later if she's interested, all right? I'm afraid I'm rather busy. I need to get back to my work."

"I'll just tell Mary I dropped by, and she can get in touch with Diane," Bo chirped. "Sorry to have bothered you."

The house was new and the last one on a quiet street near the eastern leg of Mission Gorge Road, once the east-west trail of Indians moving between seashore and hilly high desert villages. Bo could smell chlorine from a pool behind a post-and-rail fence to the left of the house. From there an attractive expanse of rocky chaparral rose to deeply shadowed hills threaded by a footpath leading from the back of Man Deer's property. Of course. The man who opened the door looked like the sort who'd walk miles for the fun of it. Bo wished he'd invited her to explore the trail while waiting for his wife. Now it would be impossible without attracting his attention.

Later Bo would identify this moment as the point of no return, the seemingly innocuous juncture beyond which events escalated with an ominous independence of anything she could do. She wanted to go for a hike. She could have taken

Molly to Mission Trails Park and walked for miles. Instead, she drove to a convenience store pay phone and called Pete Cullen.

"Cullen," he answered with a gravelly abruptness that reminded Bo of peasants threatening to occupy a castle. That grimly forlorn resolve.

"My name is Bo Bradley and I work for Child Protective Services," Bo said, matching his tone. "I'm calling because you worked on the Malcolm case thirteen years ago. You may not remember it, but—"

"I remember it," he interrupted. "But I won't discuss it with you until I see your ID. I'll be down in San Diego tomorrow afternoon. We can talk then."

"Tomorrow's out. I'm having a Christmas party. And I can prove who I am over the phone. Just call the Child Abuse Hotline for confirmation. Then I'll call you back."

"You got a tree yet?" he growled.

"Tree?"

"Yeah. Christmas tree for your party. You got one?"

"Uh, no," Bo answered, confused by the sudden shift. "I'm going to get one tonight. Why?"

"Don't. I'll bring one down. What's your address?"

"Last apartment building on Naragansett, Ocean Beach, upstairs, number four."

Bo couldn't imagine why she'd answered him. Something about the gruff old cop seemed to demand a reciprocal bluntness. If it weren't for that Eeyore-like pathos in his voice, she thought, he'd be scary. And he was bringing her a Christmas tree. She guessed that meant he'd be coming to the party as well, which would be fine. There should always be a stranger at Christmas gatherings, her grandmother had insisted. To honor the fearful Caillech Beara, whose connection to death and madness would always seem strange to the living.

"Great, Bradley. See you tomorrow morning."

Bo heard him hang up and wondered when she'd talked to

anyone more uncomfortable with speech. Talking actually seemed to cause him pain, and the feeling was infectious.

"He's obviously not Irish," she remarked to Molly as she headed out of Mission Gorge and toward Beverly and Howard Schroder's house. Eva had been right. It made sense to check out the possible reality behind Janny Malcolm's terrified assertion that somebody had been outside her window at the foster home.

The Schroders weren't there when Bo arrived, but it seemed pointless to waste the trip. Standing beside the Pathfinder, she surveyed their property. The two-story house had been built against a hill, with the garage apartment comprising the ground floor. To the left of the wide driveway, stairs to the second-story porch were flanked by a reinforced cement wall. Its rounded cap was narrow and covered in places by runners of the popular succulent erroneously called "ice plant" in Southern California for another, smaller succulent whose resinous leaves appear to be coated with sparkling frost. When crushed, the chubby two-inch ice plant left a slick, jellylike goo. Bo decided not to attempt a climb up the narrow, rounded wall and turned her attention to the graduated cement-block wall flanking the other side of the driveway.

It, too, was draped in the ice plant that had been used as ground cover for the entire lot. But here the cement blocks made a narrow set of steps leading to the foundation of the second story, set in the hillside. The bedrooms would be on this side or in the back, Bo assumed, and began to climb.

The cement blocks stopped at the house's perimeter, so she carefully bent to lift the tangled ice plant runners before placing each step on the dead gray undergrowth as she climbed to the rear of the house. The first bedroom must be the Schroders', she thought as she peered in a window. King-sized oak canopy bed with a floral spread and mint-green dust ruffle. Pictures of children on a matching dresser. Probably foster children, Bo thought as she noticed a framed school photo of Janny Malcolm. Nice foster parents.

Next was an opaque bathroom window and then, facing the back, the window to a teenager's room. Definitely Janny's. The vampire posters were a dead giveaway. Bo turned to survey the upward-sloping ground beyond the window and felt her heartbeat escalate. The ice plant was crushed in several places near the window, and some ten feet higher it was flattened in a short trough shape that made no sense until Bo realized what had happened. Somebody had approached the house from above, tripped in the dark, and fallen. Crawling now to maintain her balance against the steep slope, Bo approached the flattened patch of succulent.

Footprints were improbable, but it was worth a try. Tugging the runners apart at the base of the flattened area, she looked at snarled gray undergrowth. Hopeless. The matting was old and well-developed, the ground at least four inches beneath it. Bigfoot, she realized, could not have made an impression in the ground here. Nor was there anything unusual stuck in the ice plant. No matchbooks, check stubs, or lockets on broken chains. But a trail of smashed patches led upward, so Bo followed it on her knees, wondering which stain remover would be best for getting the pale green ice-plant goo out of her khakis. At the top of the hill behind the Schroders' property was a high chain-link fence surrounding a school playground.

"Ha," Bo nodded, noting that the fence didn't wrap around the school ground, but merely protected the grade-schoolers and their Frisbees from falling down the steep hill. Anyone could walk around the end of the fence and slide into the Schroders' hillside backyard. And there would be no one on the school grounds at night to witness this suspicious behavior. An intruder could easily enter and exit the Schroder property without being seen, but that person would have to have surveyed the situation earlier, in daylight, to know that. And wouldn't someone have noticed a stranger walking around in a schoolyard?

Bo hunkered beneath the fence and checked the current patrons of the grassy area beyond. A man and two children playing catch. A teenage girl walking a beautifully groomed border collie. Two young women with babies in strollers watching a toddler pile grass and twigs on the rubber seat of a swing.

"Hi, Jennifer!" one of the children called to the teenager, who waved and then chatted briefly with the two young mothers. These were neighbors. People who knew each other. They would have noticed a stranger on the school property. For a moment Bo considered clambering out of the ice plant and asking them, but then remembered that she hadn't brought her CPS ID with her. And there were spider webs in her hair. Perhaps now was not the best time.

Sliding back down on the seat of her khakis, she stepped from the lowest cement block to the driveway just as a police cruiser stopped behind the Pathfinder.

"Oh, shit," she sighed. Somebody had seen her and called the cops.

"I know how it looks, but I'm here investigating a case in which somebody's stalking a child in the foster care system," she said, walking toward the black-and-white with her palms waist-high and facing outward. "Bo Bradley, court investigator, CPS. Run my plates to verify."

"Already called it in," a young female officer smiled professionally from the passenger's seat as her partner, a balding body-builder, got out and approached Bo.

"Stalker?" he asked.

"Fifteen-year-old female reported that somebody was looking through her window last night," Bo explained. "This is her foster home, the Schroders'. They aren't home, but I wanted to check it out. Somebody *was* up there, outside her window. The ice plant's smashed where they came down the hill from a schoolyard above."

"That would be Stevenson Elementary. Slope's pretty steep."

"Tell me," Bo agreed.

"Pathfinder's registered to Barbara Joan Bradley, a CPS worker," the young woman announced from the patrol car. "She's who she says she is."

"In the future wait until people are home before you go crawling around in their yards," the balding cop advised, and walked back to the black-and-white, his heavy leather belt and sidearm holster creaking.

"Sure," Bo replied, feeling their mutual disappointment that she hadn't turned out to be anything interesting. There had been times, she remembered with a rueful smile, when she would have been exactly what they expected when the dispatcher announced, "Unknown adult female climbing through ice plant to look in windows of unoccupied private home." The memory prompted her to stop for a Coke and take her meds before checking out her next destination, the home of Jasper Malcolm.

It had been one of the lesser Victorian mansions built before the turn of the last century, she realized as she parked and checked the Golden Hill address. Subsequent renovations included a hodgepodge of styles which made the three-story structure look like a child's drawing of a castle. The long, west-facing side of the house had been covered in brown shake shingles, and a door halfway to the rear was shaded by a white aluminum awning. Probably an apartment, she guessed.

Most of the huge old Victorians in Golden Hill had long ago been subdivided into oddly laid out apartments with stairs going nowhere and bedrooms accessible only through closets. The front of the house had been painted barn red, and the gingerbread millwork adorning the porch a creamy pale yellow. The porch floor and window flashings were a deep green, as was the tottering wrought-iron fence enclosing a small yard boasting no less than three cement birdbaths surrounded by now-dormant rosebushes. Bo nodded to a splashing blue jay as she led Molly up the brick walk toward a large porch flecked with golden squares of light created by the sun filtering through cream-colored lattice at the western end. A single wicker rocker near the door faced a fraying wicker footrest. The rocker was padded with an old pink blanket and several pillows. Jasper Malcolm, Bo remembered, was old.

Which probably accounted for his not answering her first ring at the solid oak door with its leaded glass window, she thought. But after trying the bell a second time she heard movement inside the house. Someone descending the oak staircase visible in the entry hall. Polished black shoes became visible beneath sharply creased gray trouser legs. Then a pale hand rested thoughtfully on the carved newel post as a pair of turquoise-blue eyes regarded Bo through thick, round glasses. After a moment the man bowed slightly, not to Bo but to something in the air above him, tugged at the pointed corners of a yellow wool vest, and approached the door.

"I am Jasper Malcolm," he said softly after opening the door. "What a well-loved young dachshund! May I ask her name?"

"Molly," Bo answered, feeling a not-unpleasant sense of falling. "Her name is Molly and mine is Bradley. Bo Bradley. I work for Child Protective Services. I'm here to discuss your granddaughter—"

"Please come inside, Bo Bradley, and have a seat in the parlor while I secure the Venerable Bede. He, of course, can scarcely be expected to welcome the lovely young Molly."

"Of course," Bo replied, hating herself for the saccharine panic in her voice. The voice people used when addressing the insane. It wouldn't do.

"Wasn't the Venerable Bede a monk who wrote about English history?" she asked, attempting a save.

"*An Ecclesiastical History of the English People*, to be precise,"
Jasper Malcolm replied. "It covered the Roman invasion to
about 731. However, *that* Bede died in 735. The one I'm
going to confine on a sun porch is my cat."

"Ah," Bo said, nodding. "Why don't I just take Molly back
to my car and——"

"Oh, no. I'm so pleased you've brought her. It will make
things nicer, you see."

Bo didn't see, but led Molly through carved woodwork into
the room he'd indicated to the left of the entry hall. It had
once been a real parlor, the formal entertaining area of the Victorian house. Later owners had covered the hardwood floor
with now-faded blue carpeting and the single white couch was
contemporary, but those facts were lost in the overall impression made by the room. Horror. Bo stood frozen on the thick
carpeting and gasped as a jester in elaborate harlequin
watched her with black glass eyes from an end table. On the
marble mantel at least thirty Kewpie dolls held their short
arms toward her, wide-eyed. Bo fought a sense that they were
about to jump, that they were daring her to save them.

*It's that baby poster, Bradley! The one everybody has at the office.
The Kewpie dolls are that poster!*

Her lifelong discomfort with dolls faded measurably. It all
made sense. Everything was really everything else, a series of
recurrent and overlapping images behind which Great Meaning hid, smiling cosmically. Knowledge of this fact, she remembered, was the special gift of those whose psychiatric
diagnoses included the term "manic." But it wasn't delusional, it was real. People who had never experienced one of
these odd flashes couldn't understand, but the experience was
"religious" in nature, transforming. A glimpse of universal
order at once confounding and reassuring. This glimpse meant
that she was where she was supposed to be, even if she had no
idea why. The awareness of secret "rightness," of special com-
plicity in a hidden universal design, she remembered, some-

times promoted an unpleasant arrogance in those with manic-depressive illness.

"But what the hell?" she whispered, enjoying the little manic rush. It was good to feel that shimmering link to the universe, to *know* she'd been chosen and was performing her task correctly, whatever it was. The thing was to keep it to yourself.

"Rose did create a timeless American icon, didn't she?" Jasper Malcolm mentioned conversationally from the parlor door. In his voice Bo heard an eerie sympathy with her brief flutter of mania. An affirmation.

"Rose?" she said, turning to face blue-green eyes magnified by thick spectacles.

"Rose O'Neil. Oh, dear, I'm so sorry. Please forgive an old man who has lived so long in solitude that he assumes all thoughts are identical to his own. Rose created the drawing on which tens of thousands of Kewpies have been modeled since the first one in 1912. They're angels, you know. Only the more recent ones lack the trademark blue wings. Do you believe in angels, Bo Bradley?"

The question carried desperation, sorrow. Bo reined in her earlier sense of cosmic sainthood, sought humility, and found it. Whatever else was happening, Jasper Malcolm had just lost a granddaughter to death.

"I am certain that we understand almost nothing of life beyond what is accessible to our brains, our narrow little band of awareness," she answered. " 'Angel' is just a word to me, but I suspect that it may represent some reality beyond my understanding. Why did you ask me that, Mr. Malcolm? Are we really talking about your granddaughter, Kimmy?"

In the dim winter light of his parlor, surrounded by the hundred glass and painted eyes of dolls whose original owners were surely dead, the slight dollmaker buttoned and then unbuttoned his gray tweed jacket, smoothed collar-length hair so white it seemed a wig, and then pressed the back of a trembling right hand against pink lips visible above his white goatee.

"Of course," he whispered, and then stood silently as tears streamed through his beard and left dark smudges on the yellow vest.

"I . . . had a dream," Bo said quietly. "Before I knew anything of this case. I think that Kimmy . . . I believe she was reaching out somehow."

The smile that broke across Jasper Malcolm's face made Bo think of Bach. The Toccata and Fugue in D Major played on a great cathedral organ beneath light spilling through a rose window created by Tintoretto.

"Thank you," he said. "You have great courage, Bo Bradley. But of course, you're Irish. I knew when I saw you and Molly at the door. But come, I have much to tell you and there's little time."

Bo followed the back of his tweed jacket through the hall toward the rear of the house. There was no point in questioning anything, and the soft clack of Molly's nails on hardwood flooring was the only sound.

Chapter 17

"My interest in dolls began as an interest in religious statuary," Jasper Malcolm explained as he led Bo through a kitchen that smelled faintly of spray starch. "My first effort, the St. Francis you see there on the counter blessing the bottle of Ivory Liquid, was a disaster. I quickly abandoned wood in favor of other media for obvious reasons."

Bo considered the misshapen carving draped in a brown washcloth. It looked more like a lizard than the patron saint of animals, and its outstretched arm seemed to threaten rather than to bless the taller dish-soap container. The rest of the kitchen's accoutrements, she noted, seemed perfectly normal.

"Why did you keep it if you didn't like it?" she asked.

"Because it was mine, Bo Bradley. I kept it because I had made it and it was mine." Weariness and anger in his voice. Over an ugly wooden statue?

"What does your St. Francis have to do with Kimmy and Janny, Mr. Malcolm? And why haven't you been available to Janny? She doesn't even know she has a family, and she's experiencing some serious problems now. She doesn't remember that she had a twin sister. But recently she's begun carrying around an old doll which I suspect is one of your creations. She calls it Kimmy.

"Janny's terrified, Mr. Malcolm. Last night she was admitted to a psychiatric hospital after she saw someone in the dark outside her bedroom window at the foster home. It may have been a run-of-the-mill neighborhood pervert, but Janny is convinced that something's coming to get her. She thinks that 'something' is Kimmy, although she doesn't know what Kimmy is. I need to know why you've abandoned your remaining granddaughter, Mr. Malcolm."

"Surely you've read your own agency's files concerning my family," he replied while ushering Bo through a door at the kitchen's rear into a large, well-lit studio. It had probably been a rear apartment, she thought, now gutted and redesigned as an artist's workplace.

Bo noted the off-white ceramic tile floor and surrounding glass cabinets from which hundreds of bisque doll heads watched with colored glass eyes or, worse, empty eye sockets. All were variants of the trademark Jasper Malcolm doll Bo had seen as Johanna in the Fashion Valley toy store. Infant dolls, each different but all sharing the exquisitely molded upper lip of a nursing baby. Against a tiled back wall a large kiln stood on firebrick, its two-twenty cord properly grounded with an extra wire running through the wall from below the switchplate. Jasper Malcolm had exercised great caution in the design of his studio, Bo thought. Wisely. The century-old wood frame house was a tinderbox.

"My supervisor doesn't want me to see the file," she told him. "I was only able to get a few addresses. She's removed the file from our office, actually. I don't know why."

"Is Mrs. Aldenhoven your supervisor?"

"Yes," Bo answered. "You remember her?"

The older man closed his eyes briefly and then merely exhaled. "I began making Infant of Prague dolls for my wife's relatives, who were from Czechoslovakia. I would design the heads and Dottie would sew the pretty robes. We used a cloth body, a rag doll body, with sewn-on china hands I bought through mail-order. But soon our Prague dolls were in such demand that I realized crafting each head individually was impossible. That's when I learned how to make hundreds of identical heads by pressing porcelain clay that had been rolled out like pie crust into a mold I made from a clay model. At first Dottie and I painted the eyes on, but I was anxious to try glass."

Here he opened a lighted metal cabinet filled with trays of eyes in varying sizes and colors. Bo felt her jaw drop and then clench.

"Some of the bronze-colored ones are actually made of cats'-eyes," he went on animatedly. "They're lovely in a dark-haired—"

"I need to know about Kimmy and Janny," Bo interrupted, pushing the cabinet door shut and leaning on a metal table where a mound of clay sat covered in clear plastic film. "I'm aware that you're a master dollmaker, and your history is fascinating. But that's not why I'm here. Please."

"I have two daughters," he went on, touching the clay through the plastic as though it were alive.

"Tamlin and Beryl," Bo filled in, watching his hands. She wasn't sure whether he wanted to caress the clay or crush it. "Why is Tamlin, a mother of three, in a convent?"

Jasper Malcolm continued to press the ball of his right thumb against the muddy plastic film. "She is safe from evil there. After Kim was hurt I made arrangements for Tamlin to join the Sisters of St. Dymphna, whom I have helped financially for years. Tamlin is not a strong person. She could not have survived otherwise."

Bo fought a growing impatience. "Could not have survived what? And who are the Sisters of St. Dymphna?"

"A small order devoted to the patron saint of the mentally ill, a young woman whose life was obliterated by evil. Her story is quite interesting. The sisters maintain a lovely facility in the mountains near Julian. Tamlin has been with them for thirteen years now."

His voice had become a whisper and Bo noticed his thumb smoothing rough facial planes in the plastic-covered clay. Without realizing it he was forming a crude face, the beginning of a doll. It seemed to have drowned beneath crumpled waves of plastic.

"Does Tamlin have a psychiatric illness?" Bo asked as something smoke-colored and terrible fell on the skin of her arms. It was like the plastic film over the clay. A somber revulsion that raised gooseflesh. Had the mother harmed her own child during a psychotic episode? The twins had been a year and a half old, statistically at low risk for a mother's untreated postpartum depression and its potentially tragic outcome. Still, that scenario would explain Tamlin Lafferty's withdrawal from all contact with her husband and children. It would also explain the paternal grandparents' swift move to Connecticut with Jeffrey, who might have witnessed the tragedy. But it wouldn't explain why everyone in the family had abandoned Janny to a life of nameless obscurity in the foster care system.

"No," Jasper Malcolm said as though the concept had never occurred to him. "Not Tamlin. Tamlin is fine. Do you know, all the baby dolls are based on a model of Kim and Janet that I made only a few months after they were born. Tamlin was so proud of them. She even sewed little matching dresses and sleepers, buttercup yellow for Kimmy and robin's-egg blue for Janny. Those were their colors, so Tamlin could tell them apart. Kim was always the more boisterous one, hence the yellow. Janet was quieter, less demanding, so she got blue, you see."

He seemed to have slipped into the past and was discussing the doomed twins with a grandfatherly vivacity that ignored the intervening thirteen years. It was like trying to interview a kaleidoscope, Bo thought. As soon as she "saw" Jasper Malcolm, got a fix on his train of thought, he changed. Yet he wasn't lying. Not quite. Neither was he revealing more than the most superficial aspects of his family's troubled history.

"Mr. Malcolm," she said, "I intend to find out what happened to Kimmy. I intend to find out who inflicted the head injury that took her life from her years ago and has finally killed her."

"It would be best if you didn't," he whispered, his aqua-blue eyes roaming the surface of her face with a sudden enthusiasm. "Please leave this situation to me and go on with your life. I am responsible, no one else."

"Do you mean that you did it? That you—"

"No," he answered, reaching to touch her cheekbone with the thumb of his right hand. "I do not mean that I have harmed anyone. I haven't."

Bo pushed his hand from her face in irritation. The touch wasn't erotic or even personal. It was simply thoughtful, as if her face were that of an unusual doll.

"You aren't helping me, Mr. Malcolm," she said. "You aren't telling me anything I need to know. And you aren't offering to help Janny, either. She needs to see you. Your grandson Jeffrey was taken in by the Laffertys, but Janny was abandoned by her parents and you as well, even though you're all right here in San Diego. Why, Mr. Malcolm? Why don't you give a damn?"

The harsh language had the intended effect. A flush of anger stained the older man's neck above his white broadcloth shirt collar, and he bit his lower lip with teeth that reminded Bo of old pearls. That yellowed wisdom.

"What do you know of evil, Miss Bradley?" he exhaled. "Don't answer; you know nothing. So let me tell you that it has no face, that it simply exists and cannot be explained, nor can it be defeated. Let me tell you that once a certainty of evil enters your life, once you *know* how alien and pure it is, you become as one blind, forever staggering through absolute dark, your arms outstretched against it. Awareness of everything else fades, is unimportant. You have no right to question my behavior. I will not permit it!"

"I am questioning your behavior whether you 'permit' it or not," Bo answered, her eyes wide and blazing. "And let me tell *you* that Janny Malcolm is not 'unimportant,' nor do I believe that fear does anything but feed evil. Beyond that I have no idea what you're talking about, not that it matters. Thank you for your time, Mr. Malcolm. I'm afraid mine is too important to waste."

In the silence that followed, Bo felt hatred in a hundred pairs of glass eyes. The doll heads, bodiless and therefore immobile even in fantasy, nonetheless seemed enraged. She had insulted their creator. Bo struggled to avoid parallel imagery involving human heads and their gods, and failed.

"I will show you to the door," Jasper Malcolm intoned, and then said nothing more as they retraced their steps through the old house. At the door Bo handed him her card and scooped Molly into her arms. The simple action brought an unaccountable sparkle of delight to the old man's face.

"And please tell Mrs. Aldenhoven she remains in my prayers," he said softly, then closed the door.

Bo chose not to consider the remark until she was safely in the Pathfinder and out of Golden Hill. When she did consider it, it seemed arcane. Obviously he'd met Madge during the original investigation, but then he'd met Mary Mandeer as well and he hadn't mentioned her. And why "prayers"? Something about the word suggested either a wistful connection or a private slur, neither of which made any sense.

"But we'll tell Madge and see how she reacts," Bo mentioned to Molly as she headed toward the central San Diego address of Beryl Malcolm, the sister of Janny's mother.

The house was one of the area's many old Craftsman bungalows, this one on a quiet street near the University of California San Diego's sprawling medical complex in the community known as Hillcrest. Bo noted with approval the long eaves shading side windows and a pleasant front porch facing the street. There were white geraniums everywhere, she noted. Rows of them in identical green plastic pots lined precisely along the porch floor where it met the wall of the house. But rather than extending a welcome, they seemed to establish a barrier. Bo wondered where in classical literature geraniums had been used as guards, and to guard what. They had that mythological sense, might even turn into serpents if one knew the magic word. Leaving Molly in the car, Bo faced the fact that she was seriously tired as she approached the house and rang the bell.

"What is it?" a breathy female voice called from inside.

"Bo Bradley from Child Protective Services," Bo answered. "I'd like to speak to Beryl Malcolm."

The woman who opened the door was short and had the most exquisite skin Bo had ever seen. A dusky peaches-and-cream complexion that glowed in matte finish from her face and the arms extending from a beige and white checked housecoat with mother-of-pearl snaps down the front. But the white terrycloth slippers on her feet were stretched and flattened from the strain of bearing her weight, which Bo guessed to be two hundred and twenty pounds at least. Framed by the doorway she looked like a Daliesque wrecking ball, melting. From within it watery aqua-blue eyes regarded Bo without interest.

"I'm Beryl Malcolm," she said. "Please come in."

Bo stepped into ankle-deep carpeting in a beige so pale it bordered on white. No pets, obviously. And no foot traffic. The carpet billowed immaculately from wall to wall, punctuated by a faux Queen Anne couch and wingback chair in cream-colored velvet and white-on-white striped brocade, respectively. Beside Beryl Malcolm the furniture seemed miniature, meant for a playhouse.

Or a theatrical set, Bradley. Because that's what this is. Meant for show. Never used.

Bo sat carefully in the wingback chair and glanced at items on the marbleized white coffee table. An art book on Fabergé eggs. A Waterford crystal lidded candy dish, empty. And three issues of a glossy gardening magazine, the top one bearing a date three years in the past.

"Ah, my aunt in Boston used to subscribe to this," Bo lied enthusiastically. "Do you garden?"

"Not much," Beryl Malcolm answered, lowering herself onto the couch as if it might slide out from under her. "What brings you here, Miss Bradley? I assume it has something to do with my niece Janet."

The words were pronounced with resignation. The woman presented the long-suffering attitude of a parent driven to exhaustion by a rebellious teenager. And yet there had been no contact between aunt and niece in years, or at least none of which Bo knew. Janny hadn't mentioned her aunt, didn't seem to know the woman existed.

"She's having some problems," Bo confirmed, keeping her voice neutral. "In fact, Janny is being treated in a psychiatric hospital. Hasn't her foster care caseworker contacted you?"

"I'm disabled," Beryl Malcolm pronounced in a soft whine, pushing thin, mouse-brown hair behind her right ear. Bo watched as the woman took a soiled paper napkin from the pocket of her housecoat and kneaded it violently in a trembling hand. "I tried to take care of my niece right after it happened, but I just couldn't manage. We have to take care of ourselves first, you know."

Bo considered the series of statements.

"We?" she said.

"Victims," Beryl Malcolm answered. "Janet is a victim, too, of course, but I'm afraid I just couldn't help her. And I can't help her now. It's best that I have absolutely no contact with any reminders of what happened. My support group is clear on this."

"Do you mean the incident in which Kimmy was brain-damaged?"

Beryl Malcolm stared at her feet, then turned to Bo. In her eyes was both irritability and a desperate boredom, as if the answer to that question were universally known.

"No, I mean my own abuse," she said. "My father incested me from the age of five until my twelfth birthday. Surely this is in Janet's file, the reason I just can't be involved with any of them. It's too painful. But if there's something she needs, I can give you a little money. Clothes or something. Let me get my purse."

Bo evinced no reaction to the jarring use of the noun "incest" as a verb, and merely watched as the mountainous woman pushed herself upright and then walked with surprising agility to a sliding wooden door at the rear of the large living room. Through it Bo caught a glimpse of coffeemaker, the back of an old-fashioned padded plastic kitchen chair in pearlized yellow. The air pushed across Bo's face by the closing door smelled faintly of rotting pizza.

And the situation had just been complicated. If Beryl had indeed been the victim of child sexual abuse at the hands of Jasper Malcolm, then the case-management profile actually made sense. Or some of it did. Two girls traumatized by the death of their mother and then abused by their father, growing up damaged. Tamlin, the younger daughter, would have been abused as well. Incestuous fathers rarely confined their diseased sexual advances to one child.

As a young adult, Tamlin would have been likely to select another abusive man as a mate unless she'd had years of therapy. If that man were Rick Lafferty, then his absence from the home on the night of the deadly incident might actually have been ordered by the courts. It was nothing unusual, the standard practice then and now. And it would have left Tamlin, a confused and dependent young woman, alone with three demanding preschool-aged children. She might have snapped.

The likelihood that she had, Bo thought grimly, was not small.

"Will twenty dollars be enough?" Beryl asked peevishly, re-closing the kitchen door behind her. "I live on my retirement and my disability allotment. I don't have much."

"It's very kind, but I didn't come here to ask you for money," Bo said, wondering what to do next. The information regarding Jasper Malcolm's abuse of his older daughter had shocked her despite the fact that she worked with such information every day. The dollmaker hadn't seemed like a child molester, but then neither did most child molesters. Trusting in what people seemed to be, she knew, was invariably a mistake.

The heavyset woman jabbed a finger at a jarring pink and green glass vase on the otherwise empty mantel, a stained straw briefcase clasped to her side. She was perspiring from her hike to the kitchen and back, wheezing softly. Bo felt her own lungs demanding air. It was as if Beryl Malcolm were absorbing all available oxygen from the room.

Aye an' it's like a cat she is, whispered the familiar voice of Bo's long-dead grandmother. *A cat suckin' the very life's breath from a baby.*

Bo was familiar with the Irish folk tale. The one warning mothers of soul-eating cats-in-the-cradle, their whiskers still as they inhale milk-scented baby breath until there is no more breath. Except according to Beryl, Jasper Malcolm was the cat, Bo reasoned. Not this obese, neurotic daughter with watery aqua-blue eyes. It didn't scan.

"Then what do you want?" the woman asked.

"I want to help Janny, Ms. Malcolm. She needs her family, some support, the truth about her past, an identity. Without any of these things she may not make it through adolescence with her sanity even though she has no real psychiatric illness. The system will assign her one anyway, and then warehouse her someplace until she becomes whatever she's told she is."

"There's nothing *I* can do for her, Miss Bradley. Surely you understand, I have to take care of myself. You deal with incest victims, don't you? You know that we have to protect ourselves at all costs."

"Mmm," Bo answered, standing. "I appreciate your time."

Back in the Pathfinder she gave Molly a dog biscuit and frowned at Beryl Malcolm's hostile army of porch geraniums.

"No, I don't understand that at all," she said softly through clenched teeth. "I'm beginning to understand what happened thirteen years ago, but I don't understand what's happening right now. I don't understand how you can just forget about Janny."

On the porch the geraniums appeared to bristle like potted terriers guarding treasure so old it had decayed into worthlessness. Like a pirate chest full of tattered doilies, Bo thought. Or a safety-deposit box crammed with deeds to long-collapsed mines. Beryl Malcolm had erected a fence of flowers around emptiness.

Chapter 18

On the drive home Bo mentally reconstructed a night thirteen years in the past, when the lives of two little girls had been damaged irrevocably. She didn't have to see the case file to imagine what might have happened. Tamlin Lafferty separated from the husband on whom she would have been absolutely dependent, separated perhaps by a court order designed to protect her and the children from his abuse. Tamlin alone with the responsibility for three small children, the house cluttered with toys, *Sesame Street* blaring from a TV, spilled grape jelly crawling with ants on the kitchen counter. Tamlin could easily have been at her wit's end when she fell into bed that night, needing her husband's embrace. And resenting the children for whose protection he had been ordered to leave.

Tamlin might have had a few drinks that night, Bo thought, or maybe a tranquilizer prescribed by her doctor for stress. She might have smoked a little marijuana, trying to calm herself and succeeding only in heightening a hunger for sugar and for sex. But whatever chemical ploy she tried would have worn off hours later, when one of the twins awoke in the night screaming, banging crib against wall as she rocked against its barred sides. It would have been Kimmy, Bo acknowledged with a shudder. Jasper Malcolm had said Kimmy was "the boisterous one."

And her demanding screams would have awakened Janny, sleeping nearby. The usually quiet twin, rumpled and confused, would have joined her reedy whine to the din. Tamlin might have awakened sick and headachy, unable to control the trembling in her arms. In the dark, not really awake but completely desperate, Tamlin might have . . .

Here Bo stopped. A worst-case scenario, it did not bear thinking. The pattern was typical for troubled and immature mothers struggling alone without supportive female relatives to teach child-rearing skills, provide respite, step in and take over when things threatened to get out of hand. Every CPS worker saw that pattern daily while investigating bruises, malnutrition, abandonment. But rarely did the pattern lead to violence and death.

"A two-story fall onto the side of a cement block," the medical report had said of Kimmy's head injury. A long fall, except there had been nowhere to fall two stories from the one-story Mission Beach cottage. A powerful blow, then, Bo thought with distaste. Had Tamlin picked up something, a book or other heavy object with a straight edge, and hit Kimmy with it? The force of the blow suggested that the object had been *swung*, like a baseball bat. A taste of bile in the back of her throat alerted Bo to the fact that this train of inquiry must stop, or she'd throw up.

On the seat beside her Molly raised one soft paw and placed it on the bend of Bo's elbow. Though still very young, the little dachshund was already beginning to exhibit the empathic abilities which distinguish dogs from all other creatures.

Bo patted the paw with her left hand and said "It's okay, Molly. Good girl," eliciting a sort of black-lipped smile on the hound face.

Bo determined not to think about Kimmy Malcolm again that night. But what about the other pieces of the puzzle? The critical events were falling into place, but there were still facts that made no sense. Why had Tamlin changed the surname of her daughters to her own maiden name when she was still married to their father? Or *was* Rick Lafferty their father? Pete Cullen's file had included no reference to any man in Tamlin's life except her husband, and Cullen, Bo was sure, would have thought of that.

Madge's role in the drama also remained inexplicable, Bo thought as she turned off Interstate 8 at its, and the continent's, terminus, and joined the slower traffic on Sunset Cliffs Boulevard. The winter beach to her right was nearly empty and limned with weak late-afternoon sun. Home. But aspects of the case seemed to hang over the mounded sand and occasional, solitary beachcomber.

If the events of Janny Malcolm's past were as grimly typical as they appeared to be, then why would Madge Aldenhoven take the uncharacteristic risk of removing the case file from the office so that Bo couldn't see it? And why hadn't supercop Pete Cullen amassed sufficient evidence to bring criminal charges against Tamlin Lafferty?

Jasper Malcolm also remained enigmatic. Trained to believe even the most far-fetched allegations by children of sexual abuse until those allegations were proven false, Bo had accepted Beryl Malcolm's story at face value. But Beryl Malcolm, she reminded herself, was not a child. Had there been any investigation of her charges against her father? Why would Beryl claim to be a victim of incest if, in fact, she were not? And if she were not, Bo told herself, the whole case again ceased to make any sense at all.

That was the cornerstone, the sickening fact of Jasper Malcolm as a child molester. From that fact all others spun out in the unwholesome design with which every CPS worker was familiar. Adult children so damaged they could never really function as adults without exhaustive therapy. Repeated abuse, although not necessarily of the same kind, of the next generation of children in the family. And that strangely flat narcissism so evident in Beryl's devotion to herself as "victim."

Bo knew better than to judge Beryl Malcolm. Her own childhood had not included abuse of any kind. Still, she thought against all her training on the subject, the woman's whining self-absorption had been a pain in the neck.

"I actually wanted to punch her in the teeth," she admitted to Molly. Saying it out loud was a relief. Too much social-worky niceness made her feel as though she were swimming in cream-of-chicken soup. In the chocolate-brown dachshund eyes was acceptance and a reminder that dinner would soon become an issue.

"We're almost home, and you can have either turkey and liver or beef chunks," Bo told her. "Then I have to clean the apartment for tomorrow."

The prospect was not appealing. Bo parked on Naragansett behind an ancient pale blue Mercedes, and stretched. She was tired, and that could be dangerous. Too much stress, not enough sleep, and symptoms of mania could seep through the restraining medications. She might talk too fast at the party tomorrow, behave too seductively with Andy or, worse, with somebody else. She might embarrass him, irritate her friends, frighten Teless. Everybody would leave early, smiling edgily as they thanked her for a wonderful time. They would glance at each other with knowing looks, and leave. It hurt her to remember other times when people had grown uncomfortable at her antics and left in droves.

"To hell with the apartment," she announced to one of the street people eyeing the Pathfinder's hood radiating heat from the engine. "I'm going to bed."

"Good for you," the man said through brown teeth, then leaned comfortably against the warm metal.

Bo hadn't noticed the light in her own kitchen window from the street below, and was surprised to open her apartment door to the sound of rap music and an odor that made her mouth water. Freshly baked biscuits and something with chicken in it simmering on the stove.

"*Sha!*" Teless Babineaux greeted her, turning off the abominable music and bending to pet Molly. "Nonk Andy give me the key and dropped me off to help get ready for the party. He said you shouldn't get too tired. So I cleaned up and made you some dinner. Chicken an' dumplings. Couldn't find no *oovkang* for dem peas, though. Peas good with dumplings."

Bo surveyed her gleaming apartment in shock, then focused on a jumbo can of peas exhibiting pride of place on her spotless kitchen counter. "Oovkang" undoubtedly meant "can opener" in Cajun, she assumed. And the absence of one in her utensil drawer had been an act of providence. Second only to raw fish, Bo hated canned peas. Canned peas, in fact, would be served daily, cold, in her version of hell. Her vision of hell would *smell* like canned peas. It had something to do with her manicky brain wiring, that propensity to assign exhaustive allegorical meaning to particular odors.

Teless beamed expectantly. Healthily. *Youngly*, Bo thought with a smile.

"I'm afraid I don't have an 'oovkang,' and besides, my religion forbids me to eat canned peas," she grinned. "But I'm famished and you're a saint! The place has literally never been this clean, Teless. Thank you so much. But how can I repay you for all your work?"

The wide blue eyes were unassuming. "Let me borrow your car to go see Janny," Teless said. "I talked to her on the phone today. She likes the ghost stories I tell, like last night at the hospital. I got a license, me. An' you gotta rest."

Bo considered the request. Janny had actually seemed to enjoy Teless's nonstop storytelling, even though both Bo and social worker Rombo Perry had shuddered at the stories' content. Haunted bayou bridges, dancing lights in antebellum graveyards, ladies-in-white who vanished from formal gardens like paper napkins blown in the wind. But rather than upsetting Janny, the stories had reassured her.

"Teless is a peer, another teenager," Rombo hypothesized.

"Maybe hearing southern ghost stories told as factual events by a peer gives Janny a framework for understanding the inexplicable things that are frightening her. In any event, Teless is good for Janny."

"I'll call Rombo and see if it's okay," Bo answered.

"I already checked. He said no problem. And Nonk'll meet me there to follow me back here and drop off your car. Then we'll go on home, *sha*. You eat, and go to bed. I gonna tell Janny 'bout *roogaroos* tonight!"

"What's a roogaroo?" Bo asked, filling a pottery bowl with chicken and dumplings, then buttering two biscuits. Teless had already cooled a plate of chicken and broth for Molly, whose tail registered delight.

"Nobody knows," the girl answered. "*Roogaroo*'s just strange things that happen, like noise in the night that don't come from nowhere."

"Sounds appropriate," Bo acknowledged while scrounging through the refrigerator for jelly. "Go ahead. There's an extra car key stuck to a magnet on the refrigerator. And Teless?"

"Yeah."

Bo feigned great interest in the label of an ancient strawberry jelly jar as she slid back onto a bar stool at the counter. "You seem to be having a terrific time here despite the fact that your boyfriend, whom you want to marry, is on his way to prison."

From the corner of her eye Bo saw the girl blush and then muster a guilty smile. "Robby Landry and me, we been friends since first grade, but he's not my boyfriend," she explained. "He knew how much I wanted to get outta there, go *someplace*. We was always gonna try it ourselves, take off together after we graduated high school, just gas up his old truck and head out, see the world."

"But you got older and Robby started getting into trouble, right?"

"Yeah, big trouble," Teless agreed, frowning. "He wouldn't

listen to nobody, not even me. So this last time when we knew he wasn't goin' nowhere for a long time, we came up with this plan. Tell everybody we'd get married before he went off to prison, see? He even went into Lafayette, tryin' to get a license, to scare my folks. Made sure everybody knew what he was doin'. You know what he said, Bo?"

"What?" Bo answered through a succulent dumpling.

"He said this was our last chance to do it together, to get out. He said I had to get out for both of us now, and using him was the way."

Bo nodded. "Smart kid."

"Yeah, *sha*, it worked! My *nanaan* freaked and paid to send me out here. I always wanted to come out here. Do you think it was wrong, what Robby an' me did?"

Bo swallowed a last bite of biscuit. Teenagers, she mused, were so damn prone to asking difficult questions. And expecting answers.

"It's never okay to deceive someone who cares about you," she answered carefully. "Never. But sometimes it happens anyway. The question is, what are you going to do about it?"

Teless scowled at the knuckles of her left hand. "You think I should tell my *nanaan*."

"What do *you* think, Teless?"

"I think I should tell her," the girl sighed. "And I think I should pay her back the money she spent for my bus fare. Except how am I gonna do that?"

"One step at a time, Teless. Just make a plan and then follow through. Now get going before you miss out on visiting hours at the hospital, and tell Janny hi for me."

With the teenager's absence the apartment felt calmer, Bo thought. Less likely to blow apart from all that unbridled energy. After a last walk with Molly, she turned the portable radio in the bathroom to the NPR station and lit a bayberry candle on the edge of the filling tub. The program was a Christmas special by a local investigative reporter, Margo

Simon. Interviews of San Diego toymakers interspersed with children's classical music. Bo slipped into the steaming water as Simon concluded an informative chat with a man who made kaleidoscopes from crushed beach glass, followed by excerpts from *The Nutcracker*. Bo directed "The Dance of the Sugar Plum Fairy" with a long-handled back scrubber, then felt her ears lay back as Simon introduced the next interviewee.

"Jasper Malcolm has delighted generations of children with his beautifully crafted bisque-head baby dolls," the reporter said, "but rumors are flying that this year's award-winning doll, Johanna, may be the last. A phoned interview, taped only hours ago, seems to deepen the mystery surrounding this reclusive local artist."

Bo listened as Jasper Malcolm's familiar, cultivated voice conceded that the end of his career was indeed in sight. But, he hinted, there might be one more doll. His masterpiece. If only he could complete the prototype in time. Margo Simon, clearly not wishing to press the possibility of terminal illness during a Christmas special meant for children, let it go. But Bo did not.

Was the old dollmaker ill? Or did his words reflect a doom closing in from elsewhere? What had Kimmy's death meant to him? The lucrative sequence of dolls had been modeled on Kimmy and Janny, he said. Thirteen baby dolls creating again and again two infant faces that no longer existed. One a frightened teenager now, and one dead. Would the dolls cease with Kimmy's death? But Jasper Malcolm had said there would be one more, if he could complete it in time. Maybe this last doll would be Janny, Bo thought. A lovely young lady doll in velvet and lace. An infant frozen in time, now allowed to grow up.

The broadcast closed with Debussy's "Serenade for the Doll," written for the composer's daughter, Claude-Emma, in the first decade of the century now ending. Bo stretched in the cooling bath water. Eventually, she pondered, everyone connected to this strange case, including Bo Bradley, would be gone. But some of Jasper Malcolm's dolls, like Debussy's music, would still exist. The thought was eerie. Bo shelved it for later and headed sleepily for her reindeer sheets until her progress was interrupted by the phone ringing.

Probably Andy, she thought, calling to confirm the arrangement for meeting Teless and returning the Pathfinder. But the voice on the phone wasn't Andrew LaMarche's.

"Ms. Bradley," Jasper Malcolm stated decorously, "by now you will have spoken with my daughter Beryl."

"I have," Bo answered. Something in his voice made her think of mice, the scritching *sound* of mice in a dark cabinet where traps are baited and waiting.

"And she told you that I sexually molested her from the time she was five until early adolescence."

"Yes."

"Did you believe her?"

"I did at first, Mr. Malcolm. Then I had questions. Why do you ask?"

"It's terribly important to me that you know the truth, Ms. Bradley. There are several reasons, but please let it suffice that this matters. I did not sexually molest or in any other way abuse Beryl or Tamlin or any other child. Evil cuts a wide swath and a blind one. I am no less its victim than poor, tortured Kimmy or her sister, whom you are championing so valiantly. Please believe me."

Bo drummed her fingers on the counter.

"Why should I?" she asked.

"Why shouldn't you?" he countered. "Good-bye, Ms. Bradley. And thank you for helping Janny."

"I haven't—" Bo began, but he'd hung up.

"Strange," she mentioned to Molly, already stretched tummy-up on her sheepskin bed. "Very strange."

In the night Bo dreamed of Goblin Market in flames, its vampire-children flying out over the sea with smoking wings.

Waking briefly, she thought she could actually smell the
charred fiberboard of the club's mock turrets, but the scent
was quickly subsumed in sleep.

Chapter 19

The reindeer sheets smelled like Christmas, Bo noted upon awakening to sunlight. Piney and crisp. Or something did. And something was clumping around on her deck. A tall man with no hips in jeans, hiking boots, and a canvas jacket. As she watched sleepily through her deck door, he shook an eight-foot-tall knobcone pine to loosen its branches and then leaned it against her deck rail.

"Got here early so I climbed over the rail, hauled it up," he said, pointing to a mess of ropes lying on the redwood floor. "Couldn't have got it up the steps and through your place anyway." The effort necessary to explain his presence seemed to drain him.

"It's eight o'clock in the morning. You must be Pete Cullen," Bo said.

"All right."

The response suggested that he'd just allowed her to assign him a name and that the name would do, although in general names were frivolous and unnecessary. Above his brown corduroy coat collar Bo took note of a wide jaw just beginning to go jowly, unmatched teeth indicating a partial plate, and blue eyes full of somber intelligence. Or one of them was. The other, the left one, moved blearily in synch with its mate but wore a caul of blindness.

"What happened to your eye?" Bo asked.

"Guy bashed it," Cullen growled, creating the impression that further demands for speech might cause him to go berserk and demolish the deck.

"Let me get dressed and start the coffee, Cullen. I'll let you in in a minute."

Bo threw on jeans and a green sweatshirt before addressing Molly.

"There's an enormous man and a tree on the deck," she pointed out. "You're supposed to be aware of these things, bark, guard. The very nature of the dog involves barking and guarding."

Molly stretched her stubby legs and then waddled to the deck door.

"Woof," she said, and then wagged her tail as Pete Cullen hunkered to hold his hand to her through the screen. His hand alone, Bo thought, would make a meal for two standard dachshunds or several generations of carnivorous beetles. Weird thought. Big guy.

"It's a beautiful tree, but it's not going to fit inside," she told him, opening the dining area deck door.

"Nope," he answered.

Bo made coffee and snapped on Molly's leash.

"I guess you're going to set it up on the deck, then. Great idea. While I walk the dog, why don't you trim off some extra branches and wire them into wreaths for inside? There's baling wire in the drawer under the coffeemaker. You don't have to say anything, okay?"

Cullen nodded, contemplating the task before him.

When Bo returned twenty minutes later there were wreaths and evergreen swags on the front door, bathroom mirror, and deck railing. The tree was upright in a bucket of water and braced by boards nailed to a triangular base. Pete Cullen seemed pleased, although it was hard to be sure. The slightly less dour set of his lips did suggest an embryonic smile, Bo thought.

"It all looks lovely," she told him. "Thank you. I hope you can come to the party tonight, Pete. It's at seven. And here's my CPS ID. Can we talk about the Malcolm case now?"

"What's your part in it?" Cullen asked, knocking a set of wooden candle holders off the coffee table in an attempt to cross his long legs while sinking into Bo's couch.

"Kimmy Malcolm died Wednesday night," Bo began. "Her twin Janny, who does not remember Kimmy, was at a Goth club on the beach when it happened. She was carrying an old doll she believes is *named* Kimmy, and went into some kind of shock. Since then she's had escalating problems, including a fear that someone is coming to get her. She's in County Psychiatric now."

Cullen's good eye had registered interest at "someone is coming to get her."

"I checked out the hill behind the foster home," Bo went on. "It's all ice plant, and steep. Janny didn't imagine somebody was outside her bedroom window, Pete. The ice plant was smashed all the way up to the school playground above the property. Somebody was there."

"Good work," Cullen muttered, causing Bo to blush with pleasure. She couldn't remember the last time anyone had actually complimented her on the way she did her job.

"Who do you think it was?" he asked.

"Probably the neighborhood Peeping Tom. The point is, Janny's being dumped into the psychiatric system and labeled with an illness she doesn't have. She's just a kid, and nobody in her family cares about her at all. They've abandoned her. They all abandoned her thirteen years ago after whatever happened in that beach cottage, and—"

"It was no Peeping Tom," Cullen interrupted. "Whaddaya say we go by and take a look at that cottage?"

"What for?" Bo asked. "It's been empty for years. It's got rats."

"It's been empty since the night somebody bashed that kid, Bradley. I want you to see it. Maybe you can figure out what happened there better than I did."

"I've already seen it and I don't really have time," Bo said, but the old cop was already at the door.

"Just take a minute," he insisted.

The Nantasket Street cottage was as ominous as it had been when Bo first saw it, curtained by dead palm fronds and tangled blueberry climber. Pete Cullen boosted Bo over the fence and then strode through plant shadows to a side window, from which he easily tore the remaining boards. The glass was broken, but jagged edges remained stuck in the glazing. Cullen knocked the rest of the glass out with his canvas-covered elbow and helped Bo over the sill before hefting himself into a ruined living room.

"Happened back here in a bedroom," he muttered, ignoring a magazine on the floor whose cover featured Ronald Reagan in a campaign debate with incumbent President Jimmy Carter. Something had gnawed the edges of the magazine.

Bo followed him through a small kitchen that reeked of rust to a rear hallway. Cullen opened a door on his right.

"In here," he said as rustlings on the trash-strewn floor made Bo's stomach lurch.

Only box springs remained on the double bed, their fabric shell eaten away in patches that made Bo think of ancient maps. The sort of maps that always included sea monsters. Things had been living in the box springs, she realized. Things probably still were living in the box springs. The air in the room felt bitter, stung her eyes.

"We shouldn't be breathing in here," she told Cullen. "Rats carry plague."

"The cribs were on either side of that dresser," he said, pointing to a waist-high chest of drawers against the wall at the foot of the bed. "Kimberly on the left and Janet on the right. The boy, Jeffrey, slept in the other bedroom."

Bo stared at the grimy glass of a boarded window near where Kimmy Malcolm's crib had been.

"Maybe somebody came through that window," she suggested without conviction.

"Screen was nailed in and undisturbed. Nobody came through it."

Something about the top of the dresser bothered Bo. Just a slab of thick pulp-composition from which the veneer was curling, it seemed to occupy more space than it actually did. It seemed somehow physically *loud*. And it made her sick.

"You never found the weapon, did you, Cullen?" she whispered through rising nausea.

He followed her gaze to the thick, straight edge of the dresser top.

"Fuck! You're right. Why didn't I see it then? Nobody hit that kid with anything, but somebody hit something with the kid! The edge of that damn dresser! Just picked her up and slammed—"

But Bo was gone, diving headlong through the rancid cottage and out the open window. Something snagged the back of her coat and she felt ripping fabric. Irrelevant. Nothing mattered but getting out of that space, away from a mental image so cruel it forever poisoned the air where its reality had occurred. Gasping against the vine-covered trunk of a magnolia tree, Bo wondered if she had the strength to tear the cottage down herself. It had to be obliterated. And so did the *thing* that had taken Kimmy Malcolm's life.

"Good eye, Bradley," Cullen said as he replaced the window boards, pounding the nails in with a rock.

"It was Tamlin," Bo whispered, still shaking. "It had to be Tamlin."

"Maybe, but I don't think so. Too violent. It was a man."

Bo inspected a foot-long flap of ripped ripstop nylon hanging from the back of her coat. "Rick Lafferty? He wasn't here. He had an alibi."

"Lafferty's parents were his alibi, which is no alibi. But I don't think it was Lafferty."

"Who, then?" Bo asked.

"The pervert," Cullen announced in a gravelly bass. "The grandpa. The little fop with his damn little dolls. He did it. I always thought he did it, but I couldn't prove it."

Bo watched a wisp of fog drift across a cluster of rattling palm fronds and evaporate over the fence. "Jasper Malcolm? Why?"

"Because he's a sick bastard. Who knows what goes on in his mind? But I think he killed his wife so he could have at those girls, have them to himself. Then they grew up and—"

"Killed his wife?" Bo interrupted. "What?"

"Supposedly she fell down the stairs in that mausoleum of a house in Golden Hill. Broke her neck."

"And?"

"And I read the medical examiner's report. She'd been carrying a tray. Tamlin was sick and the mother'd taken dinner up to her room on a tray. There were flowers on the tray in a small glass vase. Roses. Dorothy Malcolm liked to grow flowers."

It occurred to Bo that Pete Cullen could be very talkative when discussing a case.

"Many women who grow flowers are not murdered by their husbands," she said.

"There were a number of small puncture wounds in the woman's face, Bradley. The ME determined that they were from rose thorns."

"So, she fell on the roses. I don't get this, Pete."

His voice dropped to basso profundo. "There were punctures on her forehead and both sides of her face, yet the ME was certain she died instantly."

Bo breathed deeply, pondering this information. The dour

cop had presented it as a sort of riddle. Solving it would earn his respect. Bo found herself wanting that respect, realized that she liked the grisly old giant.

"Maybe her body moved after the fall that broke her neck. She dropped the tray and the flowers fell down the steps, then she fell on them, dying instantly. But gravity caused her to roll farther down and in the roll her head turned, pressing against the rose stems from the other side."

"Good, you're good," he grinned. "That's what the ME figured, too. But I don't buy it. I think somebody deliberately pushed those thorns into her face as she lay there dead at the bottom of the stairs. A kind of a mark to show he'd won. Malcolm has a thing about faces, you know. His damn dolls. It's the kind of thing he'd do, hurt her face that way."

Bo remembered Jasper Malcolm's interest in her own face, his touch on her cheekbone, and shuddered. Then she remembered a child's doll-like skull, also ruined.

"You may be right, Pete," she said. "But why would he hurt his own granddaughter?"

"Remember Tamlin said the man who broke in grabbed both twins. I think he meant to kill them both, but dropped Janet when Tamlin struggled with him. I think he had to kill them before they grew any older, before he couldn't resist them any longer. He had to keep them babies, like his dolls, or succumb to his lust for them. It was the only way he could stop himself."

"But Tamlin would have seen him, been able to identify him. Why would she protect him?"

"Money, some sick attachment to him. Malcolm's loaded. He supports that monastery she's in, and his other daughter, Beryl, as well. You know how victims are, Bradley. You work with this stuff every day. They never stop worshiping the bastard that raped them as kids, even when they grow up."

" 'Worship' isn't the right term, and Tamlin's in a convent, not a monastery," Bo began, and then remembered Jasper

Malcolm's phone call of the night before. "He called me, you know, and asked me to believe he'd never molested a child. He said it was important."

"He's a shitbag," Cullen said with finality. "Do you know his dolls are used to make kiddy-porn photos that're sold all over the world?"

"Whaaat?"

"Yeah. We've been tracking this thing for a while. Hard to prosecute, since dolls aren't people. I wanna nail him, Bo. I want it so bad I can taste it!"

There was a determined movement beneath the blueberry climber near Bo's left foot.

"And I want to get out of here," she said. "I'm having a party this evening, a Christmas party. I'm going to go out and buy wine and cookies and creme-filled chocolates with little sugar holly leaves on them. I'm not going to think about this case any more today."

"Won't work, hound dog," Cullen said knowledgeably. "But you can try. And I think I'll take you up on that invitation. Party sounds pretty good, actually. But first maybe we'll drop in on our friend the dollmaker, huh? I've got some pictures I'd like to show him. And I think you and I make a pretty good team."

Bo was flattered.

"I've already seen him," she replied. "The one I haven't talked to is Tamlin. If I were going anywhere today it would be up to Julian to interview Tamlin Lafferty, but I really don't have time."

"I haven't convinced you the old man's the perp?"

"Nobody convinces me of anything," Bo smiled ruefully. "I have to do it myself."

"Then let's do it."

"Do what?"

"Get you up there to interview Sister Sicko."

Bo looked at her watch. "Pete, it's a three-hour round trip to Julian and back."

"Not in a chopper," he answered, a genuine smile threatening to crack the panes of his face. "I need your help on this thing, Bradley. Let's go!"

Chapter 20

Daniel Man Deer inhaled deeply and chose crumb-crust apple pie with vanilla ice cream and coffee. Beside him Mary shrugged off her rust-colored down vest and ordered the same thing, but with pastry crust. The little Julian restaurant was warm and redolent with the characteristic odor that had rescued the town after the mines played out. Apples. Thousands of them from mountain orchards planted above deep veins of quartz that could be, and sometimes were, laced with gold.

Dan wasn't quite sure why they'd made the mountainous hour-and-a-half drive from San Diego except that Mary wanted to go someplace. For days she'd talked about a trip, a drive up to San Francisco or out to Palm Springs, a weekend cruise down the Mexican Baja Peninsula, maybe a week in Hawaii. Tucked in the pocket of his pajama shirt he'd found a colorful brochure on deep-sea fishing off Santa Catalina Island. Mary believed that he needed to get away, that his obsessive prowling in Mission Trails Park was unhealthy.

"Dan," she'd whispered the night before after an inspired interlude of lovemaking that left him breathless, "this Indian thing you're doing is approaching silly. You've been peeing in spray cans in the garage and then hauling them off to the park. No doubt this is some ancient Kumeyaay ritual, but face it, you're not an ancient Kumeyaay. You're a well-off retired mortgage broker of Kumeyaay ancestry. It's the end of the twentieth century now, Dan. Let's hop on a Concorde and spend Christmas in Paris!"

"I was trying to save a bobcat," he'd said, blushing in the dark. "Marking territory with urine to keep him out of the park, over across Fifty-two where it's still wild and he can live safely. I think it worked, Mary. There hasn't been any scat on the trails for days."

Her silence after this revelation suggested that she knew there was more to it.

"And?" she said finally.

"And it was a way of appealing to the Old Ones, asking for their help with the unhappy spirit I knew was approaching you. They had methods for dealing with spirits of the dead, you know. I needed their help to protect you."

Mary had smoothed his hair and kissed the top of his head, nestled against her breasts.

"You were peeing in cans to save a bobcat in order to solicit the help of your ancestors in protecting me from the spirit of Kimmy Malcolm. Do I have this right?"

"Yeah."

"Dan?"

"Yeah?"

"You are the most wonderful man in the world and I love you, but this is nonsense. Madge Aldenhoven and I buried Kimmy Malcolm three days ago. It was a terrible case, but it's over now. There is no 'spirit' pursuing me, nothing you need to protect me from. And I absolutely insist that we get out of here for a while. Preferably to someplace where there have never been Indians!"

"We'll take a drive tomorrow," he'd promised, keeping to himself an awareness that there were just some things Mary would never understand. Like the fact that he couldn't leave San Diego right now. Like the certainty that he would be called upon, finally, to stand against something alien and threatening. Something from the world of the dead crossing back not in love and courage, like David, but in bitterness.

And Mary, straightening the edge of her pillowcase before settling in to sleep, also kept certain thoughts to herself. There was one thing she hadn't told her husband about the Malcolm case, one thing she would never tell him. Men were not equipped to cope with the chaotic forces which bind life to life, she knew. Men were frightened by chaos and knew a single response to fear, a response which usually involved killing something. Only women could withstand that maelstrom and survive to maintain the illusion of order. Madge Aldenhoven had survived, so far. But the danger Daniel Man Deer imagined to be threatening his wife was in fact looming closer to Madge. And it had nothing to do with the ghost of Kimmy Malcolm.

"Let's go look at woodburning stoves," she said after Dan finished his pie and the melted ice cream in her dish as well. "The hardware store has a bunch of them—different enamel colors, soapstone, Franklin stoves, hi-tech ones, everything."

"Do you want a woodburning stove?" he asked, rising sluggishly in the overheated restaurant festooned with twinkling Christmas lights that made him sleepy. "Where would we put it?"

"I don't want one, I just want to *look* at them," Mary answered. "They're pretty. They're Christmasy."

Daniel Man Deer followed his wife onto the main street of a mountain mining town where sparse, tiny snowflakes flashed in the morning sun before dissolving on the shoulders of tourists. He had no idea why looking at woodstoves should be fun, but he didn't care. He'd stand around and look at piles of giraffe manure if she wanted him to. As long as he could be with her, woodstoves were just fine.

Overhead a Boeing Chinook helicopter clattered above the pines and then seemed to land somewhere at the edge of town.

There were a few meadows nearby large and flat enough to handle the big chopper, Dan thought. But what was it doing up here? In the distance he could hear its twin rotors slow and then stop. Probably the police or the military. People sometimes grew marijuana in the backcountry, he knew, but Julian wasn't exactly a magnet for criminal activity. Nothing there but abandoned mine shafts, apples, and tourists from San Diego looking for country atmosphere.

"I like the red one," Mary said as they entered the hardware store. "And look! You can get a cast-iron dragon to sit on top as a humidifier. I guess the steam comes out its nose."

"Nose," Dan repeated without thought. He had a funny feeling about that helicopter.

Pete Cullen had arranged for an off-duty sheriff's deputy to meet them near the field where the chopper landed as efficiently as he'd arranged for the chopper. Piloted by a friend of his, a flight instructor at Camp Pendleton, it was a two-hour "loan" from the Marines, the friend said. In exchange, Pete was to make sure the Marines got a mention when the story broke about busting the porn ring.

"Convent of St. Dymphna," Pete told the Jeep's driver. "It's off Pine Hills Road, used to be some kind of church camp until about thirteen years ago."

"It's the old Hayden property," the deputy said. "Hear those nuns fixed it up real nice."

"Or somebody did," Cullen growled, and then fell silent.

Bo relaxed and enjoyed the relative silence of the Backcountry Sheriff's Department Jeep as they drove through oaks, manzanita, and pine. The delicate snow falling was a nice touch, she thought. And Pete Cullen's bony knee cramped against hers in the Jeep's back seat felt oddly pleasant. She watched as his big hands clenched and then stretched in response to some private thought undoubtedly having to do with Jasper Malcolm and this case, an open professional sore for thirteen years. When the Jeep hit a pothole in the mountain road, he lurched against her awkwardly.

"Christ! Sorry," he muttered.

Bo smiled inanely and then bent to retie a shoelace with shaky fingers.

Bradley, you cretin, did you remember to take your meds this morning? No, you didn't! This guy's twenty years older than you and has all the charm of freeze-dried moss. Get real!

Except Pete Cullen didn't look twenty years older with his cop hair and aviator sunglasses. What he looked like was an interesting challenge. Bo mentally surfed a private list of manicky sexual encounters for the most absurd, and forced herself to remember it. The *doorman* years ago at a swank St. Louis hotel where she was working the registration table for a social worker's conference on homelessness. There had been something irresistible about his epaulets.

The memory made her smile with chagrin. Mania in its early stages promoted such ridiculous behavior and then went on to dissolve every other boundary separating rationality from emotional anarchy. She'd just get through this interview with Tamlin Lafferty, if in fact she were allowed to speak to the woman, and then be rotored home to the plastic vial of Depakote resting in her handbag beside Molly's bed. Or the other vial of the same stuff in her bathroom medicine cabinet. She had plenty. The point was to *take* it.

"Here it is, Bradley," Cullen noted, nodding to an attractive wooden sign announcing CONVENT OF ST. DYMPHNA.

Beyond a simple gate Bo could see three large shake-shingled buildings attached by a rustic post-and-beam cloister through which the winter sun fell in slanted stripes. From one of the buildings she heard chanting. Post-Gregorian, she thought as the practiced voices drifted out on cold, still air. And familiar. It was the "Rorate Coeli," the traditional introit for the fourth Sunday in Advent. For a moment the sound drew Bo back to a Boston childhood in which her mother had filled the house with music and taught her daughters—even Bo's little sister Laurie, who could not hear—its varying forms.

"You go on," Cullen said. "I don't think they want men in there."

Bo opened the gate and walked twenty yards to a bell just outside the cloister. She had known the bell would be there, and knew what to do. Ringing it briefly, she merely stood and waited. Four minutes later a plump woman of about seventy entered the cloister from an interior door and walked toward Bo, her eyes downcast. The brown fabric of her habit perfectly matched the cloister's redwood posts and made her seem merely a moving aspect of the building itself.

"How may we help you?" she asked through the redwood slats of an arched door. Beneath the habit's simple cowled hood the woman's ruddy, kind face observed Bo closely. Her glance fell on Bo's left shoulder.

"Of course," she smiled. "Someone has sent you to us for a coat, and I think I know just the one! In return we ask only that you pray for people who are hated and misunderstood because they have neurobiological diseases which affect the brain. Will you pray for them?"

"Well, I, uh . . ." Bo began, remembering that her winter coat *did* suggest indigence, "I don't need a coat. I mean, I do need a coat, but that's not why I'm here, although I certainly support the concept you've just outlined. Actually, I'd like to speak—"

"We're happy to be of help," the cheery nun insisted. "Just wait there and I'll be right back. Size twelve, right?"

"Well, yes, but no!" Bo bumbled on. "I do wear a twelve and for that matter I *have* a psychiatric illness, so I'm sort of blown away by all this, but what I'm here for is to speak to a woman named Tamlin Lafferty. My name is Bo Bradley and I work for Child Protective Services in San Diego. This concerns a client on my caseload. I'm sorry if I misled you."

"Your coat is a mess," the nun noted, smiling. "And I'm afraid none of the sisters is available for talks with outsiders. We live a cloistered life. It's best for what we do."

"Which is?" Bo asked.

"Pray. We live communally and we pray, particularly for souls troubled by psychiatric illness. Our patron is St. Dymphna, whose martyrdom at the village of Gheel, Belgium, in 650 resulted in her sainthood and the transformation of Gheel to an internationally recognized haven of compassion for those with nervous and brain disorders."

Bo saw the conceptual straw and grabbed it.

"This situation involves a child who's in a psychiatric hospital," she said. "It's very serious. I *must* speak with Tamlin Lafferty, who may be able to help. Please."

"I'll get our Mother Superior," the woman nodded into her ample bosom and left.

Minutes later another nun whose calm bearing hinted at authority approached Bo.

"My name is Mother Mary Andrew," she said. "And I know about Kimberly's death. Mr. Malcolm, who is our benefactor, informed me. I know why you're here. But Sister Martin, as Tamlin Lafferty has been called for thirteen years now, cannot help you. There is no point in your speaking to her."

Bo leveled her gaze into intelligent brown eyes set in a refined, even aristocratic, face. Mary Andrew, she thought, might be the descendant of one of Julian's original families. Southern aristocrats driven from Georgia by carpetbaggers after the Civil War, but denied employment in North-sympathizing San Diego when their accents revealed their origins. Out of her brown habit and into gray silk, Bo imagined, the nun could easily have played Melanie in *Gone with the Wind*.

"Please hear me out," Bo pleaded. "Tamlin's surviving daughter is in grave danger. If I can't ascertain what happened to that child so that I can help her deal with it, she's very likely to be shunted off into the public psychiatric system and lost. She isn't ill, but eventually she'll think she is. I need to talk to her mother."

"I'm sorry," Mother Mary Andrew said with finality.

Bo felt her ears lay back as a rage at pointless authority bubbled up from deep inside her. Who was this woman to stand between Janny Malcolm and the truth she so desperately needed to know?

"Great," Bo said. "I'll call you in a year or so when Janny, who will only be sixteen, has lost the battle for an identity and given up. She'll believe she's crazy then, damaged, a misfit nobody will ever love. But of course I'm sure you'll be happy to include her in your prayers. How very damn *precious* of you!"

"You're impulsive and cruel, Ms. Bradley," Mother Mary Andrew said, watching as several snow crystals blew onto her sleeve and then vanished.

"No, I'm Irish and manic-depressive," Bo answered, playing the ace. "I know what I'm talking about."

The nun unlocked the cloister door with slender fingers and turned away.

"Come, then," she whispered, "but I will expect an apology when you realize that Sister Martin can tell you nothing."

Bo was left unceremoniously in a nearly bare anteroom just beyond the cloister. In it were four folding chairs, a small wooden table, and a graceless crucifix made of two pine branches lashed together. Its corpus, carved also of pine, was so ungainly Bo suspected Jasper Malcolm must have created it in his St. Francis period. The room, she thought, was the visiting area. It felt musty, seldom-used.

"I'm Sister Martin," a voice announced from the hall door. "Mother Superior said you wished to see me."

Bo turned and then gasped. The face of the nun before her was Janny's, and seemed only slightly older.

"Please sit down, Sister Martin," Bo began, and then explained the reasons for her presence. "Janny needs to know what happened that night," she concluded. "She needs to know what happened to her twin and she needs to know why her family has abandoned her."

"God has not abandoned my children," Tamlin Lafferty answered calmly. "God and his Holy Mother are the only family we need."

In the eyes of Janny Malcolm's mother Bo saw nothing but an emotionless peace. The woman might have been one of her father's dolls. The nun doll, Bo thought with a shiver.

"Mrs. Lafferty," she tried again, using a different tactic, "either someone broke into that beach cottage and attacked your twin daughters or you did it yourself. If you didn't, it's time you told somebody who did. Janny's future may depend on your courage now. What happened that night?"

"So long ago. A stranger came, I struggled, then it was over. Please. The person you're asking these questions isn't the same as then. I know only peace now. My life is perpetual prayer and thanksgiving for the salvation of the world through grace."

Switch to Plan C, Bradley. You're getting nowhere.

"Grace," Bo intoned, trying to remember the Baltimore Catechism which had bored her insensate as a child. "And how do we achieve grace?"

Tamlin reproduced the formula while Bo raked her brain for a way to land this loose kite.

"And to whom is grace forever denied?" she recited.

The question wasn't part of the Catechism, but it was the one to which she wanted an answer.

"Those born without souls," Tamlin answered as if Bo had asked directions to the ladies' room. "They are unable to love God."

With that she placed a small object on the table beside Bo's hand, and left. When the door closed Bo had the odd impression that she'd been alone in the room all along. That Tamlin Lafferty had used no air, generated no body heat, occupied no psychic space at all.

And the object was an old-fashioned scapular, two holy pictures encased in plastic and tied to opposite ends of a looped cord. Catholic children used to be given these, Bo recalled, to wear under their clothing for protection. One picture over the chest and the other in back. But protection from what? On the way out Bo extended an apology to Mother Mary Andrew and then remembered the answer. For protection from evil.

Pete Cullen had created a path around the Backcountry Sheriff's Department Jeep, pacing.

"So?" he inquired with a characteristic disdain for extraneous syllables.

"So the perpetrator in this case is the one with no soul," Bo told him. "At least I think that's what Tamlin meant."

"Not exactly what I need to drag that old bastard's ass into court, but it describes him pretty well. Is that all you got?"

Bo fingered the scapular in her coat pocket. It should be given to Janny, she decided. She would tell Janny everything she knew, and then say her mother had sent this symbolic gift from a world of safety and relentless peace. Maybe it would help. At least it would give Janny something concrete to hang on to.

"Yeah," Bo answered. "Tamlin's in the ozone, just repeated a very condensed version of the story she told when it happened. But she knows, Pete. In her strange way I think she tried to tell me who it was. Except all I can deduce is that she was describing herself."

"A nun with no soul?"

"Yeah. Can we stop in town on the way back to the helicopter? I want to pick up some apple pies for the party."

"Sure," Cullen said, even his dead eye registering a thoroughly masculine disdain for anyone who could think of party refreshments in the middle of important business.

The deputy double-parked in front of Bo's favorite pie shop long enough for her to borrow forty dollars from Cullen and select five pies. On her way out she noticed a familiar figure on the sidewalk in front of the Old Julian Drugstore. It was Daniel Man Deer and an attractive middle-aged woman. He was carrying what looked like a cast-iron dragon and she was smiling. Bo remembered the voice at Kimmy Malcolm's funeral, reciting a poem by Louise Bogan. The woman would be Mary Mandeer!

"I'll be right back," Bo told Pete Cullen after shoving the five pie boxes into his arms. Then she hurried across the street, wadding her coat under an arm as she ran.

"Mrs. Mandeer? I'm Bo Bradley from Child Protective Services," she gasped. "My supervisor, Madge Aldenhoven, has told me so much about you. Could we talk for a minute?"

"What about?" Mary Mandeer asked.

"A poem called 'Statue and Birds.' "

The skin over the woman's nose, Bo noticed, grew pale and shiny even as a flush crept up her neck. The curse of pale-skinned redheads, Bo knew it well. Impossible to mask the slightest shock when your entire face was broadcasting a patchwork of color.

"I'm trying to help Janny Malcolm," Bo went on. "Do you know who killed Kimmy?"

Mary Mandeer sighed and regarded the dragon in her husband's arms.

"I've always thought it was Tamlin," she said. "But the police never really investigated that possibility. They thought it was Rick, the father, and then later one of them was convinced it was Jasper Malcolm, the grandfather. I assume you know about the other daughter, Beryl's, claim that Jasper Malcolm molested her continually after the girls' mother died. That set the police off, convinced them he'd been the one who broke in that night."

"She told me. Did you believe her at the time? Did you believe that Jasper Malcolm was a child molester?"

"*I* believed Beryl Malcolm," Mary Mandeer said thoughtfully, "at least for a while. It was a very complex case, Ms. Bradley. Nothing was ever proven, nothing was ever clear."

"What do you mean 'I' believed, Mrs. Mandeer? Was there somebody else who didn't? Who? The only other CPS worker on that case was Madge Aldenhoven, and the two of you buried Kimmy Malcolm in secret only days ago. I need to know the truth, Mrs. Mandeer. You worked for CPS and so as long as you live in California you're legally forever a mandated reporter of child abuse whenever you see it. Janny Malcolm has been and is now being abused. By the system. You've got to help her. You're *obliged* to help her."

"And you're obliged to stop harassing my wife," Daniel Man Deer pronounced in tones that meant business. The iron dragon in his arms seemed to squirm threateningly.

"Please call the hotline later when you've thought about this," Bo begged Mary Mandeer. "They'll contact me at home and I'll call you back."

"Your enthusiasm places you at great danger, Ms. Bradley," Daniel said softly. "You have no idea how much danger."

"What?" Bo queried. But the big man had already wrapped an arm about his wife and steered her away into the throng of tourists.

Only then did it occur to Bo that she might just have lost her job. Mary Mandeer would be sure to phone Madge Aldenhoven the minute she got home. She would tell Madge what had just transpired, that Bo was continuing to work on a case her supervisor had explicitly forbidden. It was grounds for dismissal.

"Whatever," Bo said to the wadded coat under her arm. It really didn't matter.

Chapter 21

The first phone call came just as Pete Cullen returned from the all-night supermarket with two more strands of tiny white lights to replace the one he'd crushed when Molly fell into the box of popcorn in his lap. He and Eva Broussard had been sitting on the couch competing to see who could string the most popcorn when the little dachshund lost her balance on his shoulder and tumbled into a dog's version of heaven, causing him to lurch forward on his knees into the tangled lights on the floor. Bo could barely hear the caller over Andrew, Dar Reinert, Teless, and Rombo Perry harmonizing on "Silent Night" from the kitchen as Estrella, ensconced in the recliner, searched for the matching chords on an old guitar Bo hadn't tuned since her black coat was new.

"Just run those around the bottom of the tree and then we can plug it in!" she called to Cullen and Estrella's husband, Henry. "Hello?"

"It's the hotline, Bradley," a male voice announced. "Sounds like you're having a party."

"You called to tell me that?" Bo yelled over the din.

"You got a message. Nothing major, just some guy named Man Deer who wants you to call him. Here's the number."

"I've already got that number, and I'll call him. Thanks."

So Daniel Man Deer wanted to talk with her, Bo thought. Why not Mary? And had Mary called Madge yet? Surveying her crowded apartment, Bo acknowledged just how far beyond professional boundaries she'd barged. A CPS worker who brought a child client into his or her home for any reason whatever was automatically fired on the spot. And sitting on Bo's bed tying wired-ribbon bows with Deb Reinert and Rombo's partner, Martin St. John, was Janny Malcolm. Beside her under a profusion of metallic gold bows was the old doll, dressed in maroon velvet and lace. Rombo and Martin had designed and sewed the outfit, modeled on a nineteenth century Kate Greenaway children's illustration.

"Martin thought a fabulous outfit for the doll might diminish some of the creepiness," Rombo had explained, "and I agreed. Janny loves it!"

Bo had nodded enthusiastically, secretly envying the doll its stylish little cape. She wondered if Rombo and Martin would be insulted if she contracted with them to create an identical one for her, in an Irish tweed. She and Rombo had discussed Janny's presence at the party in a long phone conference earlier. Teless wanted Janny to come and Janny wanted to come, Rombo had said. He'd be responsible for her on her "furlough" from the hospital. A happy evening would be good for her.

"I agree," Bo concurred, taking the leap. After all, what was the point of a Christmas party from which the one most needing warmth and friendship would be excluded? Bo was sure Irish tradition would support her decision, if San Diego County's Department of Social Services would not.

"Mr. Man Deer," she began from the bathroom where she'd taken the portable phone. "I received a message from the hotline that you'd called."

"I want to speak with you, Ms. Bradley," he said urgently. "Tonight if possible."

"I have some friends here at the moment, a tree-trimming

party. They'll be leaving at around nine, so we could talk then. Do you mind my asking why this can't wait until tomorrow? What's happened?"

There was a silence in which Bo imagined the burly Indian glowering at the phone in his hand.

"I have seen *wikwisiyai*," he said softly, "the rattlesnake shaman. I saw him in the river gorge, from a distance, after Mary and I returned today. I had gone there to walk as I often do."

"Yes?" Bo answered. Something in his voice demanded respect.

"He had covered himself with dust and carried bundles of white sage in each hand."

"He was 'smudging' something, purifying it with smoke from the sage," Bo offered.

"There has not been a rattlesnake shaman in a hundred years, Ms. Bradley."

"Then he was a ghost."

"He was a warning. I must see you tonight."

"Things will have cleared out by ten," Bo said, giving him her address. "I'll see you then."

Man Deer's language hadn't seemed strange at all. It had reminded her of her grandmother.

"Okay, let's plug her in!" Pete Cullen yelled as Bo joined the group on her deck. Janny Malcolm made one last adjustment to a swirl of gold ribbon, and everyone broke into "Oh, Tannenbaum" in English and German simultaneously as a thousand white lights blazed from the tree. Bo felt Andrew's arm circle her waist, and leaned against him.

"Oh, Andy," she whispered, "it's so bright even Caillech Beara can see it from out in the fog!"

"What?" he said, nuzzling her cheek.

"This is her feast, you know, or was before Christianity. In the longest night she gives birth to the sun, year after year. But in her travail she's especially dangerous, and so we mortals cluster around light during her season, where she can't approach."

"I wish I'd known your grandmother," he smiled. "What a heritage she left you!"

"Now, food!" Teless announced, drawing everyone immediately to the kitchen counter, where a pot of Cajun jambalaya sat steaming beside a warm stack of Martin St. John's famous whole wheat yeast rolls. Bo had sliced the apple pies and warmed them in the oven. A gallon of homemade French vanilla ice cream brought from San Diego's trendy downtown Gaslamp district by Deb and Dar Reinert waited in the freezer. There was plenty of wine, and somebody had started coffee. Bo observed her guests from the deck door and felt a rush of contentment. The party was a roaring success.

Curling on the arm of the recliner, she slid an arm over Estrella's shoulders.

"How do you feel?" she asked.

"Great! For some reason I have all this energy all of a sudden, and so does the baby."

Estrella pulled Bo's free hand to her beach-ball-shaped abdomen. There were thumps and thuds of surprising strength, Bo thought. The last one had been a kick, no question. Es and Henry's new offspring seemed to be enjoying the party, too.

"The baby can hear the voices, the music, especially the bass notes because they vibrate," Estrella explained. "I feel like dancing myself."

"Try some of Teless's jambalaya instead, Es. Let me get you a bowl."

"I've already had two," Estrella admitted. "And pie. Ravenously hungry, for some reason. Think I'll grab the bathroom while it's free.

"And have you noticed your shrink tonight?" Es grinned as Bo helped her from the overstuffed chair. "She always looks stunning, but do I detect a special glow on those Iroquois cheekbones?"

Bo glanced around for Eva Broussard, found her leaning against the edge of the deck doorway, her arms crossed elegantly across the beadwork of a chamois blouse she'd worn with a long, slender skirt. Eva held a glass of wine that punctuated her conversation with reflected light as it moved. Pete Cullen stood with his back to a bookcase, towering over the lithe and muscular woman who was both friend and psychiatrist to Bo. Above him on the bookcase a pottery vase shaped like a parrot seemed to smile.

As Bo watched, Eva laughed and then leaned to touch her head lightly against Cullen's chest. A universally understood womanly gesture of affection and interest, it had apparently escaped the hidebound ex-cop's lexicon of experience. He lurched backward against the bookcase as though Eva had attacked him, dislodging the Mexican vase and a slipcased collection of the novels of Rumer Godden, in paperback. The vase bounced off his shoulder and landed on the carpet, unbroken, as Eva Broussard shook her head.

"I'll be damned," Bo whispered to Estrella. "Eva *likes* him."

"It's perfect," Estrella agreed. "He'll never know what hit him. Boy, I feel funny, Bo. Will you wait right here while I use the john?"

"Sure," Bo answered as Teless and Janny approached with the glazed eyes of teenagers-who-have-a-plan.

"Could we just walk up to Goblin Market for about a half hour?" Janny began. "We can walk from here and I really want Teless to see it. I mean, she's never *seen* a Goth club, I guess they don't have them in Louisiana, and we could, you know, borrow some black clothes from you and stuff. You *have* to wear black, Teless. Mr. Perry said to ask you what you thought, Bo. But I mean, he doesn't really know what Goth's about, and you do. So what do you think?"

"No way, Janny," Bo answered. "I don't think it's a good idea."

Neither girl seemed surprised.

"We figured you'd say that. But what about if Mr. Perry and Mr. St. John go with us?" Teless suggested. "They'd be like escorts. And we won't stay long."

Bo regarded Janny Malcolm, a "mental patient" on furlough from a psychiatric hospital where Christmas would involve red and green Jell-O in Styrofoam cups instead of the usual orange Jell-O. A mental patient with no mental illness except that created by lies and silence. Janny Malcolm smiled expectantly.

"If you can talk Rombo and Martin into it, why not?" Bo gave in. "I'm not really in charge of your case anymore, anyway. With Rombo right there, what can happen?"

The psychiatric social worker had been a boxer in his troubled youth, but pugilistic skills were not what Bo had in mind. He was also one of the most competent and compassionate professionals with whom she'd ever worked. Rombo Perry would look after his young charge with the zeal of a mother elephant. The girls would be perfectly safe.

"Bo?" Estrella called from behind the partially opened bathroom door. "Wow, oh, *madre de dios*, Bo, I think this is it! Can you get some towels? And you'd better get Henry!"

Towels? Bo remembered the facts of reproduction, the little sea in which each mammal swam until its lungs were ready for air. Then the sea broke and rushed away, signaling the time for birth.

Bo pulled open the door to her linen closet, grabbed every towel there, and handed them to Estrella.

"Oh, Es, the baby's coming, right?"

"Definitely," Estrella grimaced.

Bo pondered logistics. Dar Reinert would have a pop-on flasher in his car; all the cops carried them. He and Deb could lead the way to the hospital, a police escort. Henry and Estrella would follow. There was plenty of time. But the scenario didn't include a role for Bo, who suddenly felt excluded. She'd stay behind and phone Estrella's sister, she decided. Except she wanted to *be* Estrella's sister, be included.

"Henry," she whispered to the blond naval officer stirring hazelnut creamer into a cup of coffee, "don't panic, but Estrella will need to go to the hospital now. The baby's coming. I'll ask Dar to give you an escort."

She wasn't surprised when Henry dropped his coffee on the little kitchen's tile floor. It was fine. She'd always hated that cup anyway. Deb Reinert hurried to clean up the fragrant spill as Bo urged Dar into his shiny blue cop jacket. Then she wrapped Estrella in her own black coat and kissed her friend on the cheek.

"Break a leg!" she said because she couldn't think of anything else to say.

"Bo, I want you to be there!" Estrella insisted. "You're the godmother, you have to be there. Eva and Rombo and everybody can stay here and finish off the party, okay?"

"Absolutely!" Bo agreed.

"I'll drive you, Bo." Andrew LaMarche joined in. "You'll be too nervous to drive."

"We're going to take the girls up to this vampire thing," Martin St. John called from the bedroom where he was tying Bo's best black silk scarf into a cravat. "But we'll be back, so call as soon as junior arrives!"

Bo heard the phone ring as she hurried to the door, and saw Eva Broussard move to answer it. It couldn't be anything important, she thought. And even if it were, it would have to wait.

Forty-five minutes later Bo was dressed in scrubs and escorted by a deliriously happy Henry Benedict to a delivery room where Estrella lay with her feet still in stirrups, holding something wrapped in a small cotton blanket. Estrella's smile, Bo thought, gave new depth to the term "radiant."

"Es?" she grinned as tears spilled down her cheeks, "can I see?"

"You're not going to believe this," Estrella beamed, pulling an edge of the soft blanket aside to reveal a tiny pink face topped by damp strands of carrot-colored hair. "Meet Patrick."

Bo felt her heart melting, felt the entire configuration of the world shift in some undefinable way. He was perfect, he was without guile or artifice, and he deserved the best. She would do her part, give him her best. She would care for him and bring him gifts. But most importantly, she would be the one to tell Patrick Benedict the stories which would frame his understanding of life.

"Red hair, Es!" she cried, touching a damp curl. "And 'Patrick.' It's an Irish laddie you've got, then!"

"The hair's just Henry's blond and my dark, mixed, I guess," Estrella smiled. "But his name is for you, Bo. An Irish name."

"Aye," Bo said as the baby wrapped an incredibly tiny hand around her little finger. "And to you, wee Padraig," she whispered, pronouncing his name in Gaelic, "the blessing of light be on you, without and within. And all the strength of heaven to bear you on your journey. Welcome!"

"Bo?" Estrella said, something dark in her eyes. "He's a boy. You don't think . . . he can't, he can't turn out like my brother, can he?"

"Not Patrick," Bo assured her friend. "We won't let that happen."

"Okay," Estrella sighed, closing her eyes. "Thanks, Bo."

In the hallway Bo and Andrew watched as Patrick was wheeled to the newborn nursery in a glass basket labeled BENEDICT, BOY, SEVEN POUNDS. Estrella would sleep while Patrick's first hours were carefully observed by professionals trained to recognize the slightest hint of trouble. There would be no trouble, Bo thought. The baby was robust. But at least Estrella could get her last full night of sleep for a long, long time.

"Ms. Bradley?" a nurse's aide called. "A Dr. Broussard

phoned and asked that you call her immediately. She said it was an emergency."

Bo knit her brows and hurried to the maternity waiting-room pay phone.

"Eva," she said when the psychiatrist answered immediately. "Patrick has arrived, seven pounds and healthy. Es is fine. What's the emergency?"

"Pete got a call just as you were leaving, Bo. Tamlin Lafferty was murdered early this evening. Someone crushed the back of her skull with a shovel as she was praying alone in the chapel at St. Dymphna's."

"I'll be right home," Bo said. "And Eva, are the kids back from Goblin Market yet?"

"No," was the answer.

Chapter 22

Eva Broussard was alone when Bo and Andrew returned to Bo's apartment, her face a mask of concern.

"Rombo, Martin, and the girls haven't returned," she announced. "I phoned Goblin Market and had Rombo paged, but there was no answer. The music was so loud I doubt that any of them could have heard a page, so it may mean nothing."

"They're probably just enjoying themselves," Andrew suggested. "Nevertheless, I'm on my way there now. Bo has told me enough about the Malcolm case to convince me that an upsetting sequence of events may have begun, potentially involving Janny and, by association, my young cousin."

Eva glanced uneasily at a thickening cloud layer which obscured the moon, then sniffed the air. "Rain," she said. "And I'm afraid there's more to be upset about. Pete left immediately after the call regarding Tamlin Lafferty. Apparently he's part of a loosely organized task force of retired police who're working with the FBI on some longitudinal tracking of various criminal activities, including a child-pornography ring which uses baby dolls as subjects in grossly pornographic photos. The dolls are actually advertised in ordinary magazines and newspapers as collectibles. Only certain key phrases in the ad text alert cognoscenti to the unwholesome industry flourishing beneath. The dolls are Jasper Malcolm's designs. Yesterday the authorities were able to arrest a key figure in the pornography distribution ring on unrelated charges. Pete feels that this arrest has frightened Malcolm, sent him over the edge. He's certain that Malcolm is Tamlin's murderer, that he's hell-bent on destroying what remains of his family before he's arrested and destroyed himself."

Bo searched for a raincoat in the closet, found one. Shiny blue plastic with a strawberry design on the lining. Undignified, but it would have to do. She wondered if Cullen had warned Beryl Malcolm.

"Pete Cullen is convinced that Jasper Malcolm murdered his wife, molested his daughters, terminally battered one of his granddaughters, and grew rich on porn photos of his dolls," Bo conceded. "And he may be right, although I'm not entirely convinced. But that doesn't mean Jasper had anything to do with Tamlin's murder or that Janny is in any danger from him. Cullen's just too sure. He thinks Malcolm eluded him thirteen years ago and he's determined to even the score."

"Cullen seems quite competent," Andrew said, dismissing Bo's point. "And Bo, I want you to stay here. There's no sense in both of us running around on a dark beach in the rain."

"It isn't raining yet and it's *my* beach," Bo pronounced through clenched teeth. "I live here. More importantly, I'm responsible for Janny being here. So is Rombo. Don't tell me what I can and can't do, Andy. You're out of line."

"I'll stay here," Eva concluded neutrally. "And Bo, Pete seemed to feel that you'd find this interesting. Tamlin's face had been dotted with ink, as if someone had randomly pressed the point of a pen against it. A black ballpoint, according to the medical examiner."

"Where's Pete now?" Bo asked as Andrew scowled in the doorway.

"I'm not sure. He may have gone to view the crime scene at

St. Dymphna's. He was quite agitated and left after the call came from the Backcountry Sheriff's Department. Apparently he'd left a message on his machine at home indicating that he could be reached here."

"Whatever," Bo replied, wondering if she should try to contact Dar Reinert, ask for a police presence at the club. If Cullen were right, Jasper Malcolm might just be there, waiting for a moment alone with his last granddaughter. But the scenario seemed out of character for the old dollmaker. Best just to get Janny back to the hospital and analyze the ramifications of Pete Cullen's theory later.

On an end table beside the couch Bo noticed Janny's doll, discarded as it should have been years in the past. Happy among friends, the teenager had momentarily escaped whatever curse lay over her.

Goblin Market was well patronized but not yet crowded as Bo and Andrew hurried past the empty lifeguard station and across fifty yards of clammy sand to its entrance. The fog, Bo noticed, lay over the beach in odd clumps that blew apart and re-formed in the growing wind. In places it was possible to see breaking black waves, far out at low tide. In others there was nothing but roiling clots of mist.

Bo felt the eerie Goth music pulsing from the club before she could understand the words accompanying it. That simple four-chord progression born in folk music and worked to death in the fifties, half buried beneath snatches of film noir choirs and echoing industrial electronic effects. The sound track for a cartoon version of Tolstoy's "The Death of Ivan Ilyich," she decided. The music managed to convey both an adolescent silliness and its concurrent longing for immutable meaning.

"What *is* this place?" Andrew muttered as a girl in military jackboots and a yellowed wedding dress hurried past, her black veil hanging in shreds.

"A stage on which alienated people merely pretend to be

alienated," Bo said, molding her answer from the remarks of a long-ago Marxist professor who was now, she'd heard, selling dental equipment in Miami. "Try to look as though you understand the decay inherent in technology."

"What?"

"What ends when the symbols shatter?" asked the voice of a British singer over a merging of creep-show musical artifacts. "What ends . . ."

Bo tried to ignore the question as she scanned the assemblage of vampires and Miss Havisham lookalikes for Rombo, Martin, and the girls. They weren't there.

"Check the tables on the beach," she told Andrew. "I'll look on the patio."

The boy named Gunther was there, dressed in a black jester's tunic.

"Have you seen Janny, er, Fianna tonight?" Bo asked him.

"Sure. And her friend, too. There were two guys with them, but one had to leave or something. She and her friend just left with the other one. Is she okay? Fianna, I mean? She looked pretty okay."

"She's fine," Bo said. "Thanks, Gunther."

When Bo found him again, Andrew was questioning a ruddy, heavyset young man whose fangs failed to create the anemic aura necessary to vampirism.

"Apparently Martin had to leave for some reason," she told the pediatrician, "or at least it was probably Martin. And Rombo and the girls have left. We can probably catch up with them if we hurry."

The Goth singer's voice followed them into wads of fog and tentative splatters of rain that made pocks in the sand.

"What ends when the symbols shatter?" the voice demanded. "What ends . . ."

"It's raining," Andrew noted miserably. "I don't know why we didn't run into them on our way over here."

"They probably walked on the beach, Andy. Let's go that

way. There's a set of steps from the tide pools past the pier. They're accessible during low tide and they lead right to my apartment building."

"They wouldn't know that, Bo. They'd walk back on the street."

"We would have *seen* them if they'd walked back on the street, Andy. Now let's go."

"Bo, it's raining and you're being difficult. Please."

Difficult. A word used to describe uncooperative children and untidy pets. Bo looked at the handsome, distinguished figure standing beside her in a windswept rain and thought of dolls. The control-freak doctor doll, to be precise. Complete with dashing mustache and antiquated attitudes about women.

"I'm walking on the beach," she said, and dived into a shelf of fog.

He didn't follow.

Bo headed toward the sea where receding water left the sand densely packed and less likely to slow her down. There were shallow footprints, she noticed, leading south. Three people, the heaviest walking between the other two, its heel impressions deeper and filmed with water. Those might be Rombo's footprints, she nodded. With Janny and Teless walking on either side. Pulling the plastic hood of her raincoat over her hair, she bent into the blowing rain and sprinted along the tracks. They were already dissolving as she ran. And then they stopped.

Bo looked up to get her bearings. The fog was denser now and moving in horizontal cartwheels caused by the interaction of cold inland air with the warmer, water-saturated air blowing off the Pacific. Moving three yards to her right, she escaped a fog-wheel and could see the Ocean Beach Pier a city block ahead. Illuminated against the black water, it was deserted. Just an artwork pier, she thought, like the one on her Christmas cards. Unreal in the slanting rain.

There had been a scuffle in the sand where the footprints stopped. Or something had happened to disrupt the orderly progress of three people south along the beach toward the pier and the barnacle-encrusted steps to her apartment building beyond. Bo stared at the wet, jumbled sand and then veered inland. There were no further tracks in the expanse of hard sand, so they must have moved upward into the littoral with its tangled kelp and difficult footing. She snagged her right toe in a nest of fishing line caught on a wet board from which three rusty nails protruded, shook the whole mess free, and hurried on. Beach crews cleaned the sand every day in summer, she remembered, but only sporadically in winter when there were few tourists to impress. And the ocean's debris could be deadly.

Ahead lay another obstacle, only momentarily visible and then obscured by a roulette wheel of spinning mist. Something limp and dark, lying atop a mass of kelp. A shark carcass, Bo thought. Not one of the little nurse sharks people caught daily off the pier, but a larger one. The size of a man.

Sweating now inside the cheap plastic raincoat, Bo skirted the object but stayed close enough to see that it was no shark, nothing left on the beach by an ebbing tide. It *was* a man, moving groggily on a mound of ropy seaweed as if he'd been asleep and only just wakened. Bo thought of selkies, the seal-people who took human form out of love but could never stay, so great was their need for the sea. The picture before her might be the birth of a selky, she imagined. That magic might happen on just such a night, and only then, safe from watching eyes. Except this selky looked oddly familiar. Too familiar.

"Martin!" she yelled, scrambling over rubbery, squeaking kelp to reach his side. "What happened? Where are Rombo and the girls?"

Martin St. John responded by vomiting into the kelp, his

right hand pressed in a fist against the back of his skull where a thin stream of blood trickled onto his neck.

"Told them . . . run!" he answered, shuddering. "Just happened. Couldn't see. Somebody behind us—"

Another spasm of retching curtailed his narrative as Bo ripped off her shoes. She could run faster that way. And she would have to run!

"Martin, you've got a concussion," she said, peering through the fog ahead. "Someone will be back as soon as possible. Whatever you do, don't let yourself drift into sleep. Stay awake!"

Far ahead Bo thought she saw two black-clad figures running through the shadows beneath the pier, toward the flat shale of the tide pool rocks with their web of eroded gutters and crab-filled sinkholes. And something else. Something lost in a spinning penumbra of fog, but something which left footprints. Something close behind the fleeing figures who were, Bo was certain, Janny and Teless.

Willing her legs to move quickly through the soft sand, Bo peeled off her raincoat and ran. But every step seemed to drag at her body, pull it downward. There was a magnetic force, she decided, generated by the pull of salt water away from the land. She knew she was covering ground. The pier was closer now. But she felt as if she were running in place against an insistent dark velvet that wanted her to stay, to sink, to give up.

"Janny!" she yelled as rain hit her teeth. "Keep going! Follow the rocks around the seawall to the steps!"

But the words merely swirled about her own ears and then were lost in the wind. The girls had run into a trap. Beyond the pier the seawall rose sharply to protect the last few feet of land between the battering sea and a row of apartment buildings, the second of them Bo's own. Below the wall, the sand ran out at a cul-de-sac of mud-colored rocks submerged except at low tides. The flat rocks were visible now, but the wind blew a shifting film of water and foam over them from the sea farther out. No one unfamiliar with the area would know they could walk around the curl of the cul-de-sac on the barely submerged shale and climb the cliffs on the other side. To a stranger it would feel like walking out to sea.

"Keep going, keep going!" Bo screamed at the distant figures as sand sucked at her ankles and another plate of fog swirled through her as if she, and not it, were insubstantial. "Dammit, *run!*"

But Janny and Teless had stopped. Bo could only see their legs below the mist, jumping desperately against the patched stone wall some eight feet high where it met the rocks. And the footsteps, generated by something shrouded in fog massed against the rising seawall, continued.

There was someone on the sidewalk above the seawall where the cul-de-sac began, she realized. Someone big. As she gasped and fell and pulled herself up again, whoever it was threw a leg over the metal railing and jumped the six feet to the tide pools below. Jumped between Janny and Teless and whatever was following them.

The footsteps reversed, but by the time Bo realized what had happened the follower was gone, vanished into the pier's shadows and the fog-riddled beach.

In seconds she felt the sand become rock under her feet, and broke through a tumble of mist to see Daniel Man Deer, rain dripping from the stone on a leather cord about his neck to run down his bare chest. Immobile, he faced the direction in which the follower had run from him. For a moment Bo saw him as part of the rock itself, as if he had been there long before seawalls and apartment buildings, before pavement and supermarkets and greed.

"It wasn't Mary at all," he said as Bo approached. "I thought I had to protect her, but that wasn't it. Who was that chasing these children, Ms. Bradley? What's going on here?"

"I don't know," Bo answered as Janny and Teless stumbled

across the tide pools and clung instinctively to the big man. "But if you hadn't been here—"

"I *was* here," he interrupted softly. "I saved the cat and the Old Ones showed the way. Mary will never understand."

"Yes, she will," Bo said, not understanding, either. "I'll tell her."

Chapter 23

"Andy!" Bo yelled minutes later as she and the big Indian ushered Teless and Janny into her apartment. "Martin was hit by someone as they walked back from the club. He's still down on the beach and I think he has a concussion. Look near the pile of kelp just north of the pier."

"I'll go with you," Daniel Man Deer said. "He may not be able to walk."

Implicit in the Indian's statements was a danger that might still lurk on the darkened beach. Eva Broussard nodded her approval as she nudged the girls into Bo's bedroom for dry clothes. Janny, Bo noticed, had seized the old doll from its place on the end table and was clutching it to her side.

"Kimmy," the girl whispered in that high, breathless child's voice, "Kimmy's *gone*!"

"Oh, shit," Bo breathed, wadding her raincoat into the kitchen sink.

The girl couldn't take much more, that was obvious. And more was unquestionably on the way. Bo secured the deck doors and then pulled the drapes over them. No point in advertising Janny's presence to whoever might be outside, looking in. And a decision had to be made. Either let Janny in on the available truth about her life, or continue to hide it from her as her psychological resources crumbled under the weight of intolerable stress.

"Eva?" Bo said softly from the bedroom door. "I think it's time Janny knew what's going on."

"Risky," the psychiatrist answered, watching Teless drying Janny's hair with Bo's terrycloth bathrobe. "But it might work. Quickly, though. And no affect. Teless and I will be right here."

Teless had heard the exchange, and nodded.

"'Affect' in this case means drama," Bo told her. "You are about to hear a shocking story. Don't react as you normally would. Just help Janny by saying calm things, okay?"

"*Oui, sha,*" Teless whispered in affirmation, and then pulled the thick fabric from Janny's ears.

"This is just a doll," Bo began, sitting beside Janny Malcolm on the bed and touching the bisque face the girl's grandfather had designed fifteen years in the past. "But there really was a Kimmy, and you're right, Kimmy is gone. It's a very sad story, but it's your story, Janny. I want you to know what it is."

The girl's face, smudged with its ruined Goth makeup, watched Bo intently. "There was a Kimmy? I'm not crazy?" she asked.

"No, dear, you are not," Eva Broussard said quietly. "You are hurt and confused and possibly aware of a recent death in some way, but you are not crazy. You're a healthy, bright young woman who needs to hear some painful truths so you can make sense of the things that have happened to you."

"What things?" Janny asked, gripping Teless's hand.

Bo listened to rain pelting the deck doors, then turned to Janny.

"You had a twin sister," she began, "and her name was Kimberly. She was called Kimmy. When you and your sister were eighteen months old something terrible happened.

Someone hit Kimmy's head, causing an injury to her brain from which she died only four days ago. In the thirteen years since it happened Kimmy has had no awareness. She has been in no pain. For all practical purposes, she's been in a kind of coma, cared for at a facility in Los Angeles. Then the time finally came for her to die. It happened the night you were at Goblin Market. And you may have felt her death in some way, but it's over now. Your twin sister is at peace and you are just fine. That's the way it is, Janny."

"Then Kimmy is the *roogaroo*," Janny said, turning wide-eyed to Teless.

"No, *sha*," Teless smiled and wrapped an arm around the other girl. "*Roogaroo*'s just a made-up thing mamas use to scare their kids, like 'Better behave or *roogaroo*'s gonna get you.' This here thing Bo's told you is just the truth. Dead folk don't walk, 'cept in stories."

"But somebody really is trying to get me!" Janny insisted. "Everybody thinks I made it up, but there was somebody outside my window at the Schroders'. I saw—"

"There was somebody there, Janny," Bo agreed. "I checked it out and the ice plant was crushed all the way up the hill to the schoolyard. I don't know who it was, but there are sick men who sneak around looking at women through open windows. You know about Peeping Toms, right?"

"Yeah," Janny sniffled, "but what about my *parents*? What happened to them? How could they just leave my sister in a place like that and leave me in all these shitty foster homes? Are they dead? Where are they?"

Bo traced a small reindeer on one of her pillowcases. Janny couldn't handle everything at once, she knew. And Eva was exuding a force field that said, *Stop*. Bo rose and took the scapular Tamlin Lafferty had given her from the dresser drawer where she'd put it when she got home.

"I'm afraid your mother has passed away, Janny. She lived in a convent until her death. These holy pictures are from that convent. I thought you might like to have them."

"Hey, I had one of these when I was little," Teless said. "Father Donneaux made all us kids wear 'em. They're supposed to protect you, Janny."

"My mother was Catholic?" Janny said, puzzled. "Does that mean I am?"

Bo smiled at the rather ordinary struggle for identity taking place before her. The fact that it was ordinary made it a miracle. Janny would have a great deal to process before this was over, but her initial reactions were ego-centered and age-appropriate. Eva, also smiling, stretched and looked at her watch.

"You will have many more questions later, but for now you have enough to digest," she told Janny. "And we do have something of a problem with which you may be able to help. First, why did your social worker, Mr. Perry, leave?"

Janny hung the scapular over her shoulders and studied the picture in front, a pretty girl in a golden scarf, holding a lily and a Bible with a shamrock on the front.

"Well, it was sort of strange, I guess. He called the hospital to let them know what time we'd be back. I mean, it was going to be a little bit later than we said, since going to Goblin Market and all. And then I heard him tell Mr. St. John that somebody had called the hospital and said there was an emergency, some kind of crisis thing, and they wanted Mr. Perry to come and nobody else. Except he told Mr. St. John he'd never heard of the people that called, or the address."

"Psychiatric social workers sometimes go out on crisis intervention calls," Bo explained. "When one of their clients, somebody they know well, is hallucinating or having other problems at home, sometimes a familiar professional face can be reassuring. Rombo was called to do a crisis intervention. It's an emergency. Of course he would go immediately, assuming Janny would be safe with Martin."

Eva Broussard had found a pair of sweatpants and a sweatshirt in Bo's dresser. "The other question we must ask both of you is this," she went on. "Did either of you see the person who attacked Martin St. John?"

"No, ma'am, I didn't," Teless said. "Mr. St. John was singing, sort of making fun of the Goth songs, you know? He was singing this made-up song about a vampire decorating service, and we were really laughing, and then something happened and he yelled 'Run!' and we did."

"Is that how you remember it, Janny?" Bo asked.

"Yeah. I was so scared, I thought it was, you know, Kimmy. I just ran. I didn't even look back, but I felt like it was following us!"

"Someone was following you," Bo confirmed. "Until Daniel Man Deer showed up. Then whoever it was ran away. You weren't imagining it, Janny."

"But *who* . . ." Janny began.

"We honestly don't know," Eva said, smoothing the girl's damp hair. "There are some strange things connected to your situation, but the police are handling them. What's important at the moment is that you and Teless are safe and that Martin is receiving medical care from Dr. LaMarche. It will be best for you to return to the hospital as quickly as possible tonight, Janny. It's the safest place for you. And Bo," she added, taking the borrowed sweats into the bathroom to change, "I'll be staying here."

"Good," Bo agreed as Andrew and Daniel led Martin St. John through her door, followed by an ashen Rombo Perry. The former boxer's hands were knotted in fists and Bo could see the shoulder muscles tensed beneath his wet shirt.

"I was set up, Bo," he announced miserably. "I should have known it when I didn't recognize the name or address on that crisis intervention call. A wild goose chase, just to get me out of the way. It was a vacant lot in Pacific Beach. And now Martin—"

"I'm going to live," Martin St. John smiled gamely as Andrew held a dishtowel full of ice against the lump on his head. "I just wish I'd seen it coming!"

"Rombo, you'll need to keep an eye on this for the rest of the night," Andrew interrupted professionally. "Wake him up briefly every two or three hours, make sure his pupils aren't dilated, that he's oriented. If there's any more vomiting, take him to an emergency room."

"I just wish I'd been there," Rombo sighed, taking a punch into thin air that made Bo wish he'd been there as well. Although a punch like that, she thought, would probably have killed Jasper Malcolm. If the follower *were* Jasper Malcolm.

"Teless and I are going back to Del Mar," Andrew told Bo without meeting her eyes. "You're welcome to come."

"Thanks, Andy, but Eva's going to stay here with me. I'll talk to you tomorrow."

"Of course," he answered crisply, and then ushered Teless into the night as though she were made of delicate crystal.

"*Nonk* Andy . . ." Bo heard the girl begin what would unquestionably be a meaningful talk on "Attitudes Toward Women," but the closing door precluded any further enjoyment of the teenager's lecture.

Rombo and Dan were right behind, urging Martin and Janny to stay close as they all hurried down Bo's apartment stairs to their cars. Eva and Bo watched until both sets of taillights were lost in the rain.

"You know, Eva," Bo said thoughtfully, "the footprints of whoever was down there on the beach will be gone by morning."

"They're gone now, Bo," the shrink replied, rubbing a hand through her cropped white hair. "And I'm quite tired. I hope you won't mind if I just turn off the lights and curl up on the couch. Do you have a blanket and extra pillow?"

Bo procured the required items, smiling. Eva Broussard, she knew, existed on very little sleep and was no more tired than inclined to tap dance through the rain to an all-night diner where she'd sing show tunes to an assemblage of soggy winos. But the appeal to Bo's Boston-trained sense of courtesy would assure quiet now. Not for the wiry, energetic shrink, but for her patient. Bo wondered why Andrew LaMarche couldn't see how easily she could be constrained by her own set of values rather than his overbearing protectiveness. Or if he ever would see.

After a warm shower Bo stretched comfortably between reindeer sheets and listened to Molly's soft snore from her basket. The rain was pleasant, soporific. In a while, Bo was asleep. Until something began pounding.

Groggily she propped herself on an elbow and heard Eva's voice, the door opening. Then a smell of burning wood, electric sparks, wet ashes. Muted voices, Eva's and a man's.

"What's going on?" she called, rousing Molly to growl half-heartedly.

The burnt smell reminded her of the dream she'd had. Goblin Market in flames. Except the restaurant which became Goblin Market at night was a cement-block and stucco building that couldn't really burn. A kitchen fire, maybe. But nothing drastic.

"Go back to sleep, Bradley," Pete Cullen's voice boomed from the living room. "It's all over."

Sure. With a come-on like that she'd just doze right off. His voice held an edge of vindication, of justice satisfied.

"*What's* all over, Pete?" she asked, dragging herself fully awake and into the kitchen. "Let's nuke up some coffee."

"Malcolm's dead," Cullen pronounced. "Coffee sounds good."

He appeared exactly as he had earlier, Bo noticed, yet he reeked of smoke and ashes. And as usual he was not bubbling over with a need to explain his remarks.

"Jasper Malcolm?" she asked.

"Roasted," Cullen said comfortably. "Burned that dried-out

old Victorian to the ground and himself with it. Probably shot himself or something before the fire got too hot. Medical examiner's got the remains. We'll know tomorrow."

"Start at Point A," Bo told him. "What happened up at St. Dymphna's? Go from there."

"Here's what happened," he boomed into the microwave from which he was pulling a large cup of coffee. "The old pervert got wind of an arrest the FBI made in Chicago. One of the honchos in the doll-porn scheme. Seems like this network of baby rapers, a few of 'em ex-cons but mostly run-of-the-mill business types, found each other on the Internet. One, a guy named Dwight Bliss—can you believe a pervert name like that?—runs this outfit in New Orleans making Mardi Gras gimcracks. You know, beads and masks and stuff. So Bliss gets a contract for a couple thousand fancy Mardi Gras dolls and discovers there are dolls out there that look so real you can photograph 'em through a scrim or a little out of focus and nobody'll know they're not the real thing. He and his little friends are one extended hard-on when their guy in Denver, who's a court reporter, does some research and finds out you can sell pictures of dolls doing anything, and it's perfectly legal."

"Pete," Eva insisted, "what happened *here*?"

"Don't know yet how Malcolm was involved in this, but police in Chicago got the guy there on something else entirely, a bunch of little shit—suspicion of mail fraud, nonpayment of child support, an old car-theft warrant from a hundred years ago in Milwaukee—that stuff. It was set up. So Malcolm gets word of this, right? And goes butt-up. He's dead, and he knows it. Only a matter of time until he's wearing denim behind a razor-wire fence, selling his jaw to the only scum higher than him on the totem pole for the dubious pleasure of staying alive. Not a pretty—"

"Pete, your enjoyment of these imagined details is becoming tedious," Eva interrupted, "as well as repugnant. What actually happened?"

"Uh," Cullen grunted. "I really hate that little bastard. Sorry. Anyway, I think he meant to do this all along, take out the rest of his 'little girls'—Tamlin, Beryl, then Janny—before taking himself out. The head nun up in the Julian place said they received a special-delivery shipment late last night. A ton of old dolls, she said, valuable and all packed and labeled. Enough to sell and keep the convent going for years. He had it all planned, see? Had his ducks in a row."

"What ducks?" Bo asked. "Why would he donate his collection to St. Dymphna's if he's this monster? And what happened to Beryl?"

"She lucked out, was at some meeting most of the evening, a support group. When the cops came by later to tell her the old man was dead, she laughed. Said her support group would probably throw a party. Malcolm may have come by looking for her, but he missed. And the guy's got this religious streak, used to make some kind of Catholic dolls. In his wacked-out mind he probably bought his way out of hell by giving a bunch of dolls to a bunch of nuns. These creeps think like that."

Bo slumped on a barstool and stirred sugar into her coffee. "So how did he get Tamlin?" she asked.

"He knew the drill up there. They take turns praying all night. There's always one of them praying in their chapel, around the clock. They take hour shifts. All he had to do was wait until his daughter showed up. The shovel, incidentally, was from the convent tool shed. He grabbed it, waited in the trees, and then whacked her. It was about eight o'clock when the next one came in and found her. It could have happened anytime between seven and eight. She died instantly."

"But *why*?" Bo insisted. "Why would he want to kill off his family?"

"Why do nuts do anything?" Cullen shrugged. "They don't

live in the same world we do. Malcolm was a nut, a sicko. End of story."

Bo toyed with the idea of pouring her coffee over Pete Cullen's head as Eva rose to stand between them.

"Thank you for coming by, Pete," she murmured. "At least we can rest comfortably in the knowledge that Janny is safe."

"Hey, can I finish my coffee?" he said as Eva pushed him toward the door.

"No, you can't. And thank you again for bringing us the news of Jasper Malcolm's death. It's been a very difficult evening. Good night."

Pete Cullen looked stricken. "What did I say?" he asked. "I've never been any good at talking."

"Really?" Eva smiled. "Perhaps we can work on that. Later."

When he was gone Bo walked Molly briefly on the rainslick street, thinking about the old dollmaker. He *was* strange. Cullen's dislike of him wasn't surprising. But had he been the cunning sociopath the ex-cop described? Bo remembered aqua-blue eyes, the slender hands working at clay under plastic film. Maybe, she nodded to herself. But she hadn't sensed it. Neither had she sensed anything else about the old man. Or had she?

The case might be over, but there was something more to discover, Bo realized. Something about an ugly carving of St. Francis. And something about Madge Aldenhoven. There would be no rest, Bo decided, until she knew the whole story.

Chapter 24

At five A.M. Bo heard Eva Broussard open the apartment door and pad barefoot down the steps to the street. Molly stirred at the sound, then circled irritably in her sheepskin bed and went back to sleep.

"Some guard dog," Bo whispered. "What does it take? FBI storm troopers in strapless pink chiffon?"

After coffee and a bowl of leftover jambalaya, Bo dressed in paint-stained sweater and jeans, forced Molly briefly outside, then hurried to the Pathfinder. The morning air was clean and strewn with gulls inspecting the beach for delicacies washed ashore during the night. Bo watched as a large herring gull flapped skyward trailing fish entrails from its beak.

"Ycchh!" she yelled at the bird even though what she was about to do might arguably fall in the same category. Scavenging, she admitted, was scavenging.

Fifteen minutes later she surveyed Jasper Malcolm's ruined home. Or the charred sculpture that was left of it. The fire crew had erected a chain-link barrier fence from which yellow warning tape flapped in the chilly breeze.

DANGEROUS KEEP OUT, it announced every two feet.

The roof had collapsed when the walls could no longer support it, Bo observed. But most of it had been hauled in pieces to the back of the lot. Probably to facilitate location of Jasper Malcolm's body. Nothing remained of the attic or second story but the towering brick chimney which had vented four fireplaces when the house was heated by burning coal. Against the winter sky the blackened bricks seemed to sway, threaten to fall. A hazard, it would be pulled down by wrecking crews from the city within hours, Bo thought. But for now it merely stood bleak and exposed, howling softly as the cold wind moved through it. Walking to the end of the temporary fence, she pushed it away from its wooden pole support. Then she stepped inside.

A damp, acrid warmth rose from the rubble and stung her eyes. The same smell Pete Cullen had brought to her apartment. For a moment she stopped as an unpleasant series of questions arose in her mind. Why had Cullen been here last night? Had he actually gone up to Julian as Eva assumed, or had he merely repeated for their edification the story he'd heard from the Backcountry Sheriff's Department during the phone call he received as the rest of them were leaving for the hospital and Patrick's birth? Where *had* Pete Cullen been during those hours?

Bo stepped gingerly across the frame of the side door to Malcolm's studio, which had collapsed with its aluminum awning still attached. Cullen, she realized, was no less strange than the man he had watched so bitterly for over a decade. An aging ex-cop working off-record with the FBI to track doll pornography? As a board hissed and creaked at her feet, she realized how peculiar that story was. And even if it were true, how far would Pete Cullen go to bring down his quarry? He'd hated Jasper Malcolm for years. Too many years. What would he have felt when he knew his nemesis had murdered once again, and once again escaped detection?

Ahead on its side was the metal cabinet Malcolm had shown her, its paint now a landscape of black blisters. From its fallen drawers a hundred perfect spheres spilled onto the blackened tile floor. Bo picked one up and rubbed the grime from it against her jeans. A blue eye looked back at her. An angry blue eye. Bo dropped it and shuddered as it bounced against the still-intact tile and came to rest against something damp and gray. A cat.

"Venerable Bede!" Bo cried happily. "You're alive!"

The bedraggled feline eyed Bo suspiciously and then moved to rub against her leg. He was filthy, Bo noted, and patches of his fur were singed to the skin. Gently she picked up the shivering animal and tucked him under her sweater.

"I don't know what I'm going to do with you, but don't worry, Bede," she told him. "I'll find you a home."

The cat fastened claws into the thick waistband of her jeans and pushed against her, making himself easy to hold with one hand. Bo was honored by his trust. She'd never been a cat person.

The firefighters had obviously cleared the fallen upper-story rubble from Jasper Malcolm's studio, she realized. This must be where they expected to find his body, and probably had, since no other area was cleared. On the ashy floor she saw a thousand shards of bisque, tiny noses, bits of painted lips. The doll heads, shattered when the house fell on them.

Shivering, Bo began a random perusal of the wreckage. Charred boards, the remains of Malcolm's design table, a mound of baked clay, two little books. Curious, she kicked at the books and watched as the one on top fell open and blew apart, its pages turned to ash. But the one beneath it was partially intact, its title discernible.

The Hours of Divine Office in English and Latin. The prayer book of a Roman Catholic priest.

Bo nudged the burnt, leather-bound book with her foot, then picked it up. Old and well used, its colored marker ribbons still lay within its pages, one red, one yellow, one green, and one black. Gently Bo opened the ruined volume to its black marker. Ash Wednesday. Of course. The Christian day of penance when priests in sackcloth smudge the foreheads of the faithful with ashes as a reminder that all must die. And of what had Jasper Malcolm such a need of repentance that he read the Office of a priest? Bo wondered. The violation of his own innocent children? Sequential murder? Personal wealth gained from the purveyance of abject depravity? Which was the worst? And which of them was true?

Riffling the pages, she felt something lodged between them. A snapshot, its edges melted to the book's binding glue. Bo tugged it loose and stared in shock. The face looking back was younger, but familiar. It was the same face Bo had seen on her supervisor's desk in a dusty photo of Madge and her husband and two sons, probably taken at about the same time. The snapshot was of Madge, and of Jasper Malcolm.

He had taken the photo, holding the camera at arm's length. His extended arm was visible in the picture, and his other arm was around Madge. The dollmaker would have been over sixty at the time, Bo guessed, but his face was handsome, radiant. And the look in Madge Aldenhoven's eyes was unmistakable as she smiled at him.

"I don't believe this!" Bo whispered. "She was in *love* with him!"

The realization was on a par with seeing your first-grade teacher at the beach in a bikini, Bo thought. That sense of shocked betrayal when a one-dimensional image is revealed to be complex, human. Had Madge, married and a mother of two, conducted an affair with a man connected to one of her cases? A man accused of molesting his own daughters? It was unthinkable.

Bo scrutinized the photo again. Madge's arm was around his waist, her face too close to his for mere professional courtesy. When things turned out well, clients sometimes asked to have their social workers join them in pictures. Bo had done it more than once. Pictures of smiling children, reunited families. This was not one of those. This was a snapshot of lovers, preserved by a deliriously happy Jasper Malcolm in perhaps Madge Aldenhoven's lifelong weakest moment. Bo was sure he had turned to kiss her in the second after the shutter clicked. And that she had kissed him back, eagerly. It was that kind of picture.

"Hey! What are you doin' in there?" a male voice shouted. "Get outta there!"

Bo slipped the photo into her jeans pocket beneath the grip of Bede's paw, and turned to face a man in full-body white plastic protective gear, gloves, and an air-filtering face mask.

"Just curious," she answered, ducking through the fence. "I live up the street, knew the old guy who lived here. A shame, huh? Say, what's the space suit about?"

"Hazardous cleanup," the man grunted importantly. "Did you touch anything?"

"No," Bo lied. "Why?"

"Irradiated blood from chemotherapy. Your friend who died in there? He had cancer. The blood's dangerous. I gotta clean that area where you were before the wrecking crew gets here to take that chimney down. Can't you read? Look, it says 'dangerous keep out.' That means you."

"No problem," Bo agreed, heading for the Pathfinder. "I was just leaving."

So the old dollmaker had cancer, she thought as she sped back to Ocean Beach. Was receiving chemotherapy. May have been dying. That would explain the distribution of his doll collection, the enervation that left him sitting in a padded rocker on his porch for hours every day. Bo remembered the rocker. An artifact of extreme age. Would Jasper Malcolm have been *able* to drive all the way to St. Dymphna's in Julian, wait around in the cold until Tamlin entered the chapel, swing a garden shovel with sufficient force to kill her, then drive all the way back to San Diego in time to lure Rombo Perry to a vacant lot and stalk Janny on the beach? It seemed unlikely.

At home Bo took Molly to her neighbor, secured the Venerable Bede in the kitchen on a bed of towels, then showered and dressed for work, wondering about Pete Cullen's role in the sequence of events. He couldn't have killed Tamlin; he was with Bo the entire day and had no motivation to do so in any event, although the same could not be said of Jasper Malcolm's death. So who had killed her? Or had anybody? With a shiver of chagrin she realized that they had only Cullen's story of that event, which might have been merely a ruse. It made no sense, but Bo had to be sure.

"May I speak to Sister Mary Andrew?" she said into the phone minutes later. "Thank you."

"This is Bo Bradley," she said when the Mother Superior answered. "I'm calling to extend my sympathy to you and the other sisters. What a shocking event."

"Yes," the nun replied softly, confirming Cullen's story. "Such violence cannot be understood. Her funeral mass will be held tomorrow in the chapel. If you feel that it would be appropriate, you may bring her daughter. I've already contacted Beryl, the sister, but her father's phone seems to be out of order. The sister agreed to go to his home and tell him."

"I'm afraid Jasper Malcolm died last night when his house burned," Bo said. "That's why his phone isn't usable. I'm sorry to burden you with more bad news. And I'll consider Janny attending the funeral, although at the moment I think it would be too much for her. Good-bye, Sister."

Slipping the old snapshot into her purse, Bo drove to work and parked in front rather than near her own office at the back of the building. The copy room was in front, just behind the reception area. For once it wasn't occupied by a repairman dismantling any of the three chronically malfunctioning copiers. Bo ducked in, made an enlarged copy of the photo, then tucked both in her purse as she hiked the ramps and corridors leading to Court Investigations, her professional home. Madge Aldenhoven, casual in a denim skirt and penny loafers, was in the hall showing something to one of the other supervisors. It was a little quilt, Bo saw. A log cabin design in green and white calicos. A crib quilt.

"Look, Bo," she said, "it's for little Patrick! I've been working on it for months. Estrella's husband called this morning with the news. Do you think she'll like it?"

"You made this? Madge, it's fabulous!" Bo smiled. "And the color's just perfect. He's got red hair, you know."

Edging into her own office, Bo watched as various other workers came out to admire Madge's handiwork. The supervisor's violet eyes were bright with pleasure. How could this be the same woman who routinely trampled the lives of strangers because the rules demanded it? How could Madge turn her back on Janny Malcolm and a thousand other lost children, then go home and lovingly stitch a quilt for Estrella's baby? Bo sighed and glanced at the old snapshot tucked in her purse. There was another Madge, she acknowledged. A human Madge who had, at least once, broken every rule in the book.

"There's a message from the social worker over at women's detox," the supervisor called cheerily through Bo's open office door. "Police brought the mother of your Friday case in last night, again. The worker says she's in pretty bad shape, showing some brain damage as well as hepatitis, a collapsed lung, and acute colitis. She'll probably sign a termination of parental rights. The social worker's recommendation is to go for a pre-adopt placement on both kids. Just transfer the case over to foster care. We're not going to have to fight on this one."

"Good," Bo replied, remembering the gray-skinned baby boy half dead in a sea of dirty clothing. The mother's story was undoubtedly a sad one, but the chain of ruined lives had to stop somewhere. Adopted and loved, the baby and his older sister might at least have a fighting chance.

"And Bo," Madge went on from the doorway, "I know you've continued to work on the Malcolm case. Mary Mandeer phoned me yesterday afternoon. I'm not going to upset Estrella by bringing disciplinary action against you, although I should. A decision has been made regarding Janny Malcolm's placement in a group home for mentally ill youngsters up in the mountains near Big Bear. I hear it's a very nice facility. The foster care supervisor and I both agree that this is best."

"Mmm," Bo replied as Madge turned toward her own office.

Two supervisors? Even a juvenile court judge would be wary of overruling such a decision. Two CPS supervisors together could, Bo knew, pretty much make their own rules. Although not this time.

But before the inevitable confrontation, Bo decided to try ancillary measures. Pulling Estrella's copy of the Yellow Pages from a bookcase, she looked under "bricklayers." Rick Lafferty's name was there.

"Mr. Lafferty, I don't have time to pad this," Bo explained after introducing herself. "Your daughter Janny is about to be carted off to a psychiatric facility for the next three years even though she's not suffering from any psychiatric illness. You can stop it, rescue her. Will you?"

"No," Rick Lafferty answered. "That's all from a long time ago. The other one, Kimmy, and now her mother—they're dead. I've had enough trouble, Ms. Bradley. Leave me out of this."

"Strike one," Bo said while drawing brick designs on a flier announcing free body-fat testing in the lunchroom the following Thursday. But what was Rick Lafferty afraid of?

Next she called information in Redding Ridge, Connecticut, only to learn that there was no listing for the senior Laffertys, George and Dizzy. Apparently they'd moved sometime within the last thirteen years. Janny's brother, Jeffrey, would be eighteen now, Bo mused. Probably a senior in high school. Did he know he'd had twin little sisters? Did he remember? Did he ever have strange dreams of a child crying, a sickening thump, and then silence?

Bo paced between her desk and Estrella's, thinking. Madge clearly wanted to put the Malcolm case behind her. She was willing to overlook Bo's insubordination and outright defiance in order to do so. But she'd made the wrong decision about Janny, a decision that could only destroy the girls' precarious emotional stability. Bo took the copy of a photo showing her supervisor in the arms of a client from her purse and folded it into her skirt pocket.

Bradley, you've hit bottom. Do this and you're as coldhearted as she is. It's not right. Don't sell your soul!

There had been numerous events in her own life, Bo remembered, which did not bear close scrutiny. She could blame a psychiatric disorder for every one of them, and how convenient. But other people didn't have the shield of a medical diagnosis to hide behind. Other people just closed the door and hoped their mistakes didn't come back to haunt them. Still, a child's life hung in the balance.

"Better the trouble that follows death than the trouble that follows shame," her grandmother's voice warned from within her mind.

Bo smoothed her curling hair behind her ears, checked her makeup in the mirror on the door, and walked briskly to Madge Aldenhoven's office.

"I feel very strongly that a psychiatric placement for Janny Malcolm is inappropriate," she said, closing Madge's door behind her. "I know the whole story, Madge. Everything except what's behind it, that is. And Janny's taken the fall for everybody involved. She's a scapegoat. But she's a *person*, Madge. Packing her off now to a psychiatric group home in the middle of nowhere may just smash that."

"Smash" had a nice ring, Bo thought. Evocative under the circumstances.

"Bo, I've told you I'm willing to overlook your unprofessional behavior regarding this case," the supervisor replied. "However, I expect you to demonstrate your desire to keep your job by respecting a professional decision made by not one but two of your superiors."

"No deal," Bo said softly, then took the framed photo of Madge and her family from behind a stack of case files on the desk. "When was this taken, Madge? About thirteen years ago?"

"I suppose so. Really, Bo, I have work to do."

"Why was there no one at Kimmy Malcolm's funeral but you and Mary Mandeer?" Bo asked, staring at the picture. "That was a lovely thing to do, but why didn't you invite her mother, or her father, or her *grandfather*?"

Only a tremor in her right hand, holding a county-issue pen against a memo pad, suggested the older woman's response to the emphasized last word.

"I insist that you drop this, Bo," she said, glaring at the wall beyond her desk. "It's no longer your case. It's out of your hands."

Bo jammed her hands into the pockets of a brown knit skirt she'd worn because it matched the habits of St. Dymphna's nuns. A folded edge of paper in one pocket made her thumb twitch.

"No, it isn't," Bo whispered. "But before this goes any further I want to tell you I think Patrick's quilt is wonderful. I'm proud to work with someone who's capable of such a loving gesture. But I will not allow you to further damage an already confused child in order to protect yourself from your own past. The woman who made that quilt would help Janny Malcolm now, not hurt her. I know who you are, Madge, even if you don't. Even if you chose a long time ago to hide from yourself behind the asinine set of rules this place generates and call it 'professionalism.' Help me out here, Madge. Let me read that case file. I know you took it home. Help Janny."

"It's not that simple, Bo," Madge said quietly. "Oh, for somebody like you it is, of course. You're impulsive, ruled by feeling. You're sure you're always right. But sometimes—"

"Did you know that Tamlin Lafferty was murdered yesterday evening as she prayed alone in a chapel for the world's mentally ill?"

"No, I—"

"Then you probably don't know that Jasper Malcolm died last night as well when his home burned around him. And oh, by the way, the last thing he said to me when I interviewed him last week was to tell you you're always in his prayers."

Bo saw the older woman's shoulders hunch inward, the sharp gasp, the beginning of tears. Perfectly orchestrated, this was the moment to reveal the gleaming, conceptual knife. Show Madge her own face alight with illicit, unprofessional, ruinous love. Break her.

In her head Bo felt a roaring of Celtic blood which loathed dishonor infinitely more than it feared death. A Celtic identity which held each individual soul accountable for its every act in life.

"I'm sorry, Madge," she said, and left.

Back in her own office she crumpled the photo and its copy into a manila envelope, carried it outside to the far edge of the parking lot, and set the envelope aflame with a cigarette lighter. When it had burned, she stirred the ashes into the ground beneath a pyrocantha shrub with a ballpoint pen. She'd come too close to doing evil, she acknowledged, shaking. Irreparable evil, to herself. Something about Janny Malcolm's case infected everyone associated with it. And Madge was going to be no help. Madge was just another pawn, broken and frightened by guilt. And by something using that guilt.

Bo gave herself the rest of the day to track that something. There would be no more time. Because by tomorrow morning, Janny Malcolm would be gone.

Chapter 25

The fax machine on Pete Cullen's desk beeped and droned as additional information arrived. The medical examiner's report, faxed up to Julian a half hour earlier, said the old man had probably died of smoke inhalation. There were no indications of suicide, although the arson squad had easily determined that the fire was set. Someone merely doused the porch and the wooden side door to Malcolm's studio with five gallons of gasoline and struck a match. Even dampened by rain, the old Victorian house had gone up in minutes.

An exterior door off a storage room at the house's rear northeastern corner had not figured in the arsonist's plan and could have provided escape if the old man had been able to reach it before being overcome by smoke in his studio. The gasoline had been transported in gallon plastic milk bottles, found on the scene without fingerprints. They were from a regional dairy and distributed through all three major food store chains serving San Diego. They had originally contained chocolate-flavored whole milk.

Cullen jammed the heel of his right hand against his twitching dead eye and read the new fax as it fed in jerks from the machine. It was from Jasper Malcolm's attorney, hard copy to follow by mail.

"The design for each Jasper Malcolm doll is purchased out-right by a single buyer, Palm Valley Doll Works," it said,

> Palm Valley holds the copyrights as well as the sub-sidiary rights to these designs. At the discretion of Palm Valley's marketing director, individual doll heads, although not the wigs, costumes, accessories or packag-ing which were attached to the dolls when first released as "collectibles," may be and routinely are sold to a va-riety of other toy manufacturers. This practice effec-tively recoups for Palm Valley the sizable fees paid to Mr. Malcolm for his designs.
>
> Neither Jasper Malcolm, his estate, nor Palm Valley Doll Works is in any way liable for damage caused by inappropriate use of these heads by subsidiary buyers. Jasper Malcolm designed and sold toys. Any public suggestion that the work to which he devoted his life was, in its intent, salacious, harmful to children in any way, or criminal will be met by aggressive legal action on behalf of his estate.

"So sue my ass," Cullen snarled at the photograph of a let-ter.

Things weren't falling into place as he'd thought they would. Malcolm should have been a suicide, but wasn't. And despite months of work in five states and three foreign coun-tries, no direct link between Jasper Malcolm and the doll porn network had been established. What it looked like was what Malcolm's lawyer said. The old guy just designed the damn dolls and sold them.

None of which meant the murdering bastard hadn't shoved his wife down the stairs, diddled his daughters, and smashed the brains out of one of his granddaughters. It sure as hell didn't mean he hadn't dispatched her mother the same way only yesterday evening. The little dots on Tamlin

Lafferty's face were proof, and a message meant for Pete Cullen alone. Nobody else still around would remember that Dorothy Malcolm's face had been tattooed with rose thorns. It was Jasper Malcolm's way of thumbing his nose one last time at the bloodhound who'd snuffled behind him for thirteen years.

Rage seeped from Cullen's gut to the rest of his body like ink in a sponge. It had been a battle of wits, and he'd lost. The need to walk, to pound the bitterness into mountain trails with his feet, was desperate. But not yet. He was still a cop, would always be a cop, and a final crime had been committed. Somebody had torched Jasper Malcolm, cooked him like the pig-in-a-hole he was. Cullen felt sure he knew who'd slopped gasoline against that old house and then dropped a match. The question was whether to keep the information to himself. Malcolm's death met Pete Cullen's criteria for justice, but not *the* criteria for justice. And civilization, he had always believed, lay in a clear understanding of the difference.

Slipping the Sig Sauer under the waistband of his jeans, he set the house alarms and grabbed a jacket. He was going down the mountain into San Diego, although he wasn't sure why. It would become clear, he decided, soon enough.

Bo pulled the Pathfinder to a stop in front of the Mandeer residence and got out. There was only one car in the drive. She hoped it was Mary's.

"Mrs. Mandeer," she said at the door. "I need to talk to you. I need your help."

Mary Mandeer tucked a strand of graying, reddish brown hair behind her ear and nodded.

"I'm packing," she said conversationally. "You'll have to come to the bedroom. Dan's off burning sage to his ancestors in Mission Trails Park, but as soon as he gets back we're driving up to Big Sur for a few days and then spending the weekend in San Francisco. We're going to have to leave pretty soon to avoid the afternoon traffic in L.A. I'm not surprised to see you, Ms. Bradley. What is it that you want me to tell you?"

Bo followed the woman into a spectacular bedroom dressed in Indian blankets and unbleached cotton linens. Its patio doors afforded a view of low desert hills to the east. Mary Mandeer was efficiently folding her husband's shirts and socks into a small suitcase. On the floor an identical one was already packed, strapped, and ready to go.

"Why was Rick Lafferty living with his parents when Kimberly Malcolm was attacked? Why was Tamlin left alone with three small children? Was it a court order? Was CPS responsible for that?"

"Yes," Mary said, eyeing the frayed heel of a sock and then throwing it and its mate into a wastebasket beside the bed. "It was my case. The original referral came from a battered women's shelter. When children are involved, the shelter staff are mandated reporters."

"Of course," Bo urged.

"Tamlin Lafferty was not then the woman you saw in a Julian convent," Mary went on, the skin around her eyes crinkling in distaste. "She and Rick married young and never seemed to be able to grow up despite the births of their children. They were both immature in a way that made them vulnerable to, well, *distortions* in the usual patterns of married love."

"You mean they were into kinky sex," Bo said. "Mary, please, I work where you did. You know there's nothing I haven't seen. What happened?"

"Fights. The game fights. I'm sure you're familiar with it. They got sex mixed up with violence and had to get in fights in order to fall in bed and make up. After a while, of course, nothing else worked and the level of violence necessary for arousal increased. They never really hurt each other, but they broke a lot of dishes and furniture. Tamlin took to diving through windows, screaming for the police. It was all part of the game, but momentarily real. By then it was out of control."

"I've seen it," Bo agreed. "So the neighbors called the police, and they took Tamlin and the kids to a shelter where she stayed two hours, refused to bring charges against Rick, and then called him to come and take her home."

"That's the one," Mary said with distaste. "After five or six emergency runs to the shelter and increasingly serious stories of abuse and fear, the shelter called the hotline and we got the case. The standard practice—"

"Is to remove the father and have the mother get a restraining order," Bo finished, "after which both parents are asked to attend parenting classes voluntarily."

"As if the problem had anything to do with parenting," Mary agreed. "Of course Rick violated the restraining order, which Tamlin never wanted in the first place. The games continued, the case was handed over from voluntary to court intervention. My recommendation was that Rick move out to avoid our placing the children in foster care. The usual, basically."

"Did Rick ever hurt the children?" Bo asked.

"Not directly. Jeffrey was cut by pieces of a thrown beer bottle, and there was some question about a liquid burn on Kimberly's arm at one point, but it was never clear who did the throwing in these instances. Later Tamlin crawled through a window carrying the twins and scraped Janny's leg in the process. That kind of thing. But neither of them ever abused the children directly. Rick wasn't close to the children, couldn't father them, but he didn't hurt them. Tamlin was torn between mothering and her out-of-control relationship with Rick, and eventually dragged the kids into the sex games as shills."

Bo studied the design of a hand-woven vest Mary was

folding into the suitcase. "Do you think Tamlin went over the edge that night and bashed Kimberly?" she asked.

"I've always thought so," Mary answered. "At first I was convinced that was what had happened. You know the pattern—immature, incompetent mother overwhelmed by the sole responsibility for small children. And in the weeks after Kimmy's injury Tamlin had that strange, glassy-eyed distance from the reality of the situation that you see in people who can't face what they've done and still *live*. Madge and I did worry about Tamlin committing suicide when it finally hit her, but it never did. The next thing we knew, the paternal grandparents had moved away with Jeffrey, Kimmy was in Kelton, and Tamlin had joined this religious community in Julian. Rick went into hiding in his parents' house and refused to attend any of the court hearings regarding Janny's custody. The police went after him pretty hard for a while, and the grandfather, too."

"Jasper Malcolm," Bo said. "I know the cop who tried to convict him of assault with intent to kill on Kimmy. He couldn't do it, but he still thinks Jasper Malcolm is guilty of Kimmy's murder as well as his wife's. He thinks Malcolm intended to kill every remaining member of his family yesterday after the FBI cracked a pornography ring involving baby dolls. Jasper Malcolm's dolls."

"I thought I'd heard everything," Mary said, shuddering. "That's a new one. Does this cop think it was Jasper Malcolm down on that beach last night when Dan was there?"

"He doesn't know about that," Bo answered. "Do you think it was? How well did you know Jasper Malcolm?"

Mary Mandeer dropped an enormous pair of athletic shoes into her husband's suitcase and then walked to the patio doors. The sun burned off the last of the morning haze as she stood looking out. In the harsh light, Bo thought, the woman looked both old and quite lovely.

"Not very well," she answered thoughtfully.

"But Madge Aldenhoven did," Bo pushed. "I know about their affair, and I assure you this is the single time I will mention it to anyone, including Madge herself. But Janny's life is on the line here, Mary. My supervisor and I are not friends. At times we literally hate each other. But despite that I cannot believe Madge would, or even could, feel affection for a man who abused children. You know about Beryl's claim that he molested her. I have to assume that Madge knew it, too, and didn't believe it. So what happened back then, Mary? Tell me what really happened so I can help Janny Malcolm have a life."

On a desk beside the patio doors was a framed photograph of a little boy with thick black hair and Mary Mandeer's large, pale blue eyes. Bo watched as the older woman touched the photo's sand-cast silver frame with one finger, tracing its edge as if she were touching the face of the child inside.

"A life, yes," she said quietly. "Of course, that's right."

Bo remained motionless, her eyes downcast. Mary Mandeer was going to tell her something. The thing to do was clear the air between them of every extraneous thought, make a tunnel in that space, just go blank. Not easy for a brain that could not, even when comfortably medicated, stop generating thoughts, imagery, words, and sounds. A brain that could not stop its almost palpable *interest* in absolutely everything. But Bo could do it, in an emergency. Could pull a sort of falcon's hood over the very chemistry of which she was made. In the spill of sunlight reaching in from desert hills, Bo went blank.

"I only know this," Mary said softly. "Madge and Jasper Malcolm spent one night together. At the Hotel Del Coronado."

Bo stifled an image of the seaside Victorian landmark with its cupolas and priceless woodwork, trysting place of an

English king and a divorcée named Wallis Simpson. An evocative picture, darkened.

"I participated in this by pretending to be away with Madge at a seminar in Los Angeles. What I really did was spend the night alone in a motel twenty miles from here reading a mystery called, of all things, *Generous Death*. I still have it somewhere, even remember the author's name, Pickard. The title turned out to be prophetic."

"How so?" Bo asked very quietly.

"Madge received a phone call at work the following Monday, telling her there were photographs of her and Jasper Malcolm, taken secretly in their hotel room. No evidence of these was ever produced, but Madge was terrified. She agreed to stop the sequence of official CPS demands, which were really *my* demands, for forensic analysis of the crime scene. In particular, the chest of drawers between the two cribs, where I believed there would be hair and blood. Kimmy's hair and blood. The police, you see, were certain the blow had been administered by a man. A man strong enough to wield a very heavy object with great force. They refused to consider what I believed had actually happened, although at the time I had the wrong person identified as the perpetrator. In any event, after the blackmail threat Madge begged me to let it go, and I did. Money was suddenly available for Kimmy's care at Kelton, and St. Dymphna's Convent in Julian received a generous endowment. Everybody was cared for, you see—"

"Who called Madge that Monday morning?" Bo asked, pulling the hood off. "Who blackmailed her?"

"She never told me," Mary Mandeer said, biting her lip. "She said it was too dangerous. But I know, don't you?"

"Yes."

It all fit. Everything. Bo didn't know why she hadn't seen it, but it didn't matter.

"Thank you, Mary," she said, hugging the other woman.

"I'll do what has to be done now. And thank Dan, too. Especially Dan. You've both saved Janny's life, you know. Tell him that. And enjoy your trip."

She could be there in twenty minutes, Bo calculated. And it was going to be ugly.

Chapter 26

Bo parked at a meter on Washington Street, one of the two main thoroughfares through the central San Diego community known as Hillcrest. It would be best if the Pathfinder were not seen, she'd determined. Best to maintain the element of surprise. There were a few things she wanted to confirm before deciding what to do next.

The neighborhood sidewalks were no strangers to foot traffic. Within walking distance of two major medical centers, they saw a steady flow of pedestrians wending their way from distant parking lots to dozens of outpatient clinics treating everything from bunions to schizophrenia. Bo stuffed her hands into the sleeves of her heavy Aran sweater muff-style, and hunched over, furtively watching the ground. Anyone glancing in her direction would see a woman obviously heading for the psych clinic. She knew how to do that walk.

The geraniums were still there. Bo noted their presence from the corner of her eye, but kept walking. Around the corner to the alley one could expect to find in any older neighborhood. At the alley she looked about in feigned confusion, then waved as if she'd just recognized someone in one of the yards, or at a window. Briskly now, she hurried to the back gate of Beryl Malcolm's Craftsman bungalow.

The yard was unkempt and littered with blown newspapers, a pitted aluminum chaise-lounge frame folded against the fence, and the seeping remains of a giant tutti-frutti Slurpee some child had undoubtedly tossed there within the hour. Bo eyed the bright pink liquid melting from its quart-sized paper cup. Something about it felt diseased, ominous.

The low chain-link gate wasn't locked, not that it mattered. She could easily have jumped the fence. In fact, jumping the fence might have been good, she thought. Might have drained some of the adrenaline twitching in the muscles of her forearms and hands.

The back door wasn't locked, either. Bo doubted that Beryl Malcolm saw any point in locks. She was, after all, omnipotent. Who would dare to intrude on her? Locks were for people who weren't absolutely sure of their superiority to everyone else. Locks were for people who were weak, frightened, pathetic. People who were like children, like little girls.

The kitchen was as Bo had expected. Rank, filthy, strewn with the debris generated by obsessive hunger. Beryl Malcolm apparently didn't cook, Bo noted. She bought things that came packaged in cans, boxes, bottles, Styrofoam. On one of the pearlized yellow plastic chairs Bo counted eight empty pizza boxes, stacked and reeking. On two others were a wad of dirty clothes and a grocery bag from which peeked three unopened packages of potato chips. The refrigerator was brand-new. Beryl hadn't bothered to remove the Day-Glo orange promotional sticker from its freezer. Neither had she cleaned the dried red salsa leaking from beneath its rubber seal near the floor.

"Get out of here!"

The voice made Bo jump even though she'd been waiting for it. Waiting since the night she'd dreamed of a long-abandoned subway station where one more train was expected, and then no more. The Station of the Dead.

"Hello, Beryl," she singsonged in a faux contralto, tilting

her head to one side and letting her eyes open too widely. "You've been expecting me, haven't you?"

The psychotic act, occurring nowhere in life except low-budget slasher movies, would serve to put the woman off, Bo calculated. It would scare her, even the playing field.

"You're crazy! Get out!"

Beryl was wearing another snap-front housecoat, this one in a floral print that obscured the egg-yolk stain on its bodice. In a trembling, pudgy hand she held a soup bowl of cooling coffee. Bo could smell its sickly-sweet vanilla flavoring, even over the room's preponderant odor of pizza-soaked cardboard.

"I know what you did," Bo sang, turning her head in bird-like jerks. "Killed your mommy and your little niece. Killed your sister and your daddy, too. Nobody left but Janny now, is there? When will you kill Janny, Beryl? How long does little Janny have to live?"

"I told you to get out," Beryl Malcolm pronounced in threatening tones. "I'm calling the police."

"Police, puh-lease," Bo mocked, staring with grossly exaggerated intensity into the watery aqua-blue eyes across the yellow Formica table. "We'll tell them what you did, won't we? We'll tell them how you like to hit *heads*, like the ones daddy was always making when you wanted him to pay attention to *you*. How you like to smash them, make the people inside them go away so you can have daddy all to yourself, right? So you can make daddy do exactly what you want him to do. So you can own your daddy, isn't that right?"

The immense woman seemed to shift the bulbous fat of her torso, shake it into her shoulders and arms, draw it up. Bo had never seen anything like the quivering psychic distortion taking place before her eyes. Beryl Malcolm was some kind of amoeba, she thought, who could throw the mass of curdled fat beneath her skin as the one-celled organism throws itself after a protrusion of its outer membrane. And with a blossoming

fear, Bo also knew what it meant. The coffee hit her face before she could fling a hand over her eyes.

"What ends when the symbols shatter?" a line from one of
the Goth songs echoed in her head. "What ends, what ends . . ."

"You think you're so smart, but you don't know anything,"
Beryl said with an absence of feeling that made Bo's skin
crawl. "You don't know what it's like to live with the memory
of that violation, that—"

"Spare me the party line," Bo said, dropping the lunatic act
as she wiped coffee from her face with a sleeve of the Aran
sweater. "I know a hundred women who actually *were* raped by
their fathers, uncles, grandfathers, and brothers. Brave, valiant
women who carve out decent lives for themselves despite the
pain. You're not one of them, Beryl. You're nothing but a vi-
ciously self-absorbed murderer who will go to prison now,
where you've belonged since you were a child!"

The transformation hit Beryl Malcolm's eyes then, answering the bleak Goth question. The watery film dissolved, revealing what had lain beneath all along. A peevish, demanding
arrogance refined to diamond-hard rage. Her body was that of
a grossly obese middle-aged woman, but the eyes, Bo knew,
were Beryl Malcolm as she had always been. They were the
eyes of a soulless child.

And they were moving beneath the white eyelids. Scouring
the cluttered room for something. Then they stopped abruptly
to focus on the coffeemaker as Bo grabbed three pizza boxes
and held them before her. The coffeemaker hit with surprising
force, but the boxes deflected any real damage. The Pyrex
carafe, flung sideways from its burner, shattered on the floor
in a spray of hot liquid.

"People don't really die, do they, Beryl?" Bo taunted,
watching uneasily as the woman moved across the rear door.
"You pushed your mother down the stairs and even pushed
thorns into her face to show her how you felt when she spent
time in her garden instead of catering to *you*. But part of her

stayed, didn't it? Part of her lived on right inside you, making you line your porch with flowers and buy gardening books you never read. And if you had any friends they'd tell you crystal candy dishes are really passé, Beryl. Brocade couches, too. But then that's your mother's living room, isn't it? It's your front, the little charade behind which you live in filth. You're hiding behind your dead mommy, Beryl, but it won't work anymore. You're finished!"

"*He* told you about the stairs, didn't he?" the woman screamed. "*He* told you what I did. I *HAAATE* him!"

The single, piercing word was accompanied by a crash as she overturned the stove, then leaned to rip its heating coils free and fling them wildly at Bo.

"In a way he did," Bo said, remembering the unpleasant little carving of St. Francis. "He told me he accepted responsibility for the ugliness he created. I guess he meant you, Beryl. But why did you have to hurt the children? Why did you go down to that beach house thirteen years ago and bash your own niece into the top of a dresser?"

"The dolls," Beryl answered, climbing awkwardly over the fallen stove toward Bo. "He made *them* into dolls and it should've been me. It wasn't fair. I'd already made Tamlin change their names to Malcolm instead of Lafferty, so he'd have us back, so he'd have his two little girls again. That had to be what he wanted, didn't it? I made her do that. But it wasn't enough. He had to make them into pretty *dolls* in all the stores where everyone could see, and I had to show him he couldn't . . ." she stopped, panting, pulling out cabinet drawers, "do that!"

Beryl Malcolm's face was splotched with purple now, as was the hand Bo saw curling around the black plastic handle of a cheap bread knife which had fallen from one of the overturned drawers.

Get OUT of here, Bradley! She wants to kill you!

"Tamlin saw you that night," Bo said as she began a retreat

toward the back door. "Why didn't she turn you in to the police?"

"So I wouldn't kill daddy," the woman answered in the voice of a bored child. "Daddy was rich and paid for everything, see? All Tamlin wanted was to wiggle on that boy Rick's dirty wiener. But he pulled his weenie out of her and ran away, and she had to be a nun but daddy kept paying and paying. Tamlin knew as long as Kimmy stayed a doll and no one saw her or the other one, I'd let daddy pay. Everyone knew daddy had to pay. Even my support group . . . !"

Bo saw the lunge coming and sidestepped toward the door as the bread knife slashed through air and Beryl Malcolm fell against the remaining yellow plastic chair. But Bo had forgotten the spilled coffee until her left foot, unable to find purchase on the slick, greasy floor, slid away from her weight at the wrong angle. She fell hard on the other knee as a tearing pain flashed in her left ankle. Beryl had dropped the knife and swung the chair over her head when Bo saw something enter from the living-room door behind the woman. Something silvery white and familiar. Somebody's hair, fastened back with a carved ivory clip.

"Get up, Bo!" Madge Aldenhoven yelled as she grabbed the grime-encrusted chair legs about to smash into Bo's head. "Run!"

Pulling a large piece of broken glass from a deep cut in her knee, Bo flung her hand toward Beryl's foot instead. Then she dragged the razor-sharp glass through the pale, veiny flesh covering ligaments, tarsal bones. Purple, almost black blood welled out of the cut as Beryl screamed, released the chair held over her head, and grabbed the knife left lying on the table. Bo watched as Madge Aldenhoven lurched backward with the chair, falling against the wheeled coffee cart. The knife was coming at Bo. She could protect her head, she realized, by jerking her torso under the table. But the descending knife was going to hit something. Slice something. Probably more than once.

Then Bo sensed another presence, footsteps pounding in the backyard. A sharp sound, a flash, the smell of cordite.

Beryl Malcolm sank to the floor with a sound that made Bo think of butcher shops, slabs of meat being slapped on a scale. Her eyes were merely amazed, then blank. Near the egg stain on the front of her housecoat was a neat, black-rimmed hole.

"Damn," Pete Cullen pronounced gloomily. "Didn't mean to kill her, but I had to shoot on the run. Place smells like maggot heaven. You ladies all right?"

"How did you know, Pete?" Bo asked as Madge groaned reassuringly and then kicked the coffee cart.

"Lotta stuff," he answered as if that answered anything. "Bad cut there. You're bleedin'. Gonna need stitches."

"There's an emergency room less than a block from here," Bo said, allowing him to pull her upright. "Except I can't walk. Tore the other ankle."

"Well, I gotta stay here with this ton of fly bait till the cops come and the paperwork's done, but . . ."

His eye fell on the wheeled coffee cart.

"Ma'am," he addressed Madge, "think you could push her over there on this?"

"Sure," Madge replied.

Bo couldn't remember when she'd felt as idiotic, but Madge seemed to enjoy the shocked attention from bystanders watching blood drip onto the sidewalk.

"How did you know what was going on?" Bo asked the supervisor. "How did you know where I was?"

"Mary Mandeer phoned me," Madge answered. "After your talk with her, I knew you'd go straight for Beryl. But there's something else, Bo. I watched you before you left the office. I saw you burn something in the parking lot."

"So? I'm always doing bizarre things. You remind me of them daily."

Madge stopped the cart beneath a coral tree, pulled a folded sheet of paper from her coat pocket, and handed it to Bo. It was an enlarged copy of a photo of Madge Aldenhoven and Jasper Malcolm, the camera obviously held in his outstretched arm.

"But I *burned* this!" Bo yelped. "That's what went up in flames out in the parking lot. That and the original. I swear it, Madge. I found the snapshot stuck in a prayer book at Malcolm's house this morning. I made the copy because . . ." Bo felt a flush of shame mottle her neck, but went on. "Because I wanted to make you do right by Janny. And because I wanted to have something on you, something I could use to get even every time you humiliate me with your damn incessant references to the fact that I have a psychiatric illness. But I didn't keep the picture or the copy. I couldn't. I don't understand where this—"

"One of the runners in the hotline saw you go into the copy room and then found this in a copier," Madge explained. "You know it never worked properly; it made an extra. He didn't know what it was and didn't care. I doubt that he even looked at it. But he brought it to your supervisor, as he should have."

"The best-laid plans . . ." Bo sighed.

Madge gave the coffee cart a stern shove forward as an orderly appeared in the emergency room driveway.

"I admire what you did, Bo," she said evenly. "You possess a great deal more character than I've realized. Beryl Malcolm might have killed you just now, and it would have been my fault, as Janny's plight is my fault. I don't know how to make it right."

"Keep Janny out of that group home!" Bo answered.

"Already done. I spoke with the foster care supervisor and then the Schroders this morning. They'll be pleased to take her back now that they understand the origins of her strange behavior. And I think when Rick Lafferty hears what actually happened, he'll be willing to develop some sort of relationship with Janny, although it will never be much. He's an odd, cowering sort of man. I think his relationship with Tamlin and then the loss of his children broke him completely."

"What did Beryl have on him?" Bo asked. "It seems she blackmailed everybody involved."

"Nothing that I know of," Madge replied. "It was the police who put the fear of God into Rick Lafferty, and his parents as well. Apparently there had been some questionable contracts between the city and Lafferty Construction. Kickbacks, the usual political corruption. The police dug it all up and threatened George Lafferty with prosecution if he didn't admit he was lying about Rick's whereabouts that night. The Laffertys always believed that the twins were fathered by someone other than their son, since Tamlin had legally changed their names. To avoid the whole ugly situation they took the one child they believed was their grandson, Jeffrey, and left town. Rick stayed, but has lived in fear of the police ever since."

At the door of the ER Bo handed Madge the copied photograph.

"He really *didn't* molest Beryl, did he?" she asked.

"No, the man I knew was flatly incapable of it," Madge said with conviction. "But then where did she come up with the story? Remember this was nearly forty years ago. Incest was not discussed at all forty years ago. We're never going to know what went on in Beryl's mind. And Bo?" The supervisor's smile was uncharacteristically impish.

"Yeah?"

"I wish you hadn't burned the original."

Bo could feel the light in her own eyes. A EUREKA! kind of light. "I've got something even better for you," she said.

Chapter 27

"No, I'm not going to stay," Bo told the doctor who'd just quilted nine stitches into her right knee with unattractive black thread and fastened bags of frozen blue jelly to her left ankle with an Ace bandage. "This is nothing, trust me."

"She's right," Andrew LaMarche smiled gamely from his post at the foot of her ER gurney. "Bo has taken harder knocks than this."

"Whatever you say, Doctor," the young intern sighed in deference to Andrew's medical-fraternity seniority. "But don't let her put any weight on that ankle and remember the antibacterial cream for the laceration. It's pretty ragged. I'm afraid she's going to scar—"

"*She* is right here in front of you and perfectly capable of hearing information about *her* own damn knee!" Bo seethed from her supine position on the gurney. "What is it about being a doctor that makes you incapable of talking to *people*? It's my ankle, my knee, get it?"

"Got it," the intern agreed, casting a covert glance at Andrew. A glance which, Bo noted, dripped with sympathy.

"Can you give me a ride, Andy?" she asked while struggling to fit crutches into the armpits of her baggy, coffee-stained Aran sweater. "After Madge phoned you, she ran by my place and then went back to the office and arranged for a couple of the hotline trainees to pick up my car and drive it home for me. They'll leave the keys in my mailbox. So my only problem now is getting home."

"Of course," he answered. "And we can talk."

"I just saw a woman shot dead in an ugly housecoat, Andy. Do we have to talk?"

"Yes," he said brightly.

The substance of the talk involved, as Bo had known it would, the future. Their future. He was sorry he'd been condescending and controlling the night before. It was a slip. He'd work on it, never stop working on it. Could she overlook the incident?

"Sure," Bo answered, squinting at her gaunt reflection in the visor mirror of his Jaguar. "I love you, Andy. It'll take more than one of your slips into male supremacy to change that. But I'm not sure I'm ready to move out to Del Mar. At least not quite yet. I may, I probably will, I *love* the apartment, but let's face it, it's a big step. No going back. That sort of thing. And right now I'm just not quite there."

She had expected him to register dismay. Controlled, of course. But his gray eyes merely sparkled happily as he turned off I-8 and onto Sunset Cliffs Boulevard near her apartment.

"Should I stop at the grocery?" he asked. "You're not going down those steps tonight, so we should get whatever you need now."

"No, Eva's already there. I called her from the ER after Madge called you. She'll walk Molly for me and can get anything I need. Mainly, I want to talk to her about this case. She's discovered something interesting. But Andy, I thought you'd be disappointed about . . . you know . . . my not moving right now."

"I have confidence in your judgment, Bo, despite my momentary lapses," he smiled. "Besides, Teless and I had a long chat last night after we left your place. She told me about the ruse she and her friend Robby Landry cooked up to get her out here, and about the debt she owes her *nannan*. You helped her with that, Bo, spelled out her responsibility for her. She's found a part-time job waitressing in a restaurant in Del Mar and called her godmother to arrange for repayment of the bus fare. And I think I can pull some strings to get her enrolled in the local high school for the spring semester. I want Teless to stay until summer, Bo. And your apartment is perfect for her. Well, for me. I couldn't stand listening to that atrocious music she plays, and—"

"Andy, that's terrific!" Bo broke in. "Janny will be able to see Teless, not lose another friend. You have no idea how hard that is on foster kids, the way the others just come and go. I approve!"

"I thought you would."

Eva Broussard was on the deck when Bo and Andrew struggled in, laughing from the exertion of getting Bo up the apartment stairs on crutches.

"I brought quiche and a double-fudge layer cake for dinner," she said, shaking her head at Bo's injuries. "And an interesting book on saints."

"I'm sure I must be scheduled for surgery immediately," Andrew hedged. "The cake's enticing, but I had enough of saints as a child. All those unusual tortures. I'll call you later, Bo. Stay off that ankle."

Bo fondly tossed a crutch at the closing door and sank into the couch. The afternoon was overcast and chilly, and Eva had turned on the wall furnace which was the apartment's only source of heat.

"Shouldn't we open the door a little?" Bo asked, edgy. "My parents both died because of a faulty wall heater. Carbon monoxide poisoning, just like my sister, only they didn't *intend*—"

"This one's electric, Bo," Eva pointed out. "And it sounds

as though you may need to take a nap before I tell you my theory about Beryl Malcolm. You're stressed."

"Probably," Bo answered, remembering a cheap bread knife descending. "But I'm dying to hear what you've come up with. Eva, that woman terrified her whole family for decades, had them in her thrall. And yet she was nothing but a common sociopath. It should have become obvious to her parents when she was still a child. And she should have wound up in prison as an adult like they all do."

The bakery box on the counter had become irresistible. Bo hopped toward it, balanced on a crutch and the back of the couch.

"Double-fudge layer cake reduces stress," she grinned. "Let's have some while you theorize, okay?"

Minutes later Eva Broussard was pacing in front of the couch, holding a book featuring a stained-glass window on its cover and gesturing with her dessert fork. Bo could hear the fringe on her moccasins flapping softly as she paced. A comforting sound.

"The key to Beryl, as to anyone, lies in the stories they use to make sense of life," she began. "And because of Jasper Malcolm's rather antiquated religious bent, she had access at an early age to some of the strangest, bloodiest tales available."

"The saints," Bo concluded, nodding to the book.

"Precisely. Beryl was unquestionably a sociopath, but she apparently inherited her father's knack for ritual and metaphor as well. As a child her demands for attention would have been insatiable, and her rage when those demands were not met, intense. A female, her most chaotic demands would have been directed at the male parent, and the mother perceived as an obstacle to his attention."

"I can't stomach Freud, Eva," Bo muttered into cocoa-scented cake, "even though some of it makes sense."

"I'm only dealing with the part that makes sense," the psychiatrist went on, her dark eyes flashing with an intellectual excitement that was contagious. "The child Beryl wanted her father's complete attention, but had no model for achieving that goal until someone—probably Jasper Malcolm himself—read her a story. A variant of one of the Celtic myths. Shakespeare used the myth in *King Lear*, and I've heard you relate another version, 'The Children of Lir.' St. Dymphna's tale is merely one of many variants on this ancient story. Do you know it?"

"No," Bo said, leaning forward. "I was raised Catholic, but that doesn't mean I've heard of every saint. There are thousands, you know. Actually, all the graceful dead are saints. Millions."

"The *graceful dead*?" Eva had to laugh. "*Mon dieu!*"

"People who've died in a state of grace, Eva," Bo grinned. "They get tie-dyed robes and six-stringed guitars instead of harps. So who's Dymphna?"

"A pious Irish fifteen-year-old whose mother died, after which her grief-maddened father wanted to marry her because no other woman was like his dead wife. Dymphna of course fled her father's incestuous advances—"

"*That's* where Beryl learned about incest at a time when it was not discussed. Wow!" Bo exhaled.

"She fled to Belgium with her confessor, Gerebern, also sainted, as well as the jester from her father's court and the jester's wife."

"Of course, the jester, just like in *King Lear*! Go on, Eva."

"It gets better," the psychiatrist nodded. "Dymphna's father followed her to Gheel, Belgium, where she was hiding. There he killed the jester and his wife, and Gerebern. When Dymphna still refused his advances, he beheaded her as well. This was in the year 650. Some seven centuries later, when the bones of Dymphna and Gerebern were discovered, miraculous cures began to occur there, or so the story goes. The town became a mecca and a compassionate haven for people with psychiatric illness. It still is. But the fascinating dimension to this is the way in which Beryl, when her original plan failed, assumed the role of the murdering father."

"I've heard about Gheel, and I think I'll just stick with my meds, Eva. But at least that clears up Beryl's motivation for pushing her mother down the stairs, doesn't it? Her mother was supposed to die so she could have her daddy, like in the story. But Jasper Malcolm knew. He knew Beryl had killed her mother, and he did nothing. He allowed a monster to grow to adulthood under his roof and did absolutely nothing to stop it."

Eva leaned against the wall, thinking.

"He probably tried, Bo, in that isolated way of artistic people. It would never have occurred to him to seek help from social or criminal justice agencies, and when his wife was murdered there were none of those for children in any event. What could he have done nearly forty years ago except to abandon Beryl at an orphanage and flee? He had no recourse but to mythology, religion. You forget how very thin is the scrim of 'enlightenment' about the brain and human behavior which characterizes our time. You don't know that as recently as your own birth, it didn't exist, and that even now most people would prefer any explanation for a sociopath like Beryl than the truth that such creatures occasionally occur."

"So he raised his monster, earning a living with his dolls and praying around the clock," Bo thought aloud. "Tamlin escaped into an immature marriage as soon as she could at eighteen, producing Jeffrey and then the twins. That's when Beryl went off, when her father created the new line of collectible baby dolls modeled on the twins. She said as much when she was trying to kill me. But Eva, I still don't understand why she went to the beach cottage that night and grabbed those little girls from their cribs. What happened to make her do that, and what about Kimmy's death triggered the final sequence of murders? She said Kimmy was supposed to stay a doll and the other one, meaning Janny, was not supposed to be seen. I don't get it."

Eva Broussard eyed the beach below Bo's deck with interest, then stretched.

"Everyone who might have provided answers to those questions is now dead, Bo. Beryl's distorted thought processes are lost forever. The important thing is that you worried this case like a terrier, wouldn't let it go, and saved Janny's life. Because Beryl would have killed her, Bo. I'm sure of that."

"There's someone else who reached out to save Janny," Bo mentioned softly. "Reached out in images that were all she'd known for most of her life—just a dreadful sense of waiting in a place with no sound but the clicks and hisses of life-support systems. A place like a subway station, long abandoned, where one last train is expected. . . ."

"Arguably, the dream you named 'The Station of the Dead' was connected in some way to Kimberly Malcolm," Eva agreed. "But the mechanisms of psychic phenomena are notoriously resistant to analysis, so I advise restraint in thinking about it, Bo. These phenomena cannot be understood; it's best not to try. And Molly and I are going for a long walk. I suggest that you rest until dinner, after which I have what promises to be a challenging engagement, but I'll be back later to check on you and walk Molly a last time before I go home."

"What challenging engagement?" Bo asked, lurching toward her bed.

"A seminar on enhanced verbal communication," Eva laughed. "I've invited Pete Cullen."

"Aha," Bo teased, but woman and dachshund were already out the door.

Later Bo cocked an ear at a message from Estrella on the answering machine, but didn't get up to answer the phone. The christening would be on March seventeenth, Es reported happily. St. Patrick's Day. Plenty of time for Bo to get a new coat.

Sometime after that Molly began leaping against the side of Bo's bed, indicating their return from the walk. Then Bo heard a knock at the door, answered by Eva.

"Thank you, I'll sign for it," she said.

"What is it?" Bo yelled.

"A registered overnight delivery from the Palm Valley Doll Works," Eva answered, bringing the large envelope to Bo. "Curious."

"I don't believe this!" Bo gasped, pulling a glossy color photo onto the bed.

The photo was of a doll, a Jasper Malcolm collectible. An auburn-haired baby doll with mischievous green eyes and a smattering of freckles across its nose. Topping its ivy-green velvet dress was a collar of Irish lace, matched by the trim on its white tights and booties. And tucked under its arm was a bright-eyed dachshund puppy, done in bronze velvet. In the curve of the doll's lower lip and in its cheekbones, Bo remembered the dollmaker's hand touching her face, and saw herself.

"Prototype, Final Jasper Malcolm Doll, 'Bo,'" someone had written in the photo's margin. "Per Malcolm's instructions, prototype to be shipped to Bo Bradley at this address as soon as replicated. ETA—March of next year."

The doll was adorable, Bo thought, blushing. The first one she'd ever seen that didn't give her the creeps.

Postscript

Only a few miles away in an attractive Point Loma neighborhood, a woman with snowy hair held by a tortoiseshell clip played with a gray cat. On the floor beside the pair were a catnip mouse and several balls of yarn, unravelled.

"It's going to be fine, Bede," the woman said softly. "For once Bo was right. You're much better than the picture!"